THE BLOODLINE TRAIL

The Bloodline Series

Book 8

by

Lynda Rees

The Murder Guru

lyndareesauthor@gmail.com

Website: https://lyndareesauthor.com

Publisher: Sweetwater Publishing Company

6612 Ky. Hwy. 17 North, DeMossville, KY 41033

sweetwaterpublishingcompany.wordpress.com

Edition 1, Copyright © 2018 by Sweetwater Publishing Company

Edited by Melinda Williams
ISBN# 978-1-7323116-0-2

Email: lyndareesauthor@gmail.com
Website: https://lyndareesauthor.com/
Facebook: @lynda.rees.author

This story is dedicated to Joy Jerry Rees,
who told me a true story
inspiring this one in me.
Joy, you supported and loved me unconditionally
as though I were your own daughter.
I adore you as my second dad.
Though you are long gone,
you continue contributing to our day-to-day
happiness and well-being.
I love and miss you with all my heart.

Lynda

CONTENTS

Love is a dangerous mystery.
Enjoy the ride!

Lynda Rees

About Lynda Rees

Lynda is a storyteller, an award-winning novelist, and a free-spirited dreamer with workaholic tendencies and a passion for writing romance. Her dreams come true, blessing her with a supportive family. Whatever crazy adventure Lynda congers up, her loving Mike is by her side. A diverse background, visits to exotic locations, and curiosity about how history effects today's world fuels her writing. Born in the splendor of the Appalachian Mountains as a coal miner's daughter and part Cherokee, she grew up in northern Kentucky when Newport prospered as a mecca for gambling and prostitution.

Published in contemporary, suspense, romance, and historical fiction, children's middle-grade fiction, advertising copy, and freelance, Lynda is an active member of several professional writing organizations and volunteer judge of professional writing events.

Author's Note:

I hope you enjoy my work and we become lifelong friends. Time for romance!

Lynda Rees, The Murder Guru
Love is a dangerous mystery. Enjoy the ride!

Book Deals, Exclusive Content and FREE reads—

Find out how:
Website: https://lyndareesauthor.com/
Write and ask me for your FREE copy of Leah's Story, a short story and prologue to The Bloodline Series.
lyndareesauthor@gmail.com

CHAPTER 1

Jaiden helped Mr. Bennett chase his escaping herd of cattle back through their broken fence line. "Thank goodness you brought a couple buckets of grain to entice these stubborn cows to safety." She'd blocked the road with her cruiser at one end and placed orange cones at the other to keep traffic out of danger. No strays on the road got accidentally hit.

"This ain't my first rodeo." The old farmer grinned pushing one errant cow toward safety.

Once the country road was free from danger, she helped guard his herd so they wouldn't run loose again while Mr. Bennett repaired busted fence. Finally finished, he shook her hand and wiped his brow. "Whew, thanks for your help, Deputy Coldwater."

"It's part of the job, but you're welcome." Jaiden loved working as deputy to Sheriff Wyatt Gordon of Sweetwater.

She made good time driving back to

town. Dusk was starting. She neared the deserted Barnes farm at the edge of town a light flashed from a window.

Damn, those kids must be partying again.

She'd arrested one juvenile last week—the one she caught. His buddies ran faster and escaped. Jaiden dragged the boy home. His dad was pissed at his son. Punishment was being assigned to clean police station bathrooms for a week.

He arrived like clockwork after school each afternoon with sagging shoulders and head hung low. He wasn't a bad kid. It tickled her seeing his dad come down on him that way. It'd serve him better than any other punishment.

He was making friends with other deputies. Finally he had guts to look into Jaiden's eyes. She smiled and winked. He blushed. He grinned.

She hit a button to call her office. "Sheriff Gordon here. What's up, Jaiden?" His southern twang could charm honey out of a bear's paws.

"Wyatt, it looks like vandals sneaking into the Barnes place again. I'm going to check it out."

"Okay, but be careful. Keep your body camera on and radio handy. Buzz me if you need backup. I can be there in five."

"It's probably just kids again. They'll run and I'll be home in half an hour. I'll let you know how it goes."

"You do that, Deputy Coldwater." Wyatt had confidence in her ability to handle a few youngsters looking for a good time, but if he thought real danger was present, he'd come running. He was a good friend and a great boss.

Jaiden drove into a dirt drive and circled behind a house. Surprisingly a vehicle parked there. Local kids typically walked here, not wanting to draw attention. They usually carried a beer cooler but were too young to partake of it. Sometimes they partied in back woods. Last winter they broke into the house, but didn't do it often.

A close look at the vehicle proved this wasn't kids. The fancy SUV probably cost around what she made in a year.

She stepped from her cruiser with her body camera on. Warily she approached the vehicle shining her flashlight. It was locked. With its tinted windows she made out no driver sat inside. Glancing around, she didn't see anyone. She tried the back door knob. It opened.

Using a firm authoritative voice she called, "Police, anyone here?" Dead silence. She called out again—same response. "I'm coming in." Holding the door wide, she entered the old farmhouse kitchen. It had seen better days and two years of being uninhabited left every surface covered with dust and cobwebs.

Making her way through into the sparsely furnished dining room with no sign of life, only footprints in dust proved someone recently walked through. Much the same the living room furniture had been covered with sheets, and still, no one in the house. A first-floor bedroom off the living room also filled with sheet-covered furniture but its filthy floor center held an expensive, pull-behind suitcase. A tag read C. Barnes.

Huh, apparently a Barnes heir had come to town.

Jaiden made her way back through the maze of rooms. She yanked the kitchen door shut behind her. No sign of C. Barnes or anyone else. Returning to her cruiser, she activated her radio.

"Wyatt?"

"Yep, I'm here, Jaiden. How are things at the Barnes place?"

"Quite. A fancy SUV is parked in back of the unlocked house. Footprints show on grimy floors and a suitcase in a bedroom with a tag for C. Barnes prove someone's here."

"C? I suppose that's Clay. It sounds like Clay Barnes returned home. Wonder if he's in town to stay or merely settling his mama's estate? It's been a couple years since her funeral. Too bad he let the place deteriorate during that time."

"Yep, and the kids around here looking for a party place haven't helped it any." She climbed into the cruiser. "I didn't find Mr. Barnes or anyone else around though. I suppose he's fine. Maybe he's exploring his property. Want me to search for him?"

"No, no need to do that. If there's

trouble, he'll let us know. Go home and enjoy what's left of your evening. You're off duty now, right?"

"Sure thing, boss. See you tomorrow." Before she finished writing notes on her pad, a tall, thin gentleman in too-new jeans, shiny boots and a crisp white dress shirt, with sleeves rolled to elbows strolled from the woods. His smile lit up his face engaging pale blue eyes like none she'd seen before, unless photos of that old actor Paul Newman counted.

He strode purposely toward her closed door with an arm extended—not bad looking, but not a muscular type she'd always been attracted to. Built more like Levi—he stood long and lanky. She shined her flashlight his way. Those pearly-blue eyes sparkled and a perfect set of shiny white teeth flashed a welcoming smile. His hand flipped up reflecting light. She flicked her flashlight off. Dusky moonlight approaching caught moisture as he licked his lips self-consciously. They appeared soft and sensual?

"Howdy, Ma'am. Are you the local Welcome Wagon?"

Through the opened window Jaiden accepted a hand offered with a smile. "Deputy Coldwater. Afraid not, I saw a light in your window. Figured you for a trespasser. I called out but there was no answer. Since the door stood open, I walked through. Seeing your suitcase, I wager you're the owner. Am I right?"

His hand felt warm and strong gripping

hers. He released his hold. She opened her door and stepped out of her cruiser. A good foot taller than her, his height ranged at six-four. She liked them tall, like her handsome brother, Calvin. Cal had bulky muscle on every inch of his body, and with their native Choctaw and Irish heritage, she and Cal sported tawny skin. This stranger's light complexion hinted he wasn't an out-doorsy type. His smile beckoned Jaiden to linger. She wanted to know him better. He acted genuinely friendly and open, unlike guys she usually met. Dating became a rarity lately.

She'd had one affair since moving to Kentucky—Moggie Larrs. That proved more friends-with-benefits than love. Now she couldn't even roll in hay with Moggie, since he'd fallen head-over-heels for her new pal, Dovie Fuller. Moggie spent most of his free time these days at Dovie's restaurant or Fuller House Farm since inheriting it.

The other guy she'd had hots for proved himself a stalker and murderer—a real downer. This tasty, grinning newcomer might be what she needed—if he intended to stick around a while.

"You're perceptive and gorgeous. I would've come home long ago had I realized local law enforcement had come to be so stunningly beautiful."

She grinned. "Yeah, Sheriff Wyatt Gordon is a total hunk, but then he's married and out of circulation."

The stranger guffawed. "No shit? Wyatt

Gordon came back to town and assumed a sheriff's position? How the hell is he doing? Last I heard he married and worked in Chicago." He brushed a hand over short-cropped, dark hair.

"He's doing excellent. His marriage ended, so he moved back to Sweetwater. Remarried, he and his wife, Sage, had a baby last year. Little Ty has recently started walking. He's a cutie, but then of course he is. His parents are amazing."

"That's awesome. I'll have to give him a ring. It will be good catching up. We played football together in high school. I'm sorry, Ma'am. Where are my manners? I'm pleased to meet you, Deputy. I'm Clay Barnes. I grew up on this little farm,"

"I suspected it. So you're Betty Barnes' son? She passed away around the time I moved to town."

"I knew you weren't a native. I'd remember you if we went to school together. Women like you aren't easily forgotten."

"I doubt many Native American families reside in the area. My brother and mother moved a few years back. I came a couple years ago to work for Wyatt. My brother, Cal works for Levi Madison training his race horses. You must know Levi if you went to school and played ball with Wyatt. Cal retired, soon after our dad died. Mom closed her large-animal veterinary clinic in Texas and moved to Sweetwater to live with Cal."

"You've planted quick roots in this little hick town. Heck yeah, Levi is one of the nicest guys I've ever met. He and Wyatt always treated me well. My parents didn't get involved in things at school. They were reclusive and private. So I didn't fit into the *in crowd*."

She shrugged and laughed. "Me either. I grew up somewhere between not fitting in with kids on a reservation and not fitting into a white school either. Cal and I made our own way."

He nodded understanding. "I get it. I was a bit of a nerd with limited social outlets. I spent a lot of time in books."

She raised a brow and grinned flirtatiously. "And what did you do with all that nerdy knowledge?"

"I became a doctor. I'm a resident general surgeon at St. Vincent Hospital in Chicago."

"Wow, impressive. Way to go nerd." Her flat hand rose up, and he slapped it.

"Can I invite you in for a cup of coffee?"

"Sure, why not. I'm off duty now. I could use a drink and good conversation."

He smiled. Her chest filled with a calm happiness. Funny—how you could instantly like someone without knowing much at all about them. Clay smelled similar to spearmint. His manly hand felt warm and good against the back of her uniform shirt ushering her inside.

He retrieved cloths from a drawer and wiped several kitchen chairs then offered her one. She sat watching him clean a table and countertops. He washed the stove top and pulled out an old fashioned percolator giving it a soaping in the sink. He brought in a couple bags of groceries from his SUV and placing them on a counter, filled a coffee pot with water from a gallon jug and grounds from a fresh can. While the pot heated on a burner, he chose a chair opposite her.

"Next time you visit, this place will look guest worthy. I promise."

"You want me to come back? You might want to wait until the evening's over to make that decision. We haven't even had coffee yet."

The pot began to percolate. He grinned and wagged his brows. "I've a perception about you, and I'm rarely wrong. You and I are destined to become friends." He eyed the dirty house. "Funny, I've never brought any friends home before."

Her eyes went wide. "Never?"

"No, never. I had a few friends at school. I didn't socialize outside of playing football. I never brought anyone home, or went to their houses. I didn't date until I went away to college. I haven't gotten serious about anyone. Determined to become a doctor, I knew it entailed dedication. I wouldn't tie myself to a gal to hurt her pulling away working on my career, but I dated casually."

"Why didn't you bring friends home?"

He shrugged and grimaced. "Dad didn't welcome strangers. He and mom kept to themselves and didn't socialize. Mom went to church because she could play piano there. But she was shy and backward and didn't make friends."

"It sounds sad and lonely."

"Not really. Happy with my life, I didn't know better. It was the way things were."

"Well, I'm honored being your first friend entertained. I'm Jaiden."

"Nice meeting you, Jaiden." He extended those long fingers to her again for a shake.

This time she grasped his mitt and shook it heartily. "Likewise, Clay. What brings you home to Sweetwater? Are you staying?"

"No, that's not the plan—at least I don't think so. I never gave it a thought. Recently The Spencer Development Firm contacted me with a lucrative offer. I'm not interested, but it's going to shit unoccupied—sad and starting to seriously fall apart. I've let it go, since Mom died. She didn't work our land for three years before since Dad passed. So it's experiencing serious neglect."

"Why didn't you take the offer?" She sipped the hot cup he sat in front of her.

"I don't know. The offer spurred a nerve inside me. I don't know. I had a longing for familiarity. , I wanted to come home and decide from here. The Spencer people want to divide my farm into twenty-to-thirty sites for high-end homes. Splitting the land is wrong. My property is a mere twenty-five acres—small for a local farm—but I'd love to see someone live in the house again and raise a family. I thought I'd check it out and see what needs doing. I want to bring back its old glory. Dad always kept this home shining and perfect. If I still want to sell, I'll hire a realtor and sell to an owner-occupied buyer."

"How can you do that and keep your job in Chicago?"

Emotions fought a tug of war in him. He struggled for right words to explain, like he didn't know himself. "My career came to a point where I must make key decisions. Do I want to continue on pushing for head of surgery? I'm not real fond of Chicago. Do I want to move to another hospital in a different location? Or do I start my own practice somewhere—wherever I settle? Unfortunately, I've not had ability to travel extensively. I lived here, went away to college in Lexington, and did surgical residency in Chicago. So I arranged a leave of absence for two months to figure it out."

Glancing around, she shook her head. "Well, your work is cut out for you here. This should be good for the soul."

"What about you? How did you end up here?"

"My brother, Calvin, and I grew up in El Paso on a ranch. The Madison family owns our neighboring ranch, Garrett and Adelle Madison. We knew Corrie and Levi. They visited their family's ranch next door to ours. We grew up riding together. Dad trained horses and Mom was a veterinarian. Cal went into the Navy and retired from the Seals a few years ago. Dad passed away, so Mom moved with him. He accepted a head trainer role at Mane Lane Farm."

"Did you come to be near your brother?"

"I was a Texas Ranger. Injured in a bust, I came to recoup with Mom. She fussed over me like a baby. A dude murdered Wyatt's deputy, and I assumed her position."

"Wow, you hardly ever think of Sweetwater and murder in the same breath." He shook his head dubiously. "How you like it here?"

"This work is much less hazardous— more enjoyable. I'm getting to know people I protect. I came from a call helping a farmer corral his runaway cattle. It's a good life. But we've had our fair share of crime since I came onboard. First job here, we busted a drug ring. Then a stalker murdered someone. Every community has its fair share of crime."

"You say Cal works for Levi?"

"Yes. He replaced a guy running a scam stealing valuable sperm. Levi is world renowned for breeding skill with successful race horses. Now Cal works with him making a name for his self. So far he won the biggest race last year in Louisville. Twice now he won big races in New York and Baltimore. I'm so proud I could spit. His career blossomed."

"Impressive. I suppose he'll stick with Levi then."

She grinned, thinking of family. "Cal

met a spicy, purple-haired organic farmer named Rose. She works for Wyatt's wife, Sage, on her organic farm Parsley, Sage, Rose, Mary & Wine. Rose is a real doll and a spit fire too. I like her a lot."

"That's a good thing. I've never heard of the farm." His head tilted quizzically.

"It was Reggie Casse's grandfather's farm. Widowed, Sage moved from New York, bought the farm, and developed a successful business. A focused, driven, force of nature, you'll love Sage."

"If Wyatt loves her, I'm sure to. Want to see my house? I've barely had time to walk through it because I wanted to take a quick stroll before dark. I didn't go far though." His hand reached. She placed her smaller one in his. Her dark skin looked awkwardly cozy enveloped by his palm. His long fingers wrapped around hers.

"Sure." She let him tug her to the dining room. He released her and her hand was emptier than it had been previously.

He surveyed space. She did likewise with hands on hips taking in every angle. "This room isn't so bad. Clean up. Strip ancient wall paper. Slap on a fresh coat of paint."

"I'm thinking these hardwood floors can be sanded and refinished. Maybe I can add fancy, wide molding for character."

"A new light fixture would do wonders."

He grinned and winked. "Good thing I talked you into sticking around. I like how you think. Help me with critical decisions." He snatched and brought her hand to his lips for a quick kiss. His breath tingled on her skin. Moisture from his lips sealed a connection sending a zip of electricity surging through her. Her heart sang for joy.

"Play your cards well and I might do that."

He dragged her into the living room flipping a sheet off exposing a worn, leather sofa.

"Nice. The quality furniture has obviously seen better days. Its leather dried and cracked."

"I believe so." He flopped the cushion up exposing a label. "Good eye, Jaiden. What're you thinking?"

"I don't know. If you don't want to purchase a new one, maybe it's worth reupholstering. It could cost half the price."

"Huh, I hadn't considered that. I'll check in town to see what local upholstery shops say. Maybe they can work on the couch, chair and loveseat while I work on the room."

"Good idea. This room needs the same things."

"I agree, along with two bedrooms upstairs and one downstairs. The furniture is crap, so I'll either sell it without furniture or buy new bedroom sets."

He marched to a wall beside a dresser. Peeling paper curled at corners. He snatched a strip and yanked. Paper ripped peeling a thick strip off. A layer of hundred-dollar bills glued attached to back of the strip in Clay's hand.

"What the—?"

Her mouth flopped open and her eyes widened. She moved closer to paper dangling from the wall. "It appears your parents left you an inheritance besides real estate."

"Wow, I had no clue. Their paranoia about privacy made them uncomfortable in crowds and social settings. I guess they distrusted banks too. Is hiding money illegal?"

She peeled another strip off a wall. It too, was backed with cash in hundreds. "I don't believe so. People used to hide cash in jars or cans, bury it on their property or stuff mattresses with it. Your parents were likely youths who survived the Great Depression or some other poverty circumstance, to have a bank phobia. It's not illegal keeping and protecting one's money, versus allowing a bank to hold and use it."

She carefully removed bills from wallpaper and piled them on a dresser. "Fun begins." She chortled.

He laughed along and did the same for a section he held. Peeling another chunk each they found more cash.

Together they went into the endeavor full force. A couple hours later the room bare walled, a huge stack of bills lay on a dresser.

Clay removed a covering from the bed. He picked up a pile of bills and sat on the edge of a bed counting. She leaned her butt against a dresser with feet crossed. Clay looked like an adorable, leggy kid playing with a new toy. Finally done counting, Clay had produced stack after stack of cash.

An incredulous look came over his face. His eyes met hers. "Absolutely incredible, I had no idea my parents had this kind of money. We always lived meekly and did without things we didn't absolutely need. Dad made money selling vegetables, eggs, hay and a couple beef cows a year. Mom did laundry for folks. She sewed and cleaned houses for people who didn't want full-time, live-in help. We never lived large, but from the looks of this we could've. They could've done much with this dough to make their lives easier."

"I guess it wasn't what they wanted. Maybe you can use it to pay off your college loans."

His eyes widened. "Actually, I don't have any—at least not enough to complain about. My parents helped me keep up with bills. I always figured they worked extra, cut back more somewhere and saved to help. Now I know how they did it. Extra came from their wall safe."

She giggled at his joke. "Funny."

With a grin on his face, he stared at a wall devoid of paper. "You know, I recall now. Mom wallpapered once a year. Now I understand why. Lordy, where, in hell did this cash come from?"

Her hands went up in a surrender stance. "Who knows? If your parents didn't have

friends or family, maybe they forgot to tell you.
Many aging parents become forgetful, especially
if they're suffering from Alzheimer's."

"Dad never did. He passed away in a
field one day from what a doctor called a heart
attack or stroke. I went away to school Mom's
last few years, so it's hard saying. We spoke by
phone frequently, but never talked money.
Maybe she grew forgetful. Not being with her, I
wouldn't notice."

"It's understandable, and easy to miss
signs not living with someone on a day-by-day
basis."

Mr. and Mrs. Barnes hid more than met
the eye. Sorrow seeped into her heart for a
friendless boy who struggled to make more of
life. His parents died without cluing him in on
such important facts.

"It's a shame. I'm sorry, Clay." She
placed a hand on his shoulder.

He capped her hand with his and smiled
through sadness. "Thanks, Jaiden." It felt right
comforting him, and her heart ached to alleviate
his pain.

She glanced at her watch—midnight.
They had laughed, chatted, and gotten carried
away stripping wall paper from his bedroom
walls and time had flown by.

"Wow, it's getting late. I've had a long
day. You must be exhausted after driving from
Chicago yesterday."

Reality set in. He comprehended what
he'd ignored. They'd enjoyed each other's

company.

"You're right. I finished my shift and left without taking a break."

"You didn't sleep before your long drive. Man, you must be exhausted. It's a wonder you aren't dead on your feet."

"I might be, now you mention it." He stood tall, blinking.

"I'd best hit the road so you can get some shuteye." Jaiden made a beeline toward the back door with him on her tail.

At her cruiser, he leaned onto the open window. For a second he acted like he'd kiss her goodnight. Instead, he withdrew and patted her shoulder.

"Thanks, Jaiden. I'm happy you showed up. I enjoyed our time together. I hate seeing you leave."

"I enjoyed myself, too, Clay." More than she wanted to admit, she liked newcomer Clay Barnes. She carefully kept reminding herself he was in town for a short vacation. She wouldn't deny opportunity for an affair with Clay, but didn't want to lose her heart to be dragged along to Chicago.

"When can I see you again? Are you off tomorrow?" Eagerness in his eyes fired hope in her gut for a relationship with him.

How to resist an adorable smile and enthusiasm flowing from baby-blue eyes she'd grown attached to? "I get off at three."

"Wonderful, I'd love to take you to dinner. You spent a whole evening with me, and all we did was work. I only had coffee to offer you."

"It's okay. I wasn't hungry. I had a burger before my last call. Dinner tomorrow sounds lovely—nothing fancy though. Maybe afterward I can help you strip another room. Who knows? Maybe walls are papered with thousands." Her giggle gurgled angst churning in her belly at leaving her new pal.

He laughed and nodded. "Okay, if you want, but I doubt it. Surely we've found all of it. How about The Royal Diner? Is it still there?"

"Oh yeah, Sadie's place rocks, the most popular restaurant in town. No wonder. Food is fabulous, and there's always fresh gossip to go with your burger and fries. Blackberry cobbler for dessert?"

"My favorites. I suppose I'm fodder for a gossip mill now I'm home."

"Probably. They don't miss much. But folks are good-hearted. They mean no harm. They worry about and take care of their own. I expect they'll delight you're back and happily help with anything you need."

"You're likely right." He stood erect. She started the engine. "Well, goodnight Jaiden. I'll ring you tomorrow. I can't wait to see you again."

CHAPTER 2

Wyatt's phone rang, and he snapped it up. "Sheriff Gordon."

"Hey, Wyatt, Clay Barnes here. Some things never change—like your familiar drawl. How you doing?"

"Good, Clay. Jaiden said you returned to town. It's been a coon's age. Let's get together."

"I'd like that, Wyatt." Wyatt was among the few not put off by Clay's family. Some folks liked keeping to themselves. He respected it, not letting it stand in the way of youthful friendships. Clay appreciated that.

"I told my wife, Sage, about your visit. She suggested bringing you home for dinner. You available tonight? She'd love to cook us a meal. Sage is known for her skill in a kitchen. You free?"

"I heard a New Yorker tagged town chick-magnet, Wyatt Gordon. I'm intrigued to meet the gal who settled you down. I'd love dinner, but I made plans with Jaiden."

Wyatt chuckled. "I'll have you know, I was settled long before Sage hit town. A matter of fact, she's my second wife. I left Chicago after a messy divorce and returned to Sweetwater. I became sheriff before Sage located here. She's anything but settling. Sage is a wild mustang who allows me to sniff her trail. Bring Jaiden along. She and Sage are pals. Sage will thrill to have Jaiden's company. Does six work?"

"Fine, but let me run it by Jaiden first. I don't want to speak for her. I'll call you later to let you know."

"Fine. I look forward to hearing from you."

♥♥♥♥

Jaiden left her truck at Clay's and rode with him to the Gordon's place. She'd gone several times over the last few years, but Clay never had.

He glanced around driving along a tree-lined fence. Horses grazed in a black-board, fenced corral in front of a rustic-designed house. A huge, furry German shepherd romped in a well-manicured lawn with a tan and white cocker spaniel. Hearing crunch of his tires on gravel dogs stopped playing and stood at attention observing their arrival.

A cedar home at the end of a drive

fronted by glass with a huge deck in a modified, a-frame style poised gracefully with a backdrop of pine forest. It looked to have sprouted of its own accord instead of being built—it blended well into a natural setting.

A tall, silver-haired sheriff stepped out sliding doors onto the deck and romped down a few steps to greet them. Long legs clad comfortably in jeans, he casually wore a black tee shirt. Friendly blue eyes sparkled Clay's way.

His pal rounded the SUV and clasped arms around him in a man-hug. With a squeeze and a pat on his back, Wyatt released him then stepped back to eye Clay up and down. Clay had gotten a chance to give Wyatt a once-over.

"You haven't changed a bit, Wyatt."

An amicable laugh sounded deep in Wyatt's throat and he patted his flat belly. "I'm thicker around my middle. Having a fabulous chef for a wife, a happy home does that. I'm pushing forty really hard this year, but so are you. You look well, Clay. You're taller and filled out." Wyatt rubbed his chin and neck.

"Yeah, I kept developing once I started at sixteen, straight through college. I think I'm done finally. I've worked hard over a few years and haven't put much attention into exercise. I keep meaning to. I'd like to bulk these skinny arms and chest up."

"Well, maybe now you're home you'll have a chance to do it." Wyatt gave Jaiden a quick hug and then led them to a deck. "Good to

see you, Jaiden. Sage is inside. She's thrilled
you came."

"Thanks for the invite." She smiled as
Clay's arm slid across her shoulders.

Dogs followed closely behind Wyatt's
feet. The larger one especially kept a close eye
checking Clay out. They accepted a round of
petting from Jaiden, who cooed and made over
them like old buddies.

"Doubtful. I'm working on my house.
It's a full-time job. But at least it's physical. I'm
getting more exercise than at a hospital."

"That's right. You studied medicine; I
heard somewhere."

"Yes, I'm a surgeon in Chicago. I
understand you moved from there."

A sad look swept over Wyatt's face then
he grinned. "Man, I hated living there. I'm
where I belong. I love being the sheriff in
Sweetwater."

"I'm not overly fond of the city myself,
but I was blessed with residency there. I'm at a
juncture where I need to decide which direction
to take. It's good timing to visit home and fix up
our old place."

They entered thru glass doors. A
stunning brunette with a tight ponytail sat in a
kitchen chair feeding an infant. A baby sported a
thick head of coal-black hair, a toothless grin
and wore a blue onesie. His eyes sparkled at
seeing Jaiden. She picked him up for a cuddle
and he cooed as he whispered something sweet
into his ear.

"Sage, I'd like to introduce my old pal from high school, Clay Barnes. Clay, meet my wife, Sage, and our son, Ty."

"Wow, congratulations. Ty is adorable and certainly gets his hair from both of you. Before Wyatt turned silver in his twenties, his hair was dark like yours, Sage. I'm pleased to meet you both." Sage extended a hand which he shook and released.

"Welcome to our home, Clay. You're keeping good company, I see. I'm glad you came, Jaiden." Sage kissed Jaiden's cheek as she put remains of Ty's dinner away. "We don't get together nearly enough. Wyatt, fetch our guests a glass of wine or a beer while I lay this young man down for a nap." She retrieved her drowsy son, turned, and they entered a door off a dining room.

When Sage returned, the threesome sipped cold brews in tow relaxing on a broad deck. Clay's hand swept in front of him indicating their property. "It's lovely here."

"We love it. This house was Wyatt's. I own an organic farm down the road and moved in here when we married."

"Yes, Jaiden told me how successfully you are. I understand you sell vegetables, fruits, herbs and grapes for wine making." He fingered Jaiden's hand resting in his.

"Yes and we make farmer's cheese and goat cheese. Jaiden's brother and his wife, Rose, live on my farm. Rose, my assistant and farmhand, has proved a blessing to me and my business."

"Oh, I assumed Levi provided Cal a home since he's Mane Lane Farm's top horse trainer. That's usually part of a package."

"He does," Jaiden said. "Our mother and I live there. Cal married Rose and moved out because she lives and works at Parsley, Sage, Rose, Mary & Wine Farm."

"Tell us about what you're doing here, Clay." Wyatt sucked a long draw on his icy bottle and handed one to Sage. She sat beside him.

"I had an offer for my property from a development company wanting to build a subdivision. It rubs me wrong. If I sell it, I'd like it to go to someone who doesn't intend to break land into little chunks, maybe family oriented."

"Jaiden said you're working on your house. Are you going to fix it up before selling?" Wyatt eyed him curiously.

Empty gnawing in his gut slammed him whenever he envisioned someone else living at his homestead. Clay swallowed a lump forming in his throat and thought about how to answer. "I guess so. I'm going to take it slow, do necessary renovations. Then I'll decide how to proceed. If I sell, it won't be to a developer."

"Are you considering staying?

Sweetwater could, I'm sure, use another doctor." Sage spoke softly and with a New Yorker accent. Her tone held no sharp edge. She exuded warmth and openheartedness. No wonder Wyatt fell for her. She was lovely with long, slender legs, and a body of a well-toned runner.

"I hadn't considered moving back until Jaiden suggested it. It's too soon to decide. I'm going to take my time and make sure whatever I do fits me for many years to come."

"That sounds wise. Excuse me." Sage went to a kitchen to answer a ringing phone. She left a glass door open. "Hello. Oh, honey that's wonderful. I'm so proud. Your dad will be, too. When are you coming home? We'll have a celebration." She strolled out to the deck with a phone against her ear. "We're having dinner with Jaiden and an old friend of your dad's. Here, tell him yourself." She beamed at Wyatt and extended her phone.

He grinned and took it. "Hey, baby girl. How's it going? No kidding? That's not surprising, but certainly good news. Text me details. I'll fetch you from the airport. Love you, Hailey. See you soon." He laid the phone on a table and turned to Clay with his shoulders back and his chest puffing out more than usual. "Sorry about that. It was my daughter, Hailey. She's studying chemistry at Stanford and called to say she scored top in her class. She's coming before returning to Chicago later in the summer."

"Her mom lives in Chicago?" Clay sought to understand.

"Right. Izzy and I divorced. She remarried. Her family resides in Chicago and her new husband is a native. Izzy will never move from there. She loves it. I on the other hand, hated it. I regret our divorce happened when Hailey was fourteen. It's tough being a long-distance dad. Sage helped me study up on technology to enjoy more well-rounded communication with my daughter."

"Yes, but remember. Hailey hated me at first." Sage laughed good-heartedly.

"She didn't hate you. She would've acted the same with any woman I cared for. We saw each other summer vacations and holidays, so we had piss poor little time with each other. She was jealous of you, but saw you weren't stealing me from her and began liking you. Look how tight you've grown. She's closer to you in many ways than with Izzy, but Izzy's obsessively self-centered."

Sage slid her hand beneath Wyatt's larger one. "Hailey is a daughter I always wanted. I adore her. She's a good big sister for Ty and nuts about our little fellow." Sage's gaze moved from Wyatt to her guests. "She's a lovely young woman." Jaiden grinned at her friend. Then her focus went to Clay, and her smile brightened his day.

Sage slipped inside hearing the baby monitor go off. A few minutes later she returned carrying a toothy grinning boy. Barely over a year old, Ty was long and lean like his dad with shocking black, thick hair.

Clay reached for him. Ty nearly shot out of Sage's arms into his.

"Shy little tyke, aren't you, pal?" The baby gurgled in Ty language and grabbed at Clay's ear with a chubby hand. "He inherited your and Wyatt's hair."

Jaiden laughed. "Seriously? Wyatt is much too young for his full, silver locks. I assumed he was blonde before grey took hold."

Wyatt laughed shaking his head. "Nope. Clay's right."

"Yeah. When he was a kid, Wyatt sported the same coal-black tresses, like your lovely mane, Sage."

Sage laughed with her husband. She nodded, and her long ponytail bopped with motion. Clay continued playing with the baby boy who was now fascinated with exploring his shirt pocket.

"How do you like Sweetwater, Clay?"

"Gosh, I've been back a couple days. I've spent time at home. Last time I was here was for Mom's funeral, but I didn't go out often then either. I haven't seen much of Sweetwater, but I will. I promised Jaiden a burger, fries and blackberry cobbler from The Royal Diner." He liked Jaiden mighty fine and sent her a sly wink telling her so. She grinned showing a full set of lovely whites. Sparkle in her eyes told him she was pleased.

He'd felt at odds with his visit to

Sweetwater. Being with his old friend and Sage had a calming effect. Unlike Jaiden, who was fire and ice—Jaiden sent shivers through him and a surge of heat straight to his core. Clay was enjoying her company immensely; but his heart told him to watch his step. She could have a chronic effect.

"Sadie will thrill to see you." Sage went to her kitchen for a refill of drinks. "I can recommend a good realtor."

"Sage knows everyone in town, though she's lived here a mere few years." Admiration filled Jaiden's gaze.

Sage returned a couple minutes later carrying four fresh amber bottles. She handed Clay his and slipped him a business card. He glanced at it and stuck it into his shirt pocket. It was generous of her to go out of her way to offer help.

"Thanks. I'll give her a call when I'm ready to talk business."

"Thanks." Jaiden accepted an icy bottle and swigged. She winked at Clay then turned to their friends.

"Wyatt, I wanted to tell you what we found last night. Jaiden and I were messing around in my house. I yanked down the wallpaper. Mom and Dad had papered over cash in a bedroom. I spent today cleaning house, so haven't had the opportunity to check other rooms, but wonder what more concealed. Is it legal? Does that cash belong to me? What should I do with it?"

Clay didn't believe in ghosts. But his place had an eerie aura since he returned. His parents were gone. They wouldn't purposely haunt him, but a mystique about it gave him chills. It was one reason he'd worked frantically renovating it, hoping to wipe away any mystical sense lingering about.

Jaiden shook her head. "I told him it's his, Wyatt. Apparently his mom hid her stash. It's not surprising of their generation." She patted Clay's knee affectionately allowing her hand to dawdle on his thigh. It felt good and natural lying there.

Wyatt guffawed. "Damn, your parents always were a bit on an odd side. They kept to themselves. Now they distrusted banks. Can't say I blame them, with what's happened over years. But no, it's not illegal to stash cash at home in any manner an owner sees fit. Was it a large sum?"

He'd brought it up. He might as well tell all. With a grimace Jaiden's way, her smile fortified him. "Yes, we've found over five-hundred-thousand-dollars."

"Damn, son, that's a ton of dough. It's expensive going to med school, right? Maybe this will help get you out of debt."

"It is, but honestly, my parents sent a huge check each year covering most of my expenses. I have small student loans, but nothing like you'd expect. I figured they did extra work and cut back. You know how thrifty they were."

"Yep, that's another word to describe them. It's good they helped you with expenses." Wyatt shook his head looking away in deep thought.

"I never asked them to and didn't expect it. This stash is odd. I'm curious how they came to have it and why they hid it this way. It makes me uneasy. I'll store it in a safe deposit box, until I figure out what's going on."

"Oddly, many bills run sequentially, like the Barnes' withdrew large sums at a time from an account before hiding the dough." Jaiden's face glowed in the dusky evening light. She was a sight to behold, appearing more beautiful each time he looked at her, making him wonder how lucky he'd get.

A bell dinged on a stove inside. Sage jumped and started for the kitchen. "Dinner's ready. I'll go plate the food. We can eat in five minutes."

Jaiden followed. "I'll help."

♥♥♥♥

Jaiden filled plates while Sage brought one delicacy after another out of an oven. The table was set. So they chatted while working.

"You like him. Don't you, Jaiden?" Sage eyed her friend across a kitchen island. "I knew by your eyes. I've not seen you look at anyone quite like that."

Heat flushed into her cheeks, but with

her tawny skin, Sage couldn't tell she was blushing. "I do, actually. He's not a muscular, sporty, out-doorsy type I usually fall for. But I enjoy Clay Barnes. He's smart, quick-witted and laughs easily. He's eye candy in a crisp, clean-cut kind of way."

Sage winked and smiled. "Has he asked about your tattoo yet?"

"Not yet." Jaiden's hand slipped to rub her neck where the horse picture lived. "We met yesterday, though it seems much longer. I got off work at six. We talked from then until midnight. I haven't talked so much with a man since Moggie and I teamed up.

"It's funny thinking of you with Moggie and now seeing you with Clay. Girl, you go from one end of the spectrum to the next." Sage slipped an arm around her friend and together they eased to the doorway. "Relax and let nature take her course. Have fun."

"I intend to." Jaiden observed Clay animatedly talking.

Wyatt's eyes shot wide, and his face poised to bust into a fit of laughter. Clay's long arms flailed around, and his face went from story-telling mode into full-blown chuckles.

Jaiden needed light-heartedness in her life. Clay Barnes fit.

CHAPTER 3

Jaiden jumped from the truck and those well-tanned, taunt legs flashed. She stepped to the ground causing Clay's breath to catch. His heart stopped for a second. She turned and bent toward the seat to retrieve an item. His heart swelled. Electricity jolted his racing pulse to life. He stared unashamedly at her tiny, firm upside-down, heart-shaped behind clad in tight cutoff jeans. Clay's mouth watered at his passing jealousy for frayed strings along a hem gently caressing bare, tender skin along the top of her legs, so near to her womanhood, where his tongue longed to.

She spun around proudly presenting gifts toward him. He met her at the kitchen door. He'd gathered his wits plucking a bag from her hands. Accepting it cleared the way for a clean visual of ample, pert breasts straining against a clingy red tank top snuggling against her delightful mounds. The scooped neck provided an enticing glimpse at cleavage rising and falling with each breath, begging his nose to delve into the crevice between them splaying kisses across velvety looking skin.

"Thanks for picking up pizza I ordered. I see you brought beer too."

"Yep." She slipped a hand into the crux of his elbow coming into step with his pace. They entered the house. "Didn't you know? It's illegal to eat pizza without beer."

He sat packages on a table and revealed a six pack from the bag. Opening a bottle, he handed it to Jaiden. "Want a glass?"

"No, thanks. It tastes better from a bottle." She sipped then her tongue snaked out and licked moisture from her lip.

He shivered thinking of the tender, pink muscle lovingly exploring his body. He opened his own beer. Taking a long swig, he needed for a distraction.

"I can't argue." He diverted lusty visions by pulling paper plates and silverware from a cabinet and sat a roll of paper towels on the table. Pulling a freshly cleaned chair out he held it for her to sit. "May we dine, my lady?"

She smiled sweetly and tossed her long mass of curly, dark hair off her shoulder. It swung behind her head and landed blanketing her back. She'd tamed it in a thick ponytail for dinner at Wyatt and Sage's home the previous night. When they'd met, she'd been working and had wrestled it into a tight French twist. Seeing it down, crowning her sultry splendor was a feminine vision he'd ever bore witness to.

Jaiden was no ordinary woman. A warrior, she protected her community. A doting sister and daughter discussing family, she proved a solid friend based on how Wyatt and Sage accepted her and how she spoke indulgently of Moggie and Dovie. At her core, she was a smoldering seductress, a lioness, a vixen, and he was falling hopelessly under her spell.

Whether it was for the long haul—which it probably couldn't be—or for a blissful brief period Clay wanted a chance with Jaiden; really with her; for better or for worse. He'd bet his medical degree it would prove for better rather than worse. He was all in.

Jaiden served slices of sinfully delicious, garlic pizza. He bit in allowing his tongue to savor intense flavors. He moaned pleasure. "Hmmm, the best pizza I ever ate."

His hand slid over covering Jaiden's. His thumb rubbed gently across her velvety skin. Their eyes met. She smiled sweetly. Their hearts communicated better than words could.

"Definitely the best company I've shared pizza with in a while." Her voice sounded growled roughly struggling with emotions.

"I'm curious. Why the horse artwork on your neck? Is that a remnant from your rebellious teen years?" He snickered fingering the painted, silky skin on her neck.

She snickered nodding. "It does give me a tough-looking edge. Doesn't it?" He laughed agreeing. "Nothing so furious, however—it's a drawing I did of my first and most beloved horse. I had it tattooed on after he died when I turned eighteen. Damn, I loved that old boy."

He should've known it had more sentimental than defiant meaning. Jaiden was all heart, and he was falling for hers fast.

After dinner Jaiden stretched. "You did a remarkable job cleaning this place up. I see you've already stripped carpeting."

"Yep, and an upholsterer picked up my sofa and chairs today. It was a brilliant idea to reupholster. He said it was quality built. I chose ultra-soft suede in a mellow camel. I can't wait to see how it turns out."

"Awesome, sounds elegant. You're going to have a hard time parting with those pieces. How about we start in your living room and try to remove remaining paper?"

She strode toward Clay's front room purposely with hands in back pockets. He couldn't take his eyes off her swaying behind strutting in front of him. If he lived to a hundred or more, he'd forever get a hard-on watching a woman walk away wearing hiking boots and short, cut-off jeans. He swallowed hard and followed at a trot.

"Depending on how much time it takes, we might be able to do dining room walls. The Salvation Army picked up the old furniture today. I kept was a huge carton of paperwork, mostly bills and whatever else my parents felt inclined to stuff in buffet drawers.

After two hours of steaming and pulling,

steaming again and scraping layers of glue, they nearly finished. Jaiden grabbed a ladder and placed it over a window. She climbed toward it and reached the last chuck clinging to a wall. As she tugged the aluminum step-ladder toppled. She grabbed for the highest rung trying to steady it but it tumbled sideways. Clay sped across the space in time to catch her keeping before slamming to the floor. The stepladder clanged as it landed and bounced once for.

Clay's arms securely surrounded Jaiden's shoulders with one hand on her firm, tawny legs draping across his arm. Her head snapped back then forward, and she laid it against his chest. Her arm clasped his other while he held her tight. She inhaled with a gasp. "I can't believe you caught me."

Her face lifted, and her mass of curls flew wildly around. A strand claimed the bridge of his nose. Releasing her grip on his shoulder she grinned mischievously. A long, red nail moved it carefully off his face.

"Fast work for a bookworm, nerdy doctor type—and you're not even panting from sprinting or straining from my weight."

He grinned playfully. "You may be muscular; Ma'am, but you're a tiny one. I can haul you around in one arm if need be. I kind of like it this way though." *Hell yeah*.

Her breast was pressed his ribcage. The lips that tortured him all evening, with a tendency to lick while she thought, were suddenly perfectly within kissable range. She winked and grinned. He sat her gently on booted feet.

"Thanks for saving me, Doc."

"My pleasure, deputy."

Remorse filled his heart when he released her. He'd held back and missed an opportunity to kiss her, after fantasizing about it all evening. She'd been light as a breeze holding her in his arms. As usual, over thinking and procrastinating, he'd spoiled the moment. He'd never learn.

She completely surprised him tiptoeing. Her hands came up behind his neck tugging his head so her soft, sweet lips clung to his.

Yeah, he'd died and gone to heaven.

She didn't let go after the initial kiss ended, keeping her face close. His arms slid around, braced against her back easily lifting her, securing her tightly against his frame. Her breasts pillowed adorably against his diaphragm, and her hot belly rested against his midriff heating him inside like no fire ever could. Blood flowed below, and his erection came to life. His mouth again covered hers. This kiss was deep and filled with pent-up emotions surging through his veins. She met his pace without hesitation.

Damned if she didn't taste better than any woman life—at least any he'd come this close to. Surprising, but garlic and beer became infinitely sexy; and a steaming, hot woman shredded any hesitation he'd considered about getting involved. Whatever future came, Jaiden in present was worth it.

Her hands held his face to hers, and her elbows gently relaxed against him. She pressed him showing she wanted him equally. Each more aggressive caress was met with earnest acceptance. Her breathing grew more rugged unleashing doubt she might not want him.

His hands slid beneath those tight butt cheeks lifting her legs to straddle his waist. Her boots rested easily against his ass. Carrying her slight bounce brought a grin to his face though he didn't release her. She smiled opening her eyes so close they almost met. Long strides transported his prize into his bedroom. A cleaned unmade bed sported new, crisp, white linens.

Without releasing their kiss or her, he sat on his bed. The sultry woman straddled him. Their kiss broke, and she looked at him with a soft, sensuous gaze perusal of his face. Her right hand slid atop his head and caressed the back. Both hands came to the front.

With eyes locked, she began unbuttoning his shirt. He hadn't worn an undershirt. Each button undone allowed her fingers to play against peach fuzz. Each touch sent tingles though him. He became one massive goose bump quivering against her skin. She tugged fabric loose from his jeans and slid it off his shoulders. Kneaded bare back muscles caused his rod to dance beneath her jean-clad ass. She grinned wickedly and wiggled atop his erection.

"If you don't stop squirming, I'll finish

without you."

With a teasing grin he lifted her by the waist to sit beside him, stood, unbuckled his jeans and bent slipping out of them. Her hands stroked tender flesh of his bare bottom, worshiping it. Her fingertips were followed by a blazing trail of kisses. One hand slid between his legs from behind cupping his balls. Gently massaging them in her heated palms, he thought he'd died and gone to heaven.

Kicking off shoes and socks, he faced where she knelt. His erection was rock-hard and curled toward his belly. Eyeing it she smiled broadly. "I knew you'd be long and lovely. You certainly don't disappoint, Doc." She winked tonguing her lips.

One hand stroked the tip while a digit from the other pressed against a thick vein protruding his shaft starting at base and moving purposely to the head. She fingered the slit. A bubble of delight popped out. Smiling she licked it off. Her tongue circled the head slowly one way then back before her mouth cupped it. She suckled.

Releasing him she bent and eased first one mound into her mouth, then sucked the other with extremely gently care. Following the artery trail from base to head she again consumed him with her fiery hot mouth.

Helplessly wondering if his legs would hold his weight, he enjoyed treatment the sexiest siren gave his penis. Sucking one hand pumped him rigid while the other kneaded his behind.

His hands tangled in her mass of curls splayed across her back.

He reached a pinnacle of ability to withstand torture and placed a hand on each side of her face, gently lifting it toward him. "We better change this game up, sweetheart. I have no intention of making it a one way showdown."

She smiled allowing him to push her onto her backside. Once there, he slipped her tank top over her head and laid it aside. A filmy, lace bra barely covered tips of her protruding breasts. With a flick of a finger, a catch between them released silk. He tossed it away exposing the most beautiful breasts he'd ever seen.

Taking a deep breath he grazed them, carefully at first and allowed his fingers to explore hard knobs standing at attention in delightful pink centers. Her hands came to her sides encouraging him. He manipulated them harder, exploring depth and firmness. Dipping for a taste, he licked circles around perimeter closer and closer finally reaching tips. Taking them in, he sucked while his hand continued fondling the other tit. Nipping it with a same measure of slow, careful study, he didn't want to miss any part of her.

Once he'd worshiped silky mounds to his satisfaction, and she moaned in pleasure, he trailed pecks southward to her taunt, flat belly. His hands splayed leisurely across smooth flesh and surrounded her slim hips then cupped her well-formed bottom displaying her privates upward delightfully. He examined delicious new territory with his eyes then the tongue.

She squirmed in his hands, sending shock waves to his cock, and filling it to brim. He lapped carefully every inch of precious meat then chewed ever so delicately. Finally delving his inside for a delectable, tasty treat, sweet and fine, he barely held his passion to wait.

Jaiden lay helpless in his embrace gripping him, lost in lusty pleasure, enjoying everything he gave. Nearing a cusp of explosion, her soft, husky voice panted.

"Please, I want you inside me."

Enjoying her marvelous body, he couldn't withhold the ultimate act from either of them any longer. She extracted a tiny package from her shorts pocket, ripped it open and grasped his steel erection in her hands sliding a thin layer of slick protection over him. Without hesitation, she guided him inside her.

Slowly, an iota at a time, he eased inside the woman he craved more than he'd ever wanted anything in his lifetime. Their gaze locked together and communication became unnecessary. Eyes spoke more than words.

Relishing increasing tightness to a hilt he pushed himself slower than he'd thought possible. Reaching the brink her lips opened with a sigh. Exhaling her nails bit into his hind-end gripping him tightly to her. With a wanton gasp she pressed against him urging his pace from slow to faster. They rocked together in a dance all their own.

Harder and harder they drove. Clay

rolled to his side and onto his back, bringing the sultry siren atop him straddling his cock. Her breasts pushed forward, and her back arched. Her head fell backward. The mane of wild curls flew from side-to-side. She rode him like a stallion bound and determined to win a race. Her eyes closed and her mouth opened. She gasped for air between lunges. The death grip her body held on his penis pounded harder and harder.

He could take no more. She gasped and held her breath. Her body went ridged. Her ass flexed tightly squeezing the very life from him. He spilled into the most delectable space he'd ever occupied. Her head jerked then rolled leisurely. Her arms stretched luxuriously. She collapsed on his torso.

Easing curls blanketing his face carefully aside, he breathed. A contented smile crossed his cheeks. His arms circled her naked shoulders, and he held her tight against him. His manhood remained buried deep within his woman. More than pure sex—it was the highest form of giving and receiving. He willed it to never end.

Jaiden drifted to sleep. Sure she was soundly relaxed he eased the sheet over them. Clay slept cradling Jaiden on top of him—if you call it sleeping. Mostly he lay listening to her steady breathing and watching her peacefully rest—in his bed—like she belonged there.

CHAPTER 4

Clay removed kitchen cabinets storing essentials in a carton. He contacted an electrician and scheduled an appointment for a quote. He met with a construction company and agreed to their price to replace roof and siding. They started the following day and assured him they'd complete work within a week. He repaired minor settlement cracks in walls and caulked nail holes where things had hung on walls. Once calking completely dried, he sanded repairs smooth. Walls and ceilings were ready for paint. Jaiden helped him choose a muted, off-white color for walls. He painted and finished the four rooms on the first floor.

Clay found the business card Sage had provided and rang the agent's number. "Carmen Burnett, Burnett Agency here—how may I serve you?" A female chipper voice sounded inviting.

Perfect. Clay needed a high-energy person anxious to market his property.

"Ms. Burnett, this is Clay Barnes. I want

to talk about selling my property."

"Mr. Barnes, if memory serves, you own a small farm at the edge of town. Right?"

Ms. Burnett was up on gossip. Staying informed was her job. Clay snickered at the small-town rumor mill. Nosy as *all get out*, folks meant no harm—at least most of them didn't. "That's me. My parents are deceased and left it to me. I may want to sell."

"Mr. Barnes, I was under the impression you accepted an offer from The Spence Development Firm. My client, Manley Spence, made a substantial offer."

Again he snickered. "Indeed, Mr. Spence's offer was interesting and far from insulting, but I've not accepted. I want to explore other options. I'm not anxious to sell to a developer. If I sell, I'd prefer a buyer keep the property whole. It's not a large farm, considering size of most estates in this area. It meant the world to my parents. I'd hate to see it subdivided."

"I see." Ms. Burnett sounded disappointed. Why would she care? Surely she'd make more commission selling his parcel herself, than with The Spence Development Firm selling single resident lots. Maybe not. He wasn't clear how real estate commissions are structured.

"Sage Benton gave me your card. She said you're the realtor of choice."

"Ah, Mrs. Benton is a darling woman. I helped her arrange purchase of her organic farm a few years ago. I'll thank her for the recommendation. How may I help you, Mr. Barnes?"

"I've done extensive renovations and would like you to take a look at the place. Estimate its market worth and possibly list it for sale. My crew completed a new metal roof and siding. I've refinished floors throughout and painted rooms. I hired professional remodelers to redo the bathrooms. They fitted new fixtures in both. I've replaced kitchen cabinets with quality ones and remodelers mount marble countertops this afternoon. New stainless appliances were installed and updated lighting throughout the house. I hung heavy, carved wooden doors to match the house's exterior. Wiring has been checked. So has the septic system. I've upgraded furnace and air conditioning and arranged a landscaping company to plant floral bushes and flowers and mulch wherever necessary. It's looking nice. By tomorrow it should be in perfect order for showing."

"I can come tomorrow morning for a walk through. We can talk commission and marketing. If you're ready, you can sign a listing contract to market your property."

"Sounds like a plan. How about 10 a.m.?"

"Perfect, see you then."

Clay hung up satisfied with his accomplishments, but torn about selling. Was he doing the right thing? He wasn't sure. One way to find out—keep moving forward.

♥♥♥♥

Ms. Burnett parked her luxury SUV behind the house the following day. Dressed to impress, she wore a pale-blue, linen suit showing off a slim figure and firm legs for a middle-aged woman. The attractive woman bore a hint of grey around temples of red, curly hair forced into submission into a French twist. Looking accomplished and self-confidant, she carried a navy, leather portfolio. Pale-indigo, kid-leather pumps looked inadequate for tromping across his ground to view the parcel.

"Good of you go come, Ms. Burnett. Allow me to take you on a tour of my house."

"Thank you for inviting me, Mr. Barnes. It's a pleasure having an opportunity to serve your real estate needs." She shook his hand with strength and confidence.

He led pointing out improvements. Returning to the kitchen, she laid her briefcase on a table where he paused. "May I offer you coffee or water?"

"Thank you, Mr. Barnes. I'd love a bottle of water." After serving her, Clay sat across from her. She revealed several brochures and a presentation. He sat quietly listening. She explained paperwork and described how she'd market the listing, what advantages she offered over others, and her fees. "I'd like to reserve pricing until we've completed our tour."

"Sure thing. Comparable information in your presentation helped me formulate my guess on a list price."

"Good, we'll pinpoint a price once we're done."

He led her out back. "I'm afraid muddy trails would ruin your lovely shoe." He glanced at her elegantly clad feet.

She smiled and marched to her vehicle. Opening the door, she retrieved her solution. "I've got it covered. I carry gym shoes for this purpose. One never knows when she'll be asked to walk perimeter of a property." She dropped the pair and slipped feet from her heels slipping them into leather sporty ones.

Clay was impressed with her anticipating his needs. He led to a path through woods behind a back yard. "I haven't found time to explore the acreage since returning other than a stroll my first evening before dark. I've been working on my house. No one has farmed since Dad died several years ago. I assume Mom let things grow out of hand. Likely small trees have sprouted in the garden. Pasture and hayfield need cutting. The large pond is full of cattails.

"No worries. You can pull cat tails and hire a farmer to bush hog fields and gardens."

"Sure, maybe you can recommend someone." She nodded.

Her long legs kept stride with Clay's step, pointing to features attractive to clients. A band of white pines stood to one side of a pathway. A magnificent magnolia tree centered a clearing near a pond. "This provides a lovely location for a picnic table or benches to give it a welcome, homey atmosphere."

"That's a wonderful idea." He studied his favorite boyhood swimming hole. "I love this spot."

An object caught his eye at the far bank.

"What the heck?" His voice muttered strutting around the bank. An eerie awareness washed over him. His pace quickened to running. A pile resembled a person as he neared.

His heart fell to his stomach and breath gushed from his lungs close enough to see clearly. Pounding footsteps hastened following behind then halting suddenly when he stopped with a jerk.

"What the hell?" His arms went out to each side, blocking her from passing. "This isn't good. Stay back." His voice took on a commanding doctor persona he'd perfected.

He stepped to a strange looking mound of fabric-covered flesh. Dark, red stains dried to a crisp on a white dress shirt. Dirt and falling leaves mixed with hardened goo clung to a stranger's face, chest and motionless arms. Greenish-grey textured tightening skin and stench from remains made it clear. He didn't need to test to ensure the gentleman was dead. Due diligence bent his knees. He examined the body searching for a pulse.

As he snapped his phone from its holster, he turned to Ms. Burnett. She was trying to get a glimpse of the corpse. "Is he . . . dead?" She went limp and ready to collapse.

He grabbed her arms offering support. Partially holding the distraught woman upright he nodded.

"It looks like Walter." She pushed forward a few steps to see his face. "It is—Walter Burnett—my ex-husband." Like a balloon losing air, she went limp in his arms and began trembling. He speed-dialed Sheriff Gordon.

"Wyatt Gordon." The familiar southern drawl of his friend gave Clay comfort.

"Wyatt, Clay Barnes. I found a body on my farm. We're in the woods behind my house. I'm here with Carmen Burnett. She says it's her ex-husband, Walter Burnett; and it appears he has been deceased for a few days."

"I'll be right there." Wyatt's chipper voice sprang to business mode.

Clay dragged the distraught woman to a downed tree. After brushing aside debris, he helped her to sit on the trunk. "Wyatt will arrive soon."

"Poor Walter, I wondered when someone would finished him."

That was an odd thing to say. Clay didn't want to impede Wyatt's investigation. He left it at that.

Sirens blared driving into his property. Before long several uniformed officers led by Wyatt filled the small clearing. Jaiden was in the group putting up the crime scene tape and securing the area. She smiled sadly and gave him a finger-wave. The men checked the area for clues, snapping photos and marking spots where they found, bagged and catalogued items of interest. The coroner arrived taking charge of the corpse once Wyatt and his CSI team had inspected it.

Eventually Wyatt escorted Clay and Ms. Burnett to the house where they stationed in his kitchen for questioning. It allowed the crime scene crew to finish working without witnesses under foot.

Happy in familiar ground away from the rotting cadaver, Clay inhaled his first normal breath. He'd seen cadavers during medical training. This was his first time coming in close contact with a decaying human carcass. The vision and putrid odor churned his stomach sending every nerve in his being aquiver. Even more impactful, he'd discovered the victim himself on his home ground. Deep breathing and concern for Ms. Burnett kept him from upchucking or passing out.

What was Mr. Burnett doing on his property anyway? Who killed him at Clay's home and why? Clay didn't even know Walter. It was a mystery he was sure Wyatt would solve.

Had this dead guy lain rotting the whole time since he'd returned? Was his ghost what caused Clay's angst about the farm? Maybe things would change for the better once they removed Walter's corpse.

Damn.

He hated the word.

CHAPTER 5

Clay poured cups of coffee then slumped into a seat across from Wyatt. Ms. Burnett had sat beside him quietly moaning occasionally, with dry, swollen looking eyes. She wore a pitiful look on her face.

Wyatt clasped his hands together on the tabletop and cleared his throat. "Ms. Burnett, I'm sorry for your loss." She whimpered. "Do you have any idea who might want your husband dead?"

She snickered with a sad smile then batting her eyes shook her head. "You're kidding. Right? Maybe I should list those in town who don't want him dead. The list might be shorter." Her voice cracked.

"I see. So—are you on the list?" His face was devout of emotion.

"Absolutely not." A hint at sorrow and maybe remorse clouded her eyes. Zach wished he knew what was spinning through her busy mind. "Sheriff, my ex-husband and I had our differences, but we long since pushed them aside. We shared many clients. To our advantage we buried the hatchet and got on with life. We've long ago shed anger for a cordial relationship."

"I see."

Clay understood Wyatt was skeptical but determined to check out Carmen's statement. It would be easy enough to find out how the exes actually got along.

"Do you have any idea what Mr. Burnett was doing on Mr. Barnes' property?"

"None what-so-ever, Sheriff. Other than business interactions, Walter and I led separate lives."

"What about you, Clay?"

Holding hands in front of him Clay protested. "Wyatt, I never laid eyes on the fellow before today. I wish I still hadn't. I have no clue what he was doing here. I've heard no disturbance on my property while living here and seen no one snooping around. He was dead for a while, from what I saw. What does the coroner say?"

"You're right. He won't know for sure how long until he gets Walter to his lab for more tests. Walter was definitely murdered, however. From our initial investigation, the scene doesn't appear disturbed. My men will be working the area for quite some time. Avoid the woods. If you find or see anything related, let me know; but don't disturb it."

"No worries, Wyatt. Wild horses

couldn't drag me into those woods now. I can't wait to clean up." Glancing at Carmen he eyed her wondering if it was proper under circumstances to ask her business questions.

What the hell.

"Ms. Burnett, I'm truly sorry for your loss. How might this affect my ability to sell?"

She studied floor tile for a few seconds then looked him straight in the eye. "Mr. Barnes, I appreciate the sentiment, though it's misplaced. I'd still take your listing, should you decide to sell. However, the property may have what we call a stigma attached to it. It means a certain population will walk away not considering it due to a murder on the premises. Others won't give a damn what transpired here. Also, should you decide to go with the developer who made an offer, he'll subdivide. That will more than likely eliminate buyer concerns since they wouldn't necessarily purchase the exact parcel where the killing took place."

"Well, I'd like to put it on the market soon as we clear this up and the crime scene is opened."

"Very well. I'll start an initial property search in preparation. We can list it when Sheriff Gordon gives you a right-of-way."

Wyatt allowed Carmen to leave and went back to work with his team, leaving Clay alone in the house except for ghosts he shared it with. Something had felt not right since Clay returned to his childhood home. Would the man in the woods haunt him too?

A murder on his property should have shocked him more, but he'd had a foreboding of sinister proportions since walking into the run-down farmhouse the first night. Finding money was a first odyssey raising its ominous head. Secrets filled the air.

Unproductive and in a funk since Wyatt left, he hoped he'd steer his mind and chores on track to get back to Chicago where he belonged. Or did he?

Late evening Jaiden quietly tapped on the back door startling Clay who sat staring at a cool cup of tea. He motioned her in. She opened the door and stopped. Jaiden's exotically beautiful face, dark tresses were forced into a severe bun and she wore little makeup. It would've been wasted on her, anyway. The half-Choctaw woman was stunning without aide of cosmetics.

She hesitated nervously in the opened doorway with her hands tucked in back of her utility belt. Jaiden looked marvelous regardless whether clad in jeans and a tee shirt, a feminine sun dress or her no-nonsense uniform adorned with a holstered pistol, club device and radio. His favorite would forever be Jaiden nude. Her spectacular body, even now, made his mouth water.

"Hey, how ya doing?" She spoke softly like he was fragile and might break at the slightest vibration. Her sweet Texan drawl was lyrical and welcomed as spring lilies.

Nodding he smiled. "I'm good—in shock, I guess. You finished up back there?"

"For now. Not sure how long we'll leave the crime scene tape up. That's a question for Wyatt. I'm sure he'll keep you posted. I'm supposed to be getting off shift about now, but heading to the station to go over evidence collected, organize the case and confer with the guys."

"Got time for a drink? I can make you tea or coffee."

She fidgeted nervously. "No, I best go."

Recollection set in. "Ah, I—I'm a suspect. Right? You can't socialize with a suspect."

Her sweet smile was comforting because she'd never lie to him. It wasn't Jaiden's style. "For now, but once the coroner nails down time of death, you'll likely drop out of running. You saw Mr. Burnette's corpse. It wasn't pleasant. He's been dead for a while. I'd wager since before you arrived."

"Yeah. I've seen plenty of dead bodies in my career. This guy was a sight I'll never forget—not what I'm used to. Thanks for checking on me."

"No problem. I was worried, and I wouldn't sleep well thinking of you distraught and wandering around this big old house alone."

He snickered. "Too bad you can't stay. You have talents to take my mind off anything."

Her weak smile broke into a full, blazing grin engaging sparkling, deep pools of chocolate brown in her eyes. Beneath her tawny skin pink rose on her cheeks. "Thank you, good sir. You have my permission to dream about me if it helps." She backed out tugging the door.

"No doubt I will. It's good knowing you're not opposed." He blew her a kiss, and it snapped shut. He locked the bolt as her slim hips swayed ambling to her cruiser. Safely inside she pulled from the driveway and her taillights vanished. He washed his cup and headed to bed.

He didn't sense danger though a killing had occurred on his property. He'd seen multiple wounds on a decaying corpse. Whoever killed Mr. Burnette wanted him dead with a passion. His killer wouldn't bother Clay. He felt certain.

Too bad Jaiden lie hot and wet in his bed tonight. His arms ached to hold her and his fingers tingled anticipating her silky skin. He wanted nothing more than to bury himself in the woman who had become part of him.

She must feel it too. She'd stopped to check on him. It meant something even if their fling was temporary. It was incredibly satisfying and real, nonetheless. At least after Jaiden's visit, he'd dream of her instead of ghosts and murderers. She'd join him in bed one way or another.

CHAPTER 6

Wyatt left his crew to finish working the crime scene once Walt's body was removed to the morgue. He arrived at Burnett's office surprised to find Sage's truck with her familiar *Parsley, Sage, Rose, Mary & Wine* banner on its doors. Entering a foyer he was greeted with a smile by Walter's smartly dressed assistant, Lisa Russell.

"Good day, Sheriff Gordon. What brings you to Burnette Mortgage Services?" She rounded a large wooden desk flanked by tall, frothy ferns with her hand extended. The pencil skirt displayed a slim figure with a crisp, white shirt tucked neatly in its narrow waistband. Her grip was dry and firm.

"I'm in town on business. My wife's truck's outside. Is Sage here?"

Lisa smiled cordially and waved toward Walter's closed door. "Indeed, Sheriff, she is waiting for Walter to arrive. I took her a cup of coffee. Would you like to join her? How do you take it?"

Obviously Lisa had no clue her boss was dead, and she'd be out of a job. If she knew, she was one hell of an actress. "Actually, it sounds terrific—black, please. Thank you, Lisa."

She nodded toward the door. "Go on in. I'll bring your drink." She opened a door on the opposite side and shut it quietly behind her.

Wyatt knocked. He tried the nob, and it opened.

Sage sat dressed for work in her usual uniform—cut-off jeans, socks, sturdy work boots, and tank top. She spun at the disturbance. Her black ponytail flipped around to rest against her back. A startled expression crossed the gorgeous face he'd die for.

"Wyatt, what on earth are you doing here?" She cocked her head looking confused.

"Better question—what are *you* doing here?" He strode toward where she sat. Her hands went out to him. Taking them he'd have sworn her energy shot into him like lightning, reinforcing his own strength with hers. He snuggled her into his arms and kissed those honey sweet lips he knew so well.

"I'm waiting for Walter." She glanced at her phone. "Damn it, he's half an hour late already. We have so much to do. I need to go soon. What in hell is holding him up? We scheduled this meeting two weeks ago, to start planning the fall harvest festival for the water walk park in town."

Easing his energetic, feisty wife into her

seat, his hands lingered on her arms. He knelt in front of her. Lisa chose the moment to enter with his coffee. She looked embarrassed having caught them in a personal instance.

"Lisa, I'm glad you joined us. Why don't you have the other seat there?" He nodded toward an adjoining visitor's chair beside Sage. Lisa sat with a dubious look on her face. "Good, I can tell you both at the same time. Walter won't come in today—or ever. His body was discovered today on Clay Barnes' farm."

Gushes of air hissed from the women. "Wyatt, what happened?" Sage's face morphed to gloom. Turning to the secretary she smiled sadly. "Lisa, I'm sorry for your loss."

"Body?" Was, the only word Lisa was capable of.

Nodding Wyatt took a fortifying breath. "I'm afraid, Mr. Burnett was murdered. Lisa, when did you last see him?"

"Actually, it's odd. He's been out of the office for two weeks now. He normally tells me if he's going out of town. I assumed he'd forgotten to inform me. I've kept pushing his appointments out making excuses with clients."

"How have you managed without him?"

"I know how to process most mortgage loans. I did those as usual. His special mortgages are a different story. They're delivered in envelopes marked PERSONAL," so I recognize them. I don't process those. Walter handles them himself. I've locked them in my desk drawer at night. There's a stack waiting for processing."

"I see."

"Wyatt, I found this under Walter's desk." Sage handed him a silver cat's paw charm and was engraved "*Daddy's pussy cat*," on one side. The o ring was open slightly explaining how it must've fallen off a bracelet of some sort.

"Cute." Dangling the broken charm toward her he eyed Lisa. "This yours?"

Lisa's face was blank. She shook her head. "No, but it looks familiar. I may've seen someone wearing it. But it's not mine."

Wyatt retrieved a small baggie and sealed the jewelry inside it, then slipped it into his pocket. He stepped toward Lisa's front desk.

"Sage, I'd suggest you go to work. You'll need to talk to the Mayor about getting someone else assigned to help you arrange the fall festival."

Sage followed, and he waited at the front of the building for her. Close, her soft, warm hand rested against his uniformed shirt. She fingered a pearly snap button.

"I'm sorry to hear about Walter. It's unexpected. I'll skedaddle. You have investigating to do on your case. Try to make it home early enough for a good night's sleep. I'll keep dinner warm. I love you, Wyatt." She tiptoed and kissed his lips. Sage tasted like spearmint and honey, two of his favorite things.

His hands slid around her slim runner's hips and rested against the base of her back. She leaned firm against him. He wished to lift and settle her long legs around his hips straddling what would inevitably result in an erection on contact. He could never get enough of his spicy wife.

"I love you, too, Sage. Thank you. I'll see you later." They knew it wouldn't be an early night, but hoped he'd have energy left to make love to his bride. He'd thought he was totally spent, and Sage had a way of breathing life into him. She pecked his nose then slipped out.

Lisa fidgeted nervously at her desk, acting nervous. Was she deciding whether to take her purse and go, or remain and try to work?

He took charge. "Lisa, I understand this is a shock. You'll be okay. I want your help. I will ask questions. Then I'm going to allow you to go home. Someone from the corporate underwriters will contact you soon to discuss future of this branch and your job. Okay?"

Nodding numb looking, she acted calmer. "Okay."

"Now then, tell me about your last interaction with Walter."

"Sure. It was a week ago Thursday, end of the day. Walter said goodnight. I left, locked up, and he went back into his private lair. He'd closed a large business deal, so I assumed he was working late to manage paperwork. He hasn't returned since. He hasn't called or anything. So I tried keeping things running smoothly."

"Okay, did anything happen that day or in preceding days seeming out of character or odd?"

She shook her head. "No, nothing strange, and Walter acted normal, like always."

"Any new clients you're aware of?"

"There are always new deals, but none in particular was out-of-order. It was business as usual."

"Did you sleep with your boss?" Wyatt had heard rumors Walter slept with every female in town willing to bare her thighs. Did his lechery end him?

The pale face of the lovely woman about twenty-two or three burned bright red. Her gaze left his toward the side. Her head shook. She met his gaze.

"No, sir, I did not sleep with Walter." A look of disgust came over her face and she shivered. "He was an okay boss, long as he kept his hands to himself. I made it clear when he first tried—there would be no hanky-panky. Damn, the geezer was old enough to be my grandpa. That's so . . . yucky." She shivered and blinked.

Wyatt couldn't suppress a slight laugh. He was old enough to be her dad. The fresh, spunky lady being hit on by a womanizing old fart angered him.

"Don't worry, Lisa. You won't have to endure his crap any longer. Walter won't pressure you again."

"Don't get me wrong, Sheriff. Walter was a gentleman after I made it clear we'd never be an item. He kept our relationship strictly professional."

"That's good to hear. Okay. Show me where your corporate information is. I'll notify headquarters. I suppose they'll close the branch until they audit it. Show me where your files and keys are. Then you're free to go. Lisa, if you need to leave town in the next few weeks, please notify me of your whereabouts."

"Sure, Sheriff, I'm happy to help."

After an hour going over files, contacts and rosters with Lisa, Wyatt contacted the company's CFO. The executive promised the company's Human Resources manager would reach out to Lisa and make arrangements.

♥♥♥♥

Stopping by the coroner's lab, Dr. Sanders was in the middle of his examination of Walter's body. Walter laid cold and grey on a stainless table. His chest was cut open and internal organs removed. Taking off his gloves Doc gave Wyatt a wave then walked to the sink to wash his hands. He removed his mask and approached Wyatt.

"I guess you know its murder. Right?" Sanders joked with a snicker.

"Nah, I figured Walter fired a gun into his own chest multiple times, so I'm going with suicide." Wyatt was used to the coroner's dry, abrasive humor. His counter brought a smile to Sander's face.

"He was a tough son-of-a-bitch. Ten rounds, all into his chest cavity. It was pretty much pulp."

"Did he have intercourse anytime near his death?"

"He did. You considering suicide, due to over-indulgence with the fairer sex?" He chuckled.

"Not sure if that's what killed him, but I heard rumors. I'm sure you did too. Walter was a horn dog in heat."

"Yes, I heard he'd hump anything with a split tail that stood still long enough."

"Evidence of intimacy?"

"Yes, even though decayed for some time before being found, semen showed up on his clothing. I also located a pubic hair that wasn't his inside his drawers. I'm testing both for DNA."

"Know how long he was dead yet?"

"The fifty-thousand-dollar question—and no, not yet; I need to run more tests. But he was deceased for several days, probably at least a week, maybe more. Lots of bugs and gooey critters to analyze before I nail down TOD."

"Anything significant you can tell so far?"

"I'd say he drank wine not long before he died, and this was a crime of passion. Not sure what kind, but someone hated this man enough to continue shooting long after he was dead. Passion was involved one way or another. A 22 pistol fired ten rounds at close range. This person knew him well enough to get close before pulling a weapon. The shooter was determined kill him."

Patting the shorter, balding man in on the back of his white lab coat, Wyatt grinned. "Thanks, Doc. Call me when you have a report and TOD."

Wyatt left to confer with his officers, examine and catalogue evidence collected. His work was cut out for him—a bitter task.

"People either loved or hated the murder victim, many on both sides. Maybe loved is too strong a word. Either people needed Walter, therefore associated with him, or they hated him because he was a philanderer. Was he killed by a scorned lover, a mistress's jilted partner, or did he wrong someone on a business deal? It's my job to find out."

"No worries, boss. We'll solve this." Jaiden looked confident.

Damn. "I hate these messy cases. Innocent people will inevitably be injured by what we'll uncover."

CHAPTER 7

Jaiden stood in front of a whiteboard
going over details with their team. "Walter
Burnette sold mortgages under a brokerage
Burnette Finance Company. Burnett is a final
leg in a much larger funding machine for
mortgage financing, much like most businesses
of its kind. Mortgages he arranged sold to stock

market investors. He basically packaged loans and arranged for the best source of funds among those in his access. He bundled and handed the sealed deal to a lending organization for premium collection. It's standard and not surprising."

Wyatt stood beside his deputy. "Burnette Finance Company worked under the FANCI Funding Corporation organization. I contacted their CFO last night. He agreed to send a forensic accountant to assess status and propose a plan of action to headquarters for managing and moving open deals forward."

Wyatt's phone rang at seven a.m. the following day. "Sheriff Gordon here," he muttered swallowing his first gulp of Sage's strong brewed coffee. They came together in their large kitchen after dressing for the day. Wyatt wore his standard summer kaki uniform with police gear attached.

Sage looked enticingly sexy bent over a counter in front of him. Long runner's legs supported her sweet fanny. Elbows leaned against the kitchen island. Frayed denim curled gently around the top of her slim thighs.

He ached to drag her back to bed to touch and kiss her delicate flesh once more. His hand slid across her buttocks around to her flat, firm belly. It was difficult recalling how large it had protruded the summer before carrying their son Ty inside her. Even then he'd been insatiable for Sage, finding her womanly, pregnant frame a sensuous delight.

She wiggled teasingly at his heat. His hand eased up to palm one plump breasts teasingly spilling toward the edge of her tank top. She moaned with desire and faced him deserting her cup of Joe. Her sultry grin and tongue snaked out licking her lip. She bit it gently making him long to hang up and slide inside her soft, wet crevice to relish her heat on him.

She nestled her nose beneath his chin, and her tongue lapped against his neck. Shivers of delight sizzled through him. He choked on his words. The phone still at his ear, he listened.

"Okay, so I'll see you in fifteen minutes." *Damn,* finally he hung up. His other free hand sped to its home around her backside. He cuddled his wife against his mounting erection. "See what you've done, you temptress?" He pressed himself harder against her flat tummy.

She grinned wickedly. "I'm innocent, Sheriff. I was merely drinking coffee trying to fortify myself for a day of dirty work in the field."

The diaper bag she'd packed sat on a countertop beside her under-the-bra sling holster and pistol. The weapon was part of Sage's uniform. She'd no sooner go without it as she would panties or a bra. Widowed during brutal slaying of her first husband on a New York City street. Moving to Kentucky, she had learned to protect herself and her critters.

Thank God she did. Sage was a danger magnet. She'd had defended herself and his daughter, Hailey, from a murderer the first summer; and a stalker had taken pot shots at her when Sage got too close to the truth about Wyatt's friend Dovie's problem. Sage had come to Riley's rescue when a break-in occurred at her house and a drug addict shot Riley's neighbor.

"Yep, I returned to Kentucky for the quiet life. Little did I know I'd fall for Lemon Sage Benton, and you'd rock my world and breathe life into my soul? I'll give you dirty work." His tongue buried in her ear. She trembled from his breath in the sensitive spot. "I don't have time for this."

"Sheriff, the boys can't do anything until you arrive, anyway. A few extra minutes won't hurt a damned thing." Her leg slid around his butt pinning him to her.

"You've got a point. It's my crime scene. They'll wait." His hands unlatched the buckle of her shorts and with a flick he slid them and a tiny lace thong to the floor between Sage's work-booted feet. Immediately his hand found her crotch hot and wet. He knew it would be. He eased his long fingers inside moist folds to the blazing core of the woman of his dreams.

She wriggled helping guide him. The whole while he splayed kisses across her neck causing shivers of anticipation to form goose bumps on her skin. With one hand he easily lifted her to sit on the countertop.

Her hands whipped his zipper open and exposed his throbbing rod. Merely less than an hour since he'd buried himself deep inside his woman, time didn't lessen his need. He was burning and stiff. He might explode if she didn't stop stroking with those indulgent hands of hers. How did a farmer have such smooth hands? *Thank God for work gloves and aloe.*

Sage knew his urgency and must've felt the same. She swiftly steered him to her crevice then gripped his ass with her hands meeting his lunge. A heavy sigh and her head lolled. Her eyes closed. She held him against her like life depended on it.

If the way he felt was any measure, it might. Their frenzied, forceful rhythm resolved to draw the very life from their bodies.

Nearing the brink of heaven and earth breath became a series of pants and huffs. Barely wasting seconds inhaling, their urgency for each other was so severe.

With a quiver he grew rigidly. Every muscle contracted. He completely submitted to his woman.

Sage tightened likewise. Her pussy gripped his erection like a vice forcing every drop of life-giving glory from him. He gave his entirety to her.

They clung together. Chins drooped against their lover's shoulders for a while, gaining air and alighting to earth once more. His woman's scent in all her naked glory with odor of his love on her skin was a heady fragrance Wyatt cherished.

A cry erupted from the other room. "Waaaa . . ."

They jerked and parted. She grinned and hopped down then bent to retrieve her shorts. "Your son's jealous. He wants Mommy to himself."

"The little tyke has a sixth sense. I bet he knows I haven't left yet." He kissed Sage's forehead. She zipped her shorts, and he belted his pants. "I better run. We'll continue this conversation tonight."

"Yeah, after Ty goes to bed. Love you, Wyatt. Be careful. Please?" She smiled warily and disappeared to tend their son.

"Always am, Sage. You be safe. We don't know this wasn't random yet. Take no chances. Tell Rose the same thing. I'll see you and Ty later. I love you. Kiss my boy for me."

"Love you, too." She blew him a kiss and rounded the door. He grabbed his go-cup of coffee and headed to The Burnette Finance Company.

Duty calls.

Wyatt's cruiser drove into the parking lot in front of The Burnett Finance Company. Ken Horn from FANCI Funding Corporation was sipping a coffee in his rental sedan. They exited vehicles and shook hands.

"Thanks for meeting me here, Sheriff, and for the call yesterday advising us what was going on. Apparently our CFO left several messages for Mr. Burnette during the last couple weeks. They went unanswered."

"Not a problem. I apologize for keeping you waiting." Wyatt removed Walter's key and unlocked the building. Entering he snapped light switches on leading the way.

"Not at all. I'm sure you have a full plate as sheriff of this delightful, little burg. Besides, I wasn't waiting more than a few minutes. It gave me time to answer emails."

Wyatt smiled inside wondering how Mr. Horn would take knowing he'd kept him waiting for one last fuck with his irresistible wife.

"Actually, I'd like to have dates and times for those calls. Please talk with your CFO today and ask him to email me a list. They might prove instrumental helping nail time of death."

"Will do. So this is Mr. Burnette's office. I understand from his secretary, Lisa, she handles most transactions. It's good, meaning things should've moved forward with outstanding mortgages since Mr. Burnette's demise."

"She told me much the same. However, Lisa said Mr. Burnett had a special mortgage file he managed. She called them BW files. Mortgagees drop or mail checks direct to Walter marked CONFIDENTIAL. Walter handled payments. In his absence, Lisa collected and kept them under lock and key. With Walter missing they haven't been processed."

"It's odd. I can't imagine what would warrant such action on loans we authorized."

Wyatt retrieved the bundle of sealed envelopes Lisa had shown him using Walter's keys from his pocket. "Here you go." He handed Ken a set he'd gotten from Lisa. "Here are keys for you to use—Lisa's keys. This set is evidence I retrieved from Walter's body. It's processed for fingerprints and DNA, so I brought it along. He kept an additional key on this set unlike any on Lisa's ring or extras locked in her desk. I figured it might go to the special file cabinet holding Walter's BW mortgages."

Wyatt unlocked all drawers in using the "*file*" marked key. One cabinet was left locked directly behind Walter's desk. Wyatt tried the extra unmarked key from Walter's personal bunch, and it worked. The file clicked open.

The drawer of hanging files was a neatly stored in alphabetical order by client last name. He ran his finger across tops to flutter folders apart glancing at names. Recognizing nearly every name on twenty-five-to-thirty folders, his quick glance highlighted a handful in his mind. He'd start with those.

"This must be the mysterious files. Mr. Horn, I'm leaving this to you to figure out. I want a complete report daily until you're finished with your analysis of the company's books. Call and use Lisa if you need her. Please be sensitive to the fact. This turn of events has her concerned for her job and financial future. I'd personally appreciate it if you'd try convincing your company to take care of the young woman. She's obviously devoted to her work, though she wasn't so sure about Mr. Burnette."

"That sounds fine, Sheriff. Please, call me Ken. Rest assured we'd love keeping Ms. Russell on if possible, while business is being either liquidated or sold to another manager. The new owner will decide whether to keep her on staff."

"I want a list of folks with BW loans active or paid off by end of the day. Email it to my office. When you figure out what was going on with those special liens, I want a summary in writing. Before you return to headquarters, I'll need to obtain a complete assessment of the state of affairs for this firm."

"I can do that, Sheriff. No problem. Thank you for your cooperation and help. I look forward to hearing you solved the crime."

"I'm a phone call or text away if you need me." Wyatt left the squirrely guy wearing a slim, grey suit over a crisp, white shirt, sitting at Walter Burnette's desk. The thick-glassed man seemed the type to enjoy numbers and details enough to prove highly effective at his job—a good asset to Wyatt in this case.

Wyatt spent the morning into mid-day working with a couple of his officers on details creating a murder-board and determining how to move the investigation forward. Leaning over a series of photographs from the scene, Jaiden's belly complained loudly. She grabbed her gut and turned a lovely shade of purple without complaint. He glanced at his watch. It was well past lunchtime.

"Damn, time flies when you're having fun. You must be famished. How about I run over to Sadie's and grab us a bunch of burgers and fries? Anyone up for dessert? She makes blackberry cobbler on Tuesdays." He glanced around at men working in the bullpen. None of them had taken a break from since arriving.

"Sounds good to me." Jaiden laughed. "I'll have dessert, too."

A few minutes later he was out and skipping across Main Street into The Royal Diner. He spotted his lovely wife sitting at a corner booth flipping through a seed catalogue. Sage smiled brilliantly seeing him enter. He sauntered to her table and slid his long frame into her booth after giving her sweet lips a peck.

"Hey, Baby, I'm surprised to see you here. Where's Ty?"

"I left him with Rose napping under a tree in his playpen while she weeded. We needed goat food from the feed store, so I decided to treat Rose and me with Sadie's burgers."

"No wonder this place centers our little town. No one can resist Sadie's cooking." He gazed around the retro diner. Black and white tile held vinyl and chrome chairs, stools and booths. Dazzling sparkles in white Formica® surfaced counter tops and tables. The place was packed with friends and neighbors enjoying Sadie's food.

Sadie delivered dishes to a nearby table and nodded acknowledging she'd seen his entrance. The epitome of an old fashioned waitress, Sadie fit perfectly in any café between 1920 and the present, intentionally portraying a character in pink and white uniform dress and apron complete with a tiny white cap. Red, curly locks teased into a French twist in back, and her bright, red—painted lips inevitably chewed a wad of gum. She spun around then returned to Sage and Wyatt's table delivering tall glasses of iced water and silverware.

"Actually, Sadie, I need an order to go." Wyatt handed her his list. "Can you bag this up for me to take back to the station?" He sipped the refreshing water handing her his list.

"Me too, Sadie. Two burgers with everything and two orders of onion rings to go for me and Rose then I need to return to work and Ty."

"No problem, ya 'all. Too bad you didn't bring your young'un. It's been a coon's age since I've seen the sweet young'un. How's baby Ty doing?"

"I normally would've brought him, but he was napping. I figured I'd do this errand before he woke up. He's with Rose."

"Tell sweet Rose hello for me. Will ya?

I'll bring your meals in a jiffy. Ya 'all just hang out now, and chat while I place your orders. I'll be right back. I want to talk with you since you're here." She winked at Wyatt.

"Sadie has the most pronounced southern accent and colorful vocabulary of anyone I knew, and she loves to lay it on thick." Sage laughed at the slow wiggle of the pink-uniformed, middle-aged woman waltzing away from them.

"That she does. She's sincere and good-hearted, if she is queen of local gossip." The older woman was like his second mother, and his mama's best friend their whole lives.

"Funny thing about our little town's gossip mill—they mean well. Most subscribe to it not for negative, but ensuring fellow citizens well-being. Folks jump to defense or aid of townspeople in need. With her diner being town focal point, Sadie is privy to everything going on."

"True, many times, she's provided leads helping me solve crimes." Wyatt snatched and sandwiched Sage's hand between his. He rarely resisted an urge to touch her.

Sadie returned and smiling nodded Sage's direction. Sage shifted so Sadie slid in beside her. "Thanks, hon. Wyatt, I need to talk with 'ya about Walter Burnette."

"Okay, Sadie, you sure you want to do it here?" He glanced around at the almost filled dining room.

Her gaze followed his and returned with

a smile. "No worries, hon. What I say ain't no secret around here. I wanted to tell ya 'all I'd done business with old Walter. I had problems getting access to enough cash last year. My roof started leaking, and my A/C went out. I needed a new heating and air-conditioning system. The room needed to go down to plywood replacing flooring. It came at a bad time. I tried getting money from my bank. They said I was mortgaged too high. I bitched to the mayor. He suggested I talk with Walter. Walter crunched numbers and arranged a second mortgage with a higher than bank offered rate. The old boy came through for me in a pinch. He called it a BW loan—special for such circumstances. It's the same type lien he gave the mayor to open his storage business."

"I was glancing through Walter's special file for BW loans this morning working with his corporate auditor. I noticed your name on a file. I saw Mayor Ken's name. Tell me about your loan. How does it work?"

She shrugged and scrunched her mouth for a second. "I guess like any other, except I either mail or drop off a sealed envelope at his office with payment marked *Confidential*. I didn't see any other difference."

"Yes, Lisa told me about the Confidential envelopes. Walter personally processed BW payments."

"Yeah, well, the old boy cared for my needs. That's all I wanted to say."

"And this debt will be paid off when?"

"Oh, no worries. I paid it off in ten months. I figured total owed and split it into my own even payments—way more than required each month. I wanted that sucker gone. It was worth biting a bullet and getting her done. You know?"

"I see, so that's a good thing. So you have no ill will for Mr. Burnette?"

"Heaven to Betsy, no. If anything, I'm grateful to him."

"Did he make a pass at you, Sadie?" Sage tilted her head and a brow shot up, indicating she'd accept no wishy-washy answer.

Sadie laughed and slapped her leg. "Sure enough. The old son-of-a-bitch had snooty taste. He chased women in every direction. His horn-dogging ended his marriage to Carmen. He preferred 'em younger. Hell, I'm about the same age and married. But yeah, he tried fancy moves on me." She acted impressed more than pissed.

"How did it make you feel?" Sage placed a hand over one of Sadie's older ones.

"Honey child, I've still got it. I know. It felt good knowing even an old dog in heat recognized it. It did my heart good getting a chance to turn the loose cannon down. He didn't let it interfere with our business though."

"You're something else, Sadie." Sage patted her hand and released it.

"What about the mayor? You said he has a BW loan with Burnette."

Sadie shook her head and pursed her lips. "I don't know much about it. He financed his business with a loan. I'd guess it's still active. Business has done well, but he invests proceeds into expansion, rather than paying down outstanding debt. You best ask Mayor Bailey yourself."

"I'll do it. Thanks for the information, Sadie. Anything else?"

She hopped from the booth. "Nope, and your orders are ready. I'll fetch 'em and meet you at the register."

"That was enlightening and good news. I'd hate to think of Sadie being taken advantage of. She has a good head on her shoulders and knows well how to run a successful business." Sage slid out of the booth.

Wyatt placed a hand to the small of her back guiding her toward the register. "Yep, Sadie's like you in a lot of ways. I'd pity the person who tried to wrong her. Fortunately, everyone loves her."

Sadie arrived with Wyatt's large bag and Sage's small one. He tossed her a credit card. "Take it all out of that." Turning to his wife's smiling face he grinned and kissed her sweet lips soaking up nectar to sustain him. "It's a pleasure treating you and Rose to lunch. Give her a hug and thank her for watching Ty. It was an unexpected treat seeing you in the middle of a day."

"Thanks, Sweetheart. I love you. Take care." Sage snatched her bag, tiptoed for one last sweet kiss then scampered out.

Wyatt watched her walk, enjoying the

view from behind. Long legs carried her slim frame toward her pickup truck parked outside. Her dark ponytail swayed to the tune of her hips rocking from movement—a sight he'd never tire of.

"You're one hell of a lucky bastard, Wyatt. That woman's worth your weight in gold." Sadie grinned at his undoubtedly silly expression.

"You're right, Sadie." He bent across the counter and kissed the redhead's rosy, painted cheek, causing a blush on her pale skin. "But I love you, too."

She stepped from behind the counter and flicked his ass with a dishtowel plucked from her waistband. Laughing, the sting hit the target. He jumped. She tucked the towel back into place.

"Get that sweet ass of yours back to work, you smooth talking devil."

Exiting, he wasn't sure who laughed louder—the crowd of friends and neighbors dining in the café, Sadie or Wyatt. His excursion provided a mood-lifting treat revitalizing him and fueling his investigation.

Later in the day poring over documents in his in-box from the forensic auditor and the CFO of the FANCI Funding Group, Wyatt's phone rang. "Sheriff Gordon here," he mumbled barely paying attention.

"Sheriff, you must help me. I need my money and the damned corporation froze Walter's assets. So did the bank. You must convince them to release my cash. I have bills to pay."

"What the hell? Who is this?" He recognized the voice but couldn't place it.

"Sorry, Sheriff, Carmen Burnette here, Walter Burnette's ex-wife. My alimony check should've deposited into my account yesterday. The damned company won't release Walter's check. He owes me. I depend on my check. I contacted Walter's bank in town too, to see if they'd make it up out of his savings or checking account, and they've done the same thing. How am I supposed to pay creditors if my income is severely cut by this? You must convince them to release my money."

"Calm down, Mrs. Burnette. I understand your dilemma. It is standard procedure when someone dies. Assets are frozen until a court hearing filing probate. The judge may grant an executor of the estate rights to pay outstanding debts with current proceeds, and will determine how funds will be distributed. I'm not sure who was named responsible or if there's a will involve. No one has a right to make payments with Mr. Burnette's estate at this time. Besides, since it is a finance business, the mother corporation has a fiduciary obligation to investigate all books and ensure the operation was managed properly. They'll be quick about it, I'm sure. They want outstanding loans The Burnette Funding Corporation handled promptly."

"What about me in the meantime? I have a mortgage and debtors who want payment now."

"Mrs. Burnette, I'd love to solve your problem, but I can't. I suggest you talk with your banker and arrange a short-term solution until your assets are released."

"Damn the son-of-a-bitch. He's screwing me even in death." She clicked her phone off without a good bye.

Wyatt snickered to himself. Jaiden eyed him curiously. "The grieving widow pissed the estate stopped her alimony check."

"It's always about money—this case probably is too. Follow the money. Find a murderer." Her head nodded. She went back to studying items in front of her.

♥♥♥♥

Late afternoon Wyatt received a list of BW mortgagees. He gave his team the lowdown. "Mostly mortgages but a few used businesses for collateral. Technically they're commercial loans. I counted twenty eight, including those closed. The list is of well-know, highly respected businessmen and women in Sweetwater. It in itself isn't surprising."

"No, not really. Walter Burnette ran a well-established business for many years and was among esteemed entrepreneurs in our area well-thought of—at least professionally." Jaiden glanced from her notes.

"The way BW loans were managed surprises me. Clients submitted loan request forms. Walter duplicated those changing data and boosting assets and income. Making it appear a client was doing better financially with more ability to repay a loan than existed. This allowed a client to qualify for a loan he or she was not technically suited for."

"So he was over-funding loans. How did this benefit him?" Jaiden's forehead scrunched up.

"Walter did all closings personally. He received closing documents from funding organizations backing loans. He doctored them before sharing them with a client. He charged more closing cost up front, initiated non-existing points on a loan gleaning more up-front monies from clients. And he doctored interest rates to higher ones increasing payments by one-to-two-hundred-dollars each."

"No damned wonder he managed payments coming in." A lightbulb must've gone off in Jaiden's head, understanding how cash flow benefitted Burnette.

"Yes, Walter made an additional two-to-five-thousand dollars up front. He capitalized from one-to-two-hundred-dollars extra per month from payments. Client checks were deposited into a special checking account. Then he wrote payment checks for actual amounts due to funding organizations."

"You must admit, the guy was brilliant." Jaiden leaned back, crossed her feet and laid her head into a cradle of her hands locked behind it.

Deputy Ted Carnes laughed and shoved Jaiden's elbow. She toppled sideways, and he laughed. The rest of Wyatt's crew joined in chuckling. Jaiden snickered while gaining her balance.

"Like 'em smart, huh, Jaiden? I'd loved to have seen that old coot hit on you. He wouldn't stand a chance. Bet the doctor fella, Clay Barnes, you're sweet on is smart too."

"Smarter than you, asshole." Jaiden flicked Ted the finger. Everyone hooted loudly.

"He's a suspect, you know. You can't play house with a suspect." Ted looked jealous.

Funny.

Wyatt had never noticed the guys eyeing Jaiden before. She'd come into his staff like a bang, filling Leah's position with expertise. She learned the tough way being a half-breed teenager in Texas, and the rest as a Texas Ranger. He hadn't noticed his men treating her differently or trying to romance her. They'd acted more like they admired and respected her. Jaiden had earned it.

"I'm a professional, Deputy Carnes." She glared down her nose at Ted.

"I never doubted it, Deputy Coldwater— not for a second." His sideways smile came with a couple of pink cheeks forcing him to avoid Jaiden's eyes.

She'd accepted Wyatt's offer for the

deputy position while recovering from wounds received during an impressive takedown in Texas with her partner. Living with her mother, Brightleaf Coldwater, and brother, ex-Navy Seal, Calvin Coldwater, had allowed her mom time to pamper and nurse her back to health. Jaiden healed then went undercover as a punk, drug-pushing, college girl helping Wyatt shut down a drug ring.

She hadn't dated around much since moving here. But she'd had a friend-with-benefits arrangement with Moggie Larrs, manager and now owner of Fuller House Farm. At least they were lovers. Then Moggie fell head-first for Dovie Fuller, his boss's granddaughter and assumed heir to the farm he inherited.

Boy it was a debacle Wyatt would never forget. He worried about how it would work out from a relationship standpoint.

Jaiden was quite a woman. Somehow she'd befriended Dovie. She and Moggie had morphed into being best buddies these days.

No fireworks like Wyatt had anticipated, especially knowing how explosive redheaded flirt, Dovie could be. He'd have laid odds the two females would tear each other's eyes out and old Moggie would fear for his life if he ever spoke with Jaiden again. None of that happened.

Funny how life played out sometimes.

CHAPTER 8

Jaiden sauntered into his opened door and leaned against a desk. "Got a sec, Boss?"

"You know it, Jaiden. You don't have to ask. Take a seat."

His deputy eased into a chair across from him holding a stack of files. Using the list you gave me of subscribers to Walter's BW loans, I cross-referenced it against registered gun records specifically looking for a 22. Doc confirmed a 22 shot killed Burnette. Or many shots if you will."

Wyatt felt a sick ache in the pit of his gut. "Yep, ten shots to the chest with a 22 pistol—a lot of anger there."

"Sure enough. Anyway, I discovered the ex-wife; Carmen Burnette owns a 22 pistol. So does Mayor Kenneth Bailey. They're on the list, so suspect. I checked the kids I chased from Clay's farm a couple weeks ago. After interviewing all three separately, they confirmed my suspicion. The body wasn't present the day they partied. Individually they described where they roamed around and what they did. Their stories jived."

"It's slightly better, anyway. It should help confirm an actual date of death. I'll run it by Doc later. I need his results anyway. I prefer doing it in person in case I have questions. Want to ride along? We can stop and check out the mayor's gun and Carmen's too, before seeing Doc." He grabbed his hat.

Jaiden popped up with a smile. "That would be good."

A few minutes later climbing into his cruiser he posed the question he'd hesitated asking around his staff. "You called it Clay's farm sparking of intimacy. You and Barnes were chummy before Walter was discovered on his farm. Right?"

She shrugged and blinked not meeting his eye. "Yeah, I guess you could say that. But I've not spent time with him since. I won't until we're sure he's not a suspect."

"No problem. It's what I expected of you. For what it's worth, I hope we clear it up sooner, rather than later. I doubt Clay had anything to do with it, but we must be certain."

"Yep, we do. And thanks, Boss. I appreciate your confidence."

"Jaiden, you're the most honorable woman on my force." He patted her hand.

She grinned the stunning smile that sent tough males over the brink—not Wyatt, of course. Sage was all the woman he could handle. "I'm the sole woman on your force."

Wyatt shrugged and laughed. Jaiden joined in.

♥♥♥♥

Wyatt knocked on Doc's door bracing himself for the inevitable scent of the coroner's lab.

"Enter," Doc Sander's booming voice shouted as they did. "Wyatt and Deputy Coldwater, it's good to see you. I've expected you, since I texted you about finishing the autopsy report.

"What 'cha got for me?" Wyatt moseyed toward the older gent in a white lab coat.

Doc Sanders slid a body drawer shut. He grinned with latex gloved hands on hips. He removed and dropped them into a nearby trash can then strode toward his desk in a corner. Wyatt and Jaiden followed and sat across from him in chairs he waved them toward.

Opening a folder on his desktop he smiled. Wyatt figured he was gearing up for a good-hearted razzing. He'd be more explicit than necessary attempting to gross Wyatt and Jaiden out.

"The corpse was cold and rigor mortis had subsided. The body was discovered sometime after seventy-two hours of death. Enzymes in his pancreas had digested itself, and body had reached gruesome odor and appearance."

Doc leered eagerly. Wyatt nodded acknowledging agreement before going on. Wyatt cringed recalling the putrid scent of the rotting corpse.

"Decomposition was at green substance state emitting methane and hydrogen sulfide. Insects harvesting tissue and fly eggs had hatched. Subsequent maggots feasted on tissue in second stage, burrowing into the corpse, spreading enzymes, and turning mass to goo. Maggots consumed between sixty-to-seventy-five percent of body matter. Time of death estimated at twelve-to-fourteen days before discovery, around the twenty-third."

Wyatt removed his hat and wiped sweat from his forehead with back of his arm. His gaze shifted to Jaiden who had blown out a couple of heavy signs during the grizzly description. Her dark complexion paled to light grey since entering the morgue but held her ground. Most folks, even seasoned cops, sometimes up-chucked in the trash at the reality of a body in such bad shape or listening to the minute details of decomposition. The gal was a pro, and Wyatt was lucky to have her beside him.

Wyatt would've stopped Doc sooner and asked him to get to the point, but it would delay getting what he needed from the man. He whispered to Jaiden. "The only case he spared me gruesome details of was Becky and Bonnie Henderson's death. The mother and daughter perished in a house fire a few years back. That hit too close for comfort. Justin Henderson is like my brother, and everyone in town loved Becky and Bonnie. Doc dropped dramatics and went straight to TOD and cause." Jaiden snickered and listened quietly.

"Geez, Doc, I knew you'd make me listen to gory specifics. I swear. You get a bang out of grossing the rest of us out."

Doc Sanders snickered. Wyatt and Jaiden chuckled, and he joined them.

"You can't begrudge an old man his moment in the spotlight. Can you, Wyatt?"

"What Doc says jives with our timeline so far. I chased partying kids from the abandoned farm a few days before the victim was slain."

"It's a good thing. We've more pressing lines of investigation to follow first. If we need to, we'll come back to the kids later. Hopefully we'll uncover the culprit before then."

"Agree." The look on Jaiden's face exhibited relief, exposing her good-hearted nature.

Wyatt handed the bracelet to the coroner. "You recognize this?"

A disappointed look came over Doc's face. "Sorry, Wyatt. I don't recall seeing it. Did you find it at our crime scene?"

"No, Sage found it underneath Walter's desk in his office." He pocketed the bag. "Thanks for your time and help, Doc. Send the report to my email. Will you?" He shook the examiner's hand. Jaiden followed suit and traced his steps leaving.

"You two come back anytime. I love company."

"Maybe we'll do lunch somewhere." Wyatt winked and waved. They backed out closing the door.

Jaiden giggled. "Is he always like that?"

"No, it's rare he gets to strut his stuff around here. Sweetwater doesn't see many homicides. Doc Sanders seldom sees such a case. He'll play it for all it's worth. It's best to humor the old goat and let him crow."

"He was certainly having a field day with us in there."

♥♥♥♥

A few minutes later Wyatt knocked on his office door after an assistant told him Mayor Kenneth Bailey was in and free.

"Come in." The older man's bolstering voice rang loudly through thick wood.

Wyatt swung the door wide and approached a large oak desk with his hand extended. "Thanks for seeing us on short notice, Mayor Bailey."

Kenneth shook Wyatt's hand standing and extended it to Jaiden. She gripped it firmly shaking it. No nervousness or unnecessary moisture infused Mr. Bailey's grip. He pointed to the visitor's chairs in front of his desk, and they sat.

"Not a problem, Sheriff Gordon. What can I do for you and Officer Coldwater today?"

"Ken, I need to ask a few questions regarding the Walter Burnette case."

Ken leaned back in his chair and leaned elbows on armrests. His hands came together fingering a rubber band he played with. "Certainly, how may I help?"

"Officer Coldwater checked registrations and the concealed weapon licenses against the list of folks doing business with Walter Burnett—particularly what he called BW loans. Our records indicate your ownership of a 22 pistol. Would you mind allowing us to examine the weapon?"

"Indeed, I'd be pleased to show the baby off. He whipped around and opened wooded doors on a back wall of his office. An impressive display of antique firearms was displayed behind a glass wall. He inserted a key from his desk into a lock and opened the glass. Pulling out a small pistol he handed it to Wyatt proudly.

"Here you go. This beauty is a Remington Saw Handle Vest Pocket Derringer.

I paid a thousand dollars for her at auction. It's a 22 with a three-and-quarter-inch barrel and a fair, dark bore. Metal is original nickel with most finish intact and slight scaring on the wood frame handle—not enough to deter value. She's in pristine condition."

Examining the weapon, Wyatt let out a relieved sigh. "She's an excellent piece, Ken. No wonder you're proud. When was the last time you shot her?"

"I've never shot this gun." He acted appalled with big eyes.

"It's certainly clean as a whistle." Wyatt eyed down the barrel. It was evident the weapon hadn't fired in a long time. This isn't the murder weapon.

"Mayor Bailey, do you own any other 22 weapons, maybe unregistered?" Jaiden fished.

"Absolutely not. This collection is my pride and joy. I own a couple of hunting rifles kept at home in a safe, but no 22s. Why?" Recollection showed on his face. "Walter was killed with a 22?"

They nodded. "Yes." Wyatt revealed the clear bag with the delicate charm contained inside. "You ever see this before?"

The mayor examined it with a blank stare. "Sorry to say, I can't help you. I don't recognize it. Anything else I can do for you?" His hand shook when he returned the pouch to Wyatt.

"Actually, you can." Wyatt handed the gun to its owner and waited for Kenneth to lock it up and return to his seat. "I understand you took out a BW loan with Walter to fund startup of your storage unit business. Tell me about it."

"Yes, I did. There's not much to tell. I tried getting a bank loan. Without substantial cash or free and clear property for collateral, they refused. I went to Walter. He ran numbers and said my property did not sufficiently back a regular mortgage—same thing my bank said. He had a BW loan program that would work. It was a bit more expensive to take out with a higher than normal interest rate, but it was doable. My business is thriving. I've since used income to expand. So I'm still carrying the loan. It's convenient because Walter manages the program personally. I felt I was in good hands. Why do you ask?" He acted perplexed.

"We're investigating all outstanding loans Walter managed personally making sure nothing strange connected to his death." Wyatt made notes.

"So you're happy with your BW loan and Walter's service?" Jaiden eyed the mayor critically.

"Indeed." The mayor linked his hands together on his bulbous belly.

"Great. Do you know of anyone displeased with Walter's service?" She stared into his eyes.

He sighed heavily. "Can't say I do. Several businesspeople in town used Walter's services. None of them indicated they're unhappy. Rumors circulate around town about

Walter's philandering, however. Some folks aren't keen on Walter on that account."

"Anyone in particular you know of?" Jaiden was like a dog with a bone.

He groaned heavily exhaling. "I hate to point fingers. It's probably not the people who killed him. If it'll help solve the case and ensure our citizens they're safe, I'll share what gossip I heard. Walter's and his ex-wife, Carmen Burnett's assistant wasn't too happy with him. You know her—Gwen Russo. Carmen found out and fired her. Carmen filed for divorce. Bea Sanders, the owner of Beauty and The Bea, wasn't too fond of Walter either. She broke up with her business partner, Candy Wrigley, after learning they were both sleeping with Walter. Maybe you should talk to those two."

"What were you doing on the 23rd, Mayor?" Jaiden looked up from her pad.

Kenneth removed his day planner from his lap drawer. Flipping back a few pages he ran a finger down the page Jaiden inquired about. "I had a breakfast meeting with the city council ending around eleven. Then I met with the town attorney, Clayton Fuller, for an hour. I ate lunch with my aide at Sadie's from noon-to-one. Then I drove to Bonnyville and met with several other mayors about issues our small towns share in common. We're looking for solutions. We do it once a year. We finished at five. Dinner was served. The State Representative joined us. After dinner we met with him airing concerns and talking politics. Around nine thirty I drove and arrived home around eleven. I drank a cocktail then hit the hay." His glanced met Wyatt's.

Wyatt was satisfied with what sounded like sufficient alibi to take him off his suspect list. His day was easily confirmed, and he knew Wyatt would check every detail. Jaiden captured the list of activities in her notes.

"Good to hear." Wyatt shook Kenneth's hand again. "Thanks, Kenneth. You helped."

"My pleasure. See you later, Wyatt. Kiss Sage for me. Nice seeing you, Deputy Coldwater."

"Goodbye, Mayor. It was a pleasure." Jaiden accepted his hand in a shake.

As they entered the coroner's lab door Jaiden grinned. "That was an interesting visit with the mayor."

"Indeed. We can rule him out. His weapon for sure, and it sounds like we can verify his alibi with a few quick calls. He pointed to a couple of others we can investigate sooner rather than later since it seems these BW mortgagees had affairs with Walter. We'll check out Gwen Russo and Bea Sander later."

"Sounds good."

♥♥♥♥

They drove first to visit Gwen Russo. "Gwen worked for Carmen and Walter when they were married. They shared adjoining offices in a building and an assistant—Gwen. Carmen discovered Walter was sleeping with Gwen. She broke up their business arrangement and filed for divorce. From what I understand, it was bitter and vindictive. Some say she took him for a bundle. From the way she acted on the phone, she's raking in a sizable alimony payment regularly."

Jaiden whistled, thumbing through bank records she collected. "Walter was paying her five-thou a month in alimony. Oddly, it's drawn on a business account instead of a regular checking or saving account."

"No wonder she was worried. That's an enormous figure." Wyatt mused.

"Looks like she'd be out of debt with such an income plus what she earns on real estate sales. Folks sure don't know how to live within their means. Most of them spend more when income increases." She bit inside her jaw studying papers.

"See anything else unusual?"

"Yeah, sort of. Carmen was getting some other kind of payment from Walter. Sporadic amounts varied each deposit over the last six months. Not counting alimony Walter paid Carmen a hundred-thousand-dollars." She looked confused.

"It sounds like commission or kick-back payments. Maybe he owed a large sum from their divorce settlement, paying it off over time. We'll find out."

"Yes, we need to clear it up for sure."

Wyatt parked in front of the mayor's storage facility. Mayor Ken kept an official business office opened in the front building. "Carmen fired her, and Ken hired Gwen to manage his operation and handle whatever other personal business he has. She keeps regular hours."

She was behind a desk. "Good afternoon, Sheriff Gordon." Gwen greeted them with a hand extended for a shake. Wyatt gripped it, shook and released then she extended it to Jaiden. "What brings you and Deputy Coldwater in here? Are you looking for storage or the mayor?" She sat behind her tan metal and Formica desk surrounded by tan metal file cabinets. It was a much less elegant office space than she'd managed for the Burnette's.

"Neither, Ms. Russo. We're here to see you." She indicated a couple of metal chairs along a wall. Wyatt grabbed them and yanked them toward front of her desk. Jaiden sat, and he did the same.

"What on earth for, Sheriff?" She tried hiding her tremble, visibly taken aback by their visit.

"Concerning Walter Burnette's murder, have you seen this before?" He handed her the plastic bag containing a silver cat's paw charm.

Turning it over and over she studied it. "It looks familiar, but honestly, I have no idea where I saw it. I think I've seen it before." She returned the bag.

Pocketing it, Wyatt sighed. "Let me

know if it comes to you." He passed her a business card with his phone numbers on it. Jaiden did the same. "You can contact either of us if you recall anything that might aide our investigation."

"Sure, Sheriff, I'm happy to. But you must understand, since I was fired, I've had no contact with either Mr. or Mrs. Burnette. We had an unpleasant parting of ways. That was it. We've had nothing to do with each other since."

"Are you bitter?" Jaiden placed her hand gently on Gwen's desk reaching out to her. Her words soothed, sounding caring.

"I wouldn't say bitter. I'm disgusted for allowing myself to be drawn into their drama. I fell for fancy words backed by absolutely no sincerity. I deserved to lose my job, and I deserve Carmen's hatred and distrust. I can't believe I believed that silly man's line. Hindsight is clear. I wish I had a do-over, but I can live with fall out."

"Were you angry with Walter?" Jaiden cooed in her soothing Texas drawl.

"Walter? Hell no. He was what he was— an ass. I let myself slip into his trap. It was a lesson learned. But no, I don't blame him. You can't hand feed a tiger without expecting him to bite." She snickered. "You think I killed him? I couldn't do it. I couldn't kill anyone."

"Where were you on the twenty third?" Wyatt braced his palms on thighs.

She glanced at a calendar. "I was here all day. We sold several storage containers owing back-payments. A decent crowd attended an auction. I did a ton of paperwork, came in early and left late. I ordered food from Sadie's diner. One handyman helping out ran to pick up lunch. Security cameras should vouch for my whereabouts."

"Good, that's helpful, Gwen. I'm glad to hear it. We need a copy of the security tape. Locate it and call my office. One of my deputies will pick it up." Wyatt stood to leave. Jaiden did also.

"No problem, Sheriff. I hope you find whoever killed Walter. He was a pig, but I didn't wish him dead. And it's scary thinking of a murderer roaming around free." Gwen paced to the door with them. "I'll find the tape and drop it off at the station on my way home. It's on the way."

"That'd be great, Gwen." Wyatt smiled and exited followed by his deputy.

♥♥♥♥

They drove toward Burnett Real Estate Agency. Jaiden wrote and went over notes. "We're knocking them off our list. I'd say Gwen isn't suspect. You agree, Wyatt?"

"Yep, and I sympathize with her. It's tough when your employer hits on you. Had she been a vindictive type, she could've filed an extremely lucrative lawsuit against the Burnette Finance Company and Walter Burnette specifically for sexual harassment. Courts take it seriously these days. She had what sounds like a solid beef."

"A grieving ex-widow now tops our list. You think she's good for it?" Jaiden eyed him from the side.

"Who knows? She has a temper. She's raging about her money being tied up. She was volatile during their divorce; but they shared many clients in common, with Walter lending and Carmen in real estate sales. Things seemed calmer between them, and they acted civil. We'll find out soon enough." Wyatt stopped the cruiser at Carmen's front door. "Let's knock the interview off and call it a day. I want to see Ty before Sage puts him to bed."

"Sweet, I suppose your little guy goes down early. He's a darling baby."

"Yep, I'm one lucky SOB." He grinned happily climbing from the vehicle.

♥♥♥♥

Carmen graciously invited them into her place of business, seated them and served coffee then sat at her impressive wooden desk. The office, like Walters, was designed to impress clients, oozing success giving the impression of subtle wealth. Likewise, Carmen was decked out in the uniform of a successful agent. As usual she wore a jacket and skirt suit of pricy-looking fabric, well-tailored and designer made. Tall pumps sported red soles signifying trademark of a famous shoemaker Sage rambled on about—

Jimmy something . . . He never kept track of all that rot.

"What can I do for you, Sheriff, Deputy Coldwater? You resolved my cash flow issues?" She fiddled with a shiny, silver ink pen with her elbows on armrests of her chair.

"I'm afraid not, Carmen. Jaiden and I looked into your accounts, however. Considering the sizable amount you receive in alimony, I understand urgency. Walter must've raked in dough, to be stuck with such a sizable alimony settlement."

She nodded noncommittally with a straight face. "He did well, yes."

"We noticed an anomaly in your deposits, aside from alimony. You received several substantial, varying amounts sporadically deposited from Walter's company account. We'd like an explanation for those payments." Jaiden pointed to figures on a balance sheet from her file.

Carmen snickered. "I figured you'd spot those payments. Walter and I shared many clients. Whenever I brought him a profitable account he succeeded in funding, he paid me a commission. It's aboveboard."

"I assume clients knew and agreed to such an arrangement." Wyatt eyed her suspiciously.

"They were aware. Surely folks aren't stupid enough to think I'd sway them toward my ex-husband from goodness of my heart."

"So this was not disclosed in writing and

agreed to by signature from clients?" Wyatt sought clarity.

"They signed no such documents. I'm not sure what Walter did with them. It was his business. I stayed out of it." She looked defensive and concern marred lines of her well-made-up face.

"I see. We'll look into legalities of your agreements. A forensic accountant doing the final audit of Walter's business for the mother company can direct us to their corporate attorney." Wyatt made a note. Carmen squirmed in her seat trying to hide nervousness.

Wyatt laid a plastic bag on Carmen's desk. "Do you recognize this?"

She picked it up fingering it like a delicate jewel, not a simple, silver charm. An affectionate expression came over her face. "Yes, it's mine. Where on earth did you find it? It came off my ankle bracelet. Did you find the chain? I lost it awhile back. I've looked everywhere I can think of for it."

"When was the last time you recall wearing it?" Wyatt felt nerves in his gut fall into line, like they always did when he was onto a lead.

"I remember putting it on the dresser for a closing on a deal with The Spence Development Firm a couple weeks ago." She glanced at her desktop calendar. "That was the twenty-third."

Jaiden sat erect on edge of her seat. "Where was this closing held? Was Mr.

Burnette involved?"

"Walter was the loan officer for the deal. So yes, he was."

"How much are we talking about?" Wyatt asked eyed Carmen.

"Well, not sure exactly, but it was a lot of money."

"Where did you find my charm?" Carmen fingered her jewelry admiringly.

"It was a gift from Walter for our last anniversary. It's platinum and engraved. It was the last piece of jewelry he gave me before I discovered he was a philandering sleazebag."

"I see, but you kept it though you were disgusted with him and divorced."

"I adored the bracelet. It's valuable, and I was very much in love with my husband when he gave it to me. So I kept it. Yes. What's your point?"

"You wore it to a mutual closing with your husband?" More occurred in this story than she wanted to tell. He was pulling threads so it would all flow out.

"Yes, so?" She sat stiffly erect.

"Did you still care for Walter?" Knowing where he was going with questioning, she stepped in helping steer conversation.

"I didn't still love him, if it's what you're asking. Where did you find my charm? Oh, I wish you'd located the bracelet too. It meant a lot to me."

"Actually, we didn't. My wife, Sage, saw it the day we discovered Walter's body. I went to his office while my CSI team worked the crime scene. Sage waited to talk with Walter. They had a meeting pre-planned. She didn't know he was dead and arrived, waiting for him to show up. Sage discovered your charm behind Walter's desk—not on the guest side, but on his side of the desk. Why there?"

Carmen blushed, glanced away taking a deep breath and let it out before returning her gaze. "It must've fallen off behind Walter's desk after the closing."

"Why would you hang out with Walter afterward? Why did you go behind his desk? DNA on Walter's body showed he had sex before he died. Did you have sex with Walter after the closing?" Apparently he had to spell it out. His suspicions were accurate. She blanched white then bright purplish-red.

Sitting tall she squared shoulders defensively. "There's no crime in consenting adults having a roll in the hay. Yes, Walter and I had a fling to celebrate our huge commissions. We occasionally had sex together, but it was purely physical. We weren't having a love affair. I suppose DNA you found was mine." She clasped her hands calmly on the desktop.

Wyatt made a note. "We'll have Doc check it against your DNA." He handed her a swab kit. "Mind swabbing inside your mouth? Then insert it in the plastic container."

She shrugged, snatched the kit and under their watchful eyes slowly did as directed. Jaiden pocketed the plastic container. "I'll drop it off to Doc on my way home."

"Thanks. Carmen, you and Walter had an amicable arrangement for working together. No love left between the two of you?" Wyatt scratched his jaw with his pen.

"Absolutely none." Her face was expressionless and hands clasped together.

"Were you angry with him?" Jaiden chimed in.

"Not at all. In fact, I was elated. We made a ton of money. We worked well together. Since no longer married, Walter's indiscretions stopped reflecting on me or my business. We tumbled in the hay occasionally. It was all. I had no reason to hate him."

"You were with him the day he died. When was the last time you saw him?"

"After we had sex on his desk, we drove to the Barnes land to take a look. The development firm we'd closed the loan with intended to buy and develop it. We strolled through woods and had sex again while there— near a pond. I left first because we didn't want to be seen together. He said he was going to enjoy serenity for a few minutes before leaving. I never saw him again."

"You're saying his killer arrived after you left. Whoever murdered Walter likely saw you together. You're lucky the culprit didn't approach while you were there. You could've been slain along with Walter."

She blanched to ghost white. "Damn, I didn't realize. Sheriff, do you think I'm in danger?"

"I seriously doubt it, Mrs. Burnette. I'd guess the person had a beef with Walter, so they waited for you to leave before approaching."

"I hope you're right, Sheriff."

"Keep your eyes open anyway and aware of your surroundings. One can never be too careful." Jaiden sat back in her chair. "Mrs. Burnette, we understand you have a twenty two registered to you. May we take a look at it?"

"Certainly." She spun around and opened a credenza drawer behind her. Turning around she laid a pistol on the desk.

"You don't carry it? You have a concealed carry permit." Wyatt was surprised she didn't pull it from her purse.

"No, not lately. I used to. I've developed carpal tunnel and can't shoot the damned thing. I carry a stun gun now because it has an easy trigger."

"Nice gun." Wyatt picked up and examined the unloaded weapon with a Smith & Wesson® Governor® Revolver, six-round cylinder. This is a nice, lightweight revolver, perfect for carrying in a purse or pocket." He handed it to Jaiden who examine the clean firearm inside and out then returned it to its owner.

"Thanks. I like it. It has two clips." She laid them on her desk. "One holds six rounds, and the other is a two-round, moon clip."

"Thanks Mrs. Burnett." The gun hadn't fired in some time from its looks. "We're going now. You have any idea who wanted Walter dead?"

"Check with the damned beautician he slept with. A rumor mongrel she started caused most of my embarrassment before our divorce. The bitch broadcast gossip about Walter's stunts from her shop all over town. I think her name is Bea Sanders. Maybe she's the murderer. I didn't kill him. Walter was worth more to me alive than dead."

♥♥♥♥

Wyatt and Jaiden climbed into his cruiser once more a few minutes later. "She's not the killer." Jaiden spoke methodically writing notes on her iPad.

"Agreed, how did you conclude it?" He was curious if she was on the same path, or if she'd spotted a different clue.

He drove out of the lot and headed to the station. She faced him. "For one thing, her weapon was inappropriate for number shots fired. Even in a daze Carmen would've emptied the gun into him. If it was completely loaded, she would've fired six shots. Even if she had presence of mind to reload, in that state she would've fired until empty again. So she would've shot twelve rounds. Ten doesn't make sense."

"Good thinking. What she said about Walter being more valuable alive sounds accurate. She's a smart mare and wouldn't kill off her gravy train. She'd survived the worst with her ex. If she wanted him dead, it was during the divorce a good year ago. After a cooling-off period she'd discovered a profitable arrangement with Walter made more sense."

"I suppose we're tackling Bea Sanders tomorrow." Jaiden wrote the name in her notes.

"Yes, and Candy Wrigley, too. They slept with Walter during the same period. It seems most of the town's womenfolk had a shot at him."

"Yuck," Jaiden shivered and shook her head in disgust.

CHAPTER 9

Jaiden parked by Clay's back door a couple hours later. She'd gone home to shower, wash her hair, shave and change into more feminine attire. She loved the soft brush of well-worn denim tightly wrapping her long legs.

Her feet snugly fit into favorite spike-heeled boots—the ones Cal teased her about mercilessly calling them *hooker heels*. They exposed her figure making her short legs appear longer. The curve of her petite hips looked more rounded and appealing to the opposite sex. It emphasized her natural wiggle in her walk. Moggie often commented audaciously about sway of her hips and how sensual it made her. She hoped to work the same magic on Clay tonight.

Having avoided personal contact during initial investigation, she was free to spend time with him. None too soon.

She could hardly believe how much she longed to lie in his arms with his naked body curled around her. She'd never felt so strongly attracted to any male before.

She liked men, but Jaiden didn't sleep with just anybody. Picky as hell, her standards proved difficult to meet.

She'd enjoyed one lover since moving to Kentucky over a year ago with her friends-with-benefits best pal, Moggie Larrs. Neither had taken the fling seriously. It was merely an outlet ending abruptly when red-headed vixen, Dovie Fuller-Dane returned to town and stole Moggie's heart. Jaiden liked the fiery chef and was happy Moggie found what he needed in Dovie.

Jaiden had been attracted to another fellow who was revealed as a psychopath. She'd put him away for homicide, stalking, and attempted murder. She wasn't scoring high on a love-o-meter these days.

Mom never failed to point it out. Brightleaf Coldwater was thrilled at Cal's marriage to organic farmer, Rose Casson, now Coldwater. She wanted the same for Jaiden and longed for grandchildren. Her best bet was on Cal and Rose. Jaiden had a long way to go before becoming a mom.

Cal must've heard her pull in. He met her at the kitchen door. Jaiden retrieved her packages and sauntered toward a man she hoped to see nude soon.

A seductive grin eased across her face. Their eyes locked, and words escaped both of them. She neared, and he opened the screen door. His arms widened inviting her into them. Jaiden slipped into his embrace like she'd traveled for ages and finally made it home.

He encircled her and one slim-fingered hand possessively cupped one butt cheek. Her grip on him was strong. She breathed deep enjoying a fragrance she'd come to adore exuded from a man she would never tire of. Being away from Clay had been torturous, but she'd done everything by the book and cleared him as quickly as possible.

It was time to celebrate fruit of her labor

and revel in sweetness of bliss in his caress. His digits played a symphony on her nerve-sensitive skin. It craved his touch and tingled at its arrival.

A bottle of wine she held in one hand propped atop his tight, slim ass. Her other hand presented a bouquet of spring flowers and a box of chocolates resting against his back. Her cheek lounged on his chest so she heard the pounding of his heart and was warmed by his heat.

One hand slid upward into her mane of unruly curls tangling in the mass and tilting her face upward. He bent to possess, and his lips touched down on hers.

His other hand firmly lifted her. She rose and parted her legs wrapping them around his waist. Settling her crotch firmly against his belt, his erection made itself known probing insistently upward toward her groin. A jolt in her center let her know she was readying for him. Her juices began to flow, and her bottom tightened eagerly.

Clay back-stepped into his house and allowed the door to shut behind them bringing her into the kitchen. He backed to a new island his cabinet maker had installed. With a tilt of his head, he indicated she should relive herself of her packages. She laid the roses down and sat the wine and chocolate next to the spray.

He snickered and the twinkle in his emerald green eyes shot sparks through her veins. She moaned with an exhale. "You brought all the right things to woo a lover."

"Wasn't sure which would make the best impression. My intention was to apologize and win your affection." She snickered without releasing him. They were so close his breath heated her tortured skin.

"Nothing to apologize for; baby, you had me without gifts. We'll put them to good use. I'm going to sip wine from your belly button, and your hot titties will no doubt melt chocolate on contact. I plan on eating more than candy tonight."

"Doc, you say the sweetest things." She winked.

Clay rested her behind on the bar—the perfect height for her with his tall, lean stature pressed against her. She was able to caress his erection from the angle through layers of fabric. The erotic sensation sent her to the point of exhaustion.

Man! So damned horny. His solid shaft proves it's mutual.

Clay wasted no time flinging off his tee shirt then stripping her tank over her head. Garments fell away. One hand unlatched a filmy bra, and he slid it off her shoulders.

His lips expelled a heavy sigh, and he blinked. His hands surrounded her mounds. He caressed them tenderly like priceless works of art under careful examination. His thumbs played with center nubs. Her nipples went rock-hard like pebbles in a stream.

Clay bit his lower lip eyeing them with a look of starvation. He tentatively suckled each one in turn moaning with abandon, teasing and lapping her breasts.

Her hands played a tune exploring his back and short-cropped hair, learning every inch of the man she adored.

Finally he pulled away gazing passionately at her nude top, then urged her tight against him. Her nipples pressed into him and their roundness melted against thin peach fuzz on his chest.

Her head lolled back, and his lips found her neck, splaying kisses across sensitive skin and licking her horse head tattoo. With each breath and nip she shivered, and her core tingled tightening in anticipation.

His tongue delved into the recess of an ear. He chewed a lobe easily; and she moaned his name. He drew back and grinned, a satisfied look on his adorable face.

He released her and bent to remove her boots. One at a time he sat them aside. Then he stripped his jeans and stepped out of them.

He was a splendid sight standing stark naked. He hesitated understanding her desire to gaze at him and waited patiently without coyness or guile— allowing her time to observe.

She hadn't noticed his bare feet. She smiled to herself. Those adorable, bony, bare feet held long, slim legs with a hint of blonde hair where his jeans didn't rub it off from pressure. He didn't shave his privates, but sparse pubic hair curled endearingly around his manhood causing a steel erection pointing toward his head nearly reaching his navel. A downy layer of hit-or-miss peach fuzz meandered across his slim belly and flat chest. He had an erect posture, shoulders rounded firm with muscle and strapping arms she thrilled at having around her.

Her hand reached for his chest. She tentatively stroked the firmness, slowly exploring. She eased downward across a taunt, rippling stomach. Delving into hair below, she finally cupped his balls in her hands. Ever-so-gently kneading, she slid a firm grip up his shaft. Her thumb pushed against a pulsing, rising vein along it reaching the head. Fingering the slit, a drop seeped out. She massaged it in. Her hand surrounded the crest and firmly stroked. Then it slid along the length of him, delighted in his size.

He heaved a sigh then blinked a couple times, cupping her buttocks in a hand. Quickly they unsnapped and unzipped her jeans. He lifted her and slid them off along with a thin slit of thong worn beneath. Yanking he tossed them aside. Pulling her to the edge, Clay knelt and spread her wide.

"Beautiful." He gasped before burying his face in her center. Hands held his head. His lips and tongue worked magic on her anxious core. With each movement, each breath against her hot, wet center, each probe of his tongue or finger, she clenched tighter until she could take it no more. Her pelvis tilted forward, and her feet braced against his back. She griped his head and came in a fierce, pulsing convulsion.

When so spent she couldn't sit upright alone any longer, Clay stood and lifted her. Taking a chair, he placed her upon his potent cock, and it filled her to perfection.

Jaiden's head was in a cloud of lusty passion. Had she died and gone to heaven?

She rocked with his pace slow and easy at first. Then harder she moved, shaken with a fierce need to bring her man to a climax he'd never forget.

Her breasts brushed his chest with each sway forward teasing to distraction. Her clit rubbed determinedly against his hilt increasing each move's sensation beyond its predecessor.

Their eyes locked in communication. Each breath, each movement forced them toward a crest. He pounded into her, and she took him with each vault.

Gripping his lifeblood with her womanhood firing vibrations, her muscles convulsed around him. Panting they rode a ride of lovers through the ages. His eyes told hers he found magic they sought. Release came, and he spilled his soul. Pulse of his coming brought her once more over an edge. She quivered and pulsated atop him reaching climax.

It required a while clinging together before returning to earth from their lusty voyage. Finally themselves again, Clay grinned and eased her away so they were eye-to-eye.

Jaiden should act modest or reserved. After all, they hadn't known each other for long.

Sitting erect atop a delectable nude male sun set over a tree line. She was oddly at ease and contented.

"Flowers, wine, chocolates?" He cocked his head in question.

"It was the least I could do, considering I've had to avoid you lately. You have an airtight alibi. Coroner confirmed DOD. You were in Chicago when Walter died."

"I figured. You don't go around sleeping with suspects. So you thought you'd come with a little vino, candy and posies; and we'd pick up where we left off? Huh?"

She grinned naughtily, cocked her head sideways with a brow rising. "Yep. I assumed you'd fall for my charms. I have plans for my gifts. I ply you with alcohol and have my way with you—eat chocolate off your belly—maybe lick some off your cock. What do you think, Doc?" She tickled his stomach with a finger.

He hardened inside her. "I reckon you're right about me, officer. I'm a sucker for you, woman; and I love chocolate."

She began moving atop his firm shaft. "Maybe later—we don't need added treats right now." Her head went back into Lust Land. Clay gripped her ass and rocked her world a third time.

Who needed extra calories, anyway?

Wyatt told Sage about their investigation

and his and Jaiden's plans for questioning the following day. They lay together on a hammock on their large modified-a-framed house. Sage's German shepherd, Tuffy, and Wyatt's Cocker Spaniel, Belle slept beside them on the decking.

"Damn, Wyatt, I hate this. People on your suspect list are friends and neighbors. Some you've known your whole life. I hate this murder being so close. It makes you question everyone's character and motives. It's damned scary."

He brushed back a tendril escaping her ponytail. "I know, Sage. It sucks, but it's what it is. We're a small, tight-knit community. Each citizen touches others in one way or another. It's the worst kind of mystery. I can't wait until it's solved. I can't help worrying about you and Rose, and Little Ty's with you. Who's saying this wasn't random?"

"Seriously? I never thought of it. You're right, but certainly a lot of folks around town have grievances, or a right to them against Walter."

"I know, and it's probably one of them."

"I have an appointment tomorrow morning at ten with Bea for a trim, manicure and pedicure."

"I'll stop by around then. Would you mind if Jaiden and I step in while she works on you and interview her? It'd be easier than screwing up her other appointments. She won't mind talking in front of you, and neither will I."

"No, it's fine. I'm a fair judge of

character, so if she's not leveling I'll spot it."

He swiped a gentle hand across her forehead then down to cup her chin and move her lips to his for a soft kiss. "That you are my darling, Sage. Maybe you can help with our interview. So far I've ruled many folks out. Our no-longer-suspected list is getting longer. At least we can celebrate that. I'm glad it happened before Clay arrived. He has enough on his plate with a dilapidated farm."

"I'm glad he has an alibi. I liked Clay Barnes. Have you seen his house since he's remodeling? Carmen tells me it's spectacular. New siding, gutters and roof install this week. It'll make a super home for someone. Maybe Clay will live there himself."

"I saw work he did in his kitchen. It's well-done. The gourmet cook in you would love it. You might spend most of your time on a tractor, caring for a herd of goats, making farmers and goat cheese, growing and harvesting wine, vegetables and herbs; but feeding friends is one of your favorite pastimes."

"I couldn't do it all without Rose's help." Rose Casson, her farmhand and good friend married Cal Coldwater, Jaiden's brother. They lived on Sage's property since Wyatt and Sage had married, and she moved in with him. *Like Wyatt said,* they were all interconnected one way or another.

"Clay and Jaiden were getting close before it happened. Do you think there's anything serious between them?"

"Not sure, but it'd be wonderful for both of them. Wouldn't it?" *Why fight it?* Sage would do what she wanted, anyway. Might as well accept his woman the way she was—impulsive, head-strong and a force to reckon with. So he laughed Sage's match-maker exposing its self.

Jaiden deserved someone to love. She was a fabulous woman and should be appreciated.

Clay was a standup guy, intelligent and a doctor. How strong did ties pull him toward returning to Chicago?

Time would tell.

CHAPTER 10

Jaiden received cursors glances and nods sauntering into Beauty and the Bea dressed in uniform. The beauty shop was hopping, with every chair filled. Three stylists busied at different stages of hair repair processes. One washed a woman's hair lying back with her body covered in a plastic wrap in Bea's signature color, hot pink. Another snipped curls falling at her feet giving a haircut. A third wound brightly colored curlers and paper swatches into tresses then squeezed a foul scented liquid on each one.

Sage relaxing with her feet soaking in a receptacle of steamy water, bubbling like a tiny hot tub, in a side room reserved for mani-pedi's. The door was open. Bea Sanders smiled at Jaiden while filing Sage's nails. Sage's head lay blissfully lounging against the headrest. A massaging lounge chair hummed and vibrated at a fierce pace.

"Good morning, Deputy Coldwater.

Sage said you and Wyatt would stop by. Come on in." She waved Jaiden toward a guest chair inside the small cubical.

"Wyatt's parking our cruiser. He told me to come on in."

The front door bell clanged. Every female head in the place bopped up with a smile acknowledging handsome, silver-haired sheriff sauntering inside.

"Morning, ladies. Don't let me disturb your spa day." He saluted removing his hat and glancing around at each woman warmly while strolling toward his target.

Sage proudly smiled at her adoring husband. Sage's heart filled to a brim knowing she had nothing to fear from female admiration Wyatt constantly attracted. Townswomen knew he was taken and a one-woman-man. The tight space suddenly felt minute with his huge presence filling it.

He did a side-step trying to avoid colliding with Bea's equipment and furniture. Then he eased a door shut behind him. "You don't mind if I close this. Do you, Mrs. Sanders?"

She blushed pink as her apron at the brilliant smile Wyatt threw her. Bea was used to holding court with women, but men rarely visited her shop. An occasional guy preferred a female stylist. Most men were more comfortable at a local barber.

"Whatever you need, Sheriff, but for heaven's sake call me Bea. No need standing on ceremony here. We've certainly known each other long enough."

"Thank you. If you're comfortable, call me Wyatt. We need privacy for this line of questioning."

"A lot of gossip goes on in my shop, but rarely do gals talk about me while they're here. No need to fodder a gossip mill."

"Agreed. So, Bea, hearsay is you and Mr. Burnette had an affair. When did it begin? Was it on-going? If not, when did it end?"

"Straight to a punch, huh? Well, your rumor stands correct. Chatter flows elsewhere besides here. Anyway, yes, I had a fling with Walter Burnette a year or so before his divorce. I was in love with him, or thought so. He said he loved me and would leave Carmen so we could marry."

Jaiden held her iPad in hand leaning on her crossed knee. "You believed him?"

Bea checked temperature of Sage's foot water with fingers. "Yes, I did—for a while."

"What happened to change your mind?" Jaiden held Bea's eyes.

"I saw him kissing Candy Wrigley goodnight on her doorstep one evening. I worked late and dropped a package off at her house. I left and his car pulled up. I stopped and watched. They canoodled awhile in his auto then strolled to her door where he kissed her with a passionate embrace. Instead of leaving, she drew him inside with her."

"How did you feel?" Jaiden drove for

facts.

Her hands slammed to prop on her thighs, and her elbows shot out. "How in hell do you think?" She glared. "I wanted to rip her eyes out with my bare claws. She was my business partner and knew I was seeing Walter."

"What did you do?" Wyatt assumed command trying to defuse the heat from his partner.

"I went home, drank a bottle of wine, and cried myself to sleep. The next morning I confronted Candy."

"How did she react?" Jaiden dug in.

"Candy's a quiet one. We were business partners for ten years and got on well. She held her end of a partnership. She doesn't date much. Most of her life she nursed her ailing father. He died five years before she took up with Walter. She dated a couple guys before. Confronted, she cried like a baby saying nothing serious happened between Walter and me. She claimed he was crazy about her, and she loved him. He was leaving Carmen for her."

"Wow. That's rotten. Walter told you both the same things." Jaiden's face showed sympathy. Her hand reached for Bea's and covered it sweetly.

Bea smiled at her. "Yeah, I figured it out for myself. I told Candy it was over. I gave her a large check for her part-ownership and told her I was taking a loan out to cover the rest."

"Did she accept the money and breakup?" Wyatt cocked his head, not understanding.

"She said that'd fine. She didn't want to work with me any more than I did her, afterward."

"How did you finance the rest?" Wyatt tapped his pen against his pad.

"I tried the bank, but they told me I wasn't a solid financial risk. My business was long established, but they explained how breakup of partnership made it appear I couldn't afford to pay a loan off. Walter had access to special lending designed for such a situation. I told him it was his fault I needed cash. He'd better come through with dough."

"Did he?"

"Yes, he tried saying he was sorry, but I wasn't having any of it. He proved untrustworthy. So did Candy. I wanted nothing to do with either of them"

"Walter gave you his '*special*' funds? Did he tell you what it was called?"

"Yes, it was a BW loan. I don't know what it means. It was for special circumstances like mine. I qualified for a higher interest rate than bank loans, but it was worth it to push Candy out of my shop for good."

"Did you and Walter continue seeing each other?" Wyatt sat back in his chair, stretching his legs to the side, trying not to look out of place in dainty furniture and a hot-pink and white-striped room.

"Heavens, no. He gave me money. I dropped off my payments each month to his secretary. It was an end of our relationship."

"What about Candy Wrigley?" Jaiden sat erect in her chair taking notes.

"What about her? Bitch is out of my life. Rumor has it she and Walter split too. Not sure why. I don't involve myself in such talk. But I hear things. Someone said she rents a booth at a shop over in Bonnyville."

"Did you mean Walter harm? Did you kill him?" Wyatt looked in Bea's eyes. Their gaze never faltered.

She spoke words one at a time in a believable, mater-of-fact manner. "No. I did not."

"Do you know who might have done it?" He held her gaze.

"I've no idea. It seems every female in this town has crossed Walter's sheets. Maybe it was one of his lovers. Maybe it was a jilted husband, or boyfriend of one of them."

Jaiden jotted a note then eyed Bea without expression. "Do you own a firearm, Ms. Sanders? I don't show one registered."

"Heavens, no. I've never needed a gun. I wouldn't even know how to load or fire one."

"Where were you on the twenty-third?" Jaiden leaned forward.

Bea went into a main room returning with her appointment book. "I can't keep track of such things. Here we go." She stopped paging through the book. "The twenty third I was booked solid all day. I closed at seven thirty then went for a burger with my friend Marsha

Long to Sadie's place. We went next door to the theatre and saw a new Julie Rose film. It was over-rated in my book."

Jaiden wrote the name Marsha Long with a note to follow up. Likely Ms. Long would substantiate Mrs. Sanders' claim.

Wyatt's head nearly reached the short ceiling of the confined room. He stretched then extended his hand to Bea. "Thank you, Mrs. Sanders. I mean, Bea. You were helpful."

"Thank you for your forthrightness, Mrs. Sanders." Jaiden shook Bea's extended hand then followed Wyatt.

"You're welcome. Deputy, if you ever need a beautician, you know where to reach me."

"Thanks, Bea. I'll remember."

Wyatt strolled leisurely through a maze of busy, smiling women gushing greetings as they left. His deputy trailed him.

Sage relaxed into her chair. Bea focused attention on Sage's nails. "That went well. It was good of you to level with them. Truth is always best, pleasant or not."

"Thanks, Sage. I was a nervous wreck."

"Well, Bea, I couldn't tell from how you spoke or acted. I'm glad it's over for you now. Sounds like you're cleared. It's awful what Walter put you through."

"Yeah, the old son-of-a bitch was a rutting pig. I didn't kill him. But he deserves a stretch in the hot seat. The devil has his work cut out for him with Walter." Bea sighed, and her normal relaxed, attitude reappeared.

♥♥♥♥

Jaiden tapped her pen against the notepad. "I located Candy Wrigley's employer. She's at the Hair Shack in Bonnyville. It's thirty miles from here. She usually gets off at five."

"Want to drop in on her this afternoon?" Wyatt asked in his slow southern drawl. "Let's catch her at home. I'll pick you up at the station at five. By time we arrive at her apartment, she should be home, if she comes straight from work.

"I'm going to take a couple sandwiches and check in on Clay during my lunch break. Then I'll go on my normal route this afternoon, unless a case pops up needing my attention."

"Sounds like a plan." Wyatt fired his engine and drove her back to the station to pick up her squad car. He had tons of paperwork waiting.

CHAPTER 11

Jaiden pulled into Clay's back yard. Hearing her vehicle he stepped out the kitchen door. She jumped from her auto and bolted into his arms. A carryout bag rested against his back. Her legs wrapped around his jeans waistband.

Jaiden's free hand caressed slight stubble aftermath of a morning shave then her fingers slid into his short cropped hair pulling adorably grinning lips to hers. "I was anxious to see you tonight; but I have to question a suspect early evening, so I'll arrive late. That's way too much time away from you." Her words came out in spurts between pecks and nibbles of delectable lips.

"I'm not complaining. I'll take this kind of service any day. You bring your smoking hot body and lunch, too. How do I warrant such care?"

He carried her across yard still kissing her. His hands gripped her ass bracing her twat tight and heatedly against his middle enabling him to walk. Reaching a picnic table, he sat her on top, still leaning toward her enveloped in her arms and accepting a multitude of kisses.

"Let's say you're a fine man, trustworthy and honorable. You're sexy as hell and a dynamo in the sack. And you're smart. I can't stand stupid men who can singularly converse about sports, vehicles or horses. You're a real man, Clay; and I'm enjoying hell out of you being here. I can't get enough of you and want to relish every second we're together."

"Works for me, little lady. Now what did you bring me?"

"Rueben's from Sadie's Royal Diner."

"Want a beer to wash it down with?" Standing upright he twisted his navy tee shirt back into place.

"I'd love one, but I'm on duty when we're finished. Got lemonade?"

Clay's long, lean figure ambled toward his back door. "Coming up. Your wish is my command." He disappeared inside returning a few minutes later with two icy glasses of lemonade on a tray beside napkins, paper plates and silverware.

As he sat beside Jaiden in chairs surrounding an umbrella covered table, his phone chirped. "Excuse me. It's Carmen. I need to take it."

"Sure, go ahead." Jaiden unwrapped their sandwiches and set a place for Clay. Then she prepared her lunch.

Clay listened quietly for a few minutes. He began looking dumbfounded. Finally Carmen must've run out of steam. "Seriously?" He swallowed hard. Nodding a couple more times, he continued looking more and more confused. "Okay, sure, yes, please. You do it. I will. Thanks, Carmen."

Clicking the phone off, he turned to Jaiden. His face blanched, so he looked white as the billowy clouds decorating a blue sky.

She touched his cheek with a finger, and her palm rested against his jawline. "What's wrong, Clay?"

"Jaiden, you're never going to believe it. This isn't my property. It doesn't belong to me."

"What the hell? Clay, you're not making sense. Your parents left it to you, right? You're their sole heir. Why? Was there a large mortgage? Is a bank taking the house?" It wasn't logical.

"No, no mortgage. My parents didn't own this place. Apparently they moved in and pretended they'd inherited it. They paid back taxes then kept them paid up yearly. The real estate is tied in layers of heirs from a previous owner who died in the early sixties. None of his distant relatives claimed the place. They let taxes fall in arrears, and over years must've forgotten about it."

"No joke? That's weird." Jaiden hardly believed her ears.

"Yeah, Carmen did a thorough title search going back over fifty years. She is trying to develop an heir list and contact them on my behalf. Maybe they'll allow me buy them out. Jaiden, it's a shock. My parents, recluses who didn't socialize, kept to themselves. They didn't want me bringing people home to visit. It never occurred to me they were dishonest. Who would've thought such a thing?"

"What are you going to do?"

"I'm going to see an attorney. Carmen recommended Carlton Fuller in Sweetwater. I'm going to review Carmen's title search and spend time in a courthouse myself doing research, in case there's error in her work. I doubt it. She was adamant it's accurate, having double-checked her staff's work."

"It's the strangest deals I've heard of. The place was literally abandoned. So many heirs were likely involved. They must've considered it so low in value and not worth their while to claim." She shook her head in awe.

"I hope we can locate all living heirs. It's been many years. Original ones died and their estates passed to children and grandchildren, maybe spread around the world. Who knows how many, and if we can locate them?" He looked baffled and defeated.

She ran a hand around his neck and cupped back of his head. "I wonder what the court will decide. Surely the state and county want someone to claim the property and take responsibility for upkeep and taxes. It's a liability to them sitting vacant. And you've invested so much money and time into renovating it."

"Not to mention my parents' time spent building it up and fraudulently making the place a productive farm. The law wouldn't look kindly on them."

"A judge should consider you an innocent victim, as much if not more so than actual heirs."

"I guess we'll find out. Carmen said she'd work on it, and I suppose Carlton will. Between those two professionals, I'm in good hands. I was getting ready to order supplies to have new board fence built around the border, and cross-fencing separating pastures. I'll hold up on it. I won't spend another dime before finding out what's going to happen to the place."

"I'm so sorry, Clay. It's a shock. I'm unhappy you're going through this. It must sting something awful, having your inheritance ripped from your mitts. Not to mention learning your parents fraudulently possessed the farm. I can't imagine what you're going through."

He tried smiling, but it never reached his

eyes. "I hope I can buy the property. It means a lot to me. I'd like the opportunity to make right what my parents did. Since I arrived home, farm and community reminded me how much I loved living here. While I've worked on it, I've begun considering moving here."

Her heart soared toward skyward then nosedived. She ached for her man. At the same time his mention of sticking around brought her joy. She'd enjoy having Clay around, but because he chose to live there—not for her. Her concern for his confusion and disappointment was strong.

Clay was clearly experiencing disappointment, shame, and sadness for his parents and himself. It was written all over his handsome face. She resolved to do whatever possible to help.

For now all she did was hold his head against her chest. He slumped into her arms.

CHAPTER 12

Jaiden climbed out of Wyatt's cruiser parked in Candy Wrigley's driveway. She rented an upstairs apartment above widow Bunker moving after her father died. Her beat-up sedan parked in a drive. Lights lit rooms above.

"Great, she's here." Wyatt followed Jaiden to a side door. She rang a bell. Footsteps ran down stairs.

Candy didn't look surprised at Sheriff Gordon and his deputy waiting at her door. She'd obviously expected them to turn up sooner or later with all the talk about her and Walter. Jaiden felt sorry for the plain, mousey woman who blushed as her door swung opened.

"Howdy, Sheriff. Ya 'all might as well come on in. I'll make coffee, and we can chat."

She strode heavily upstairs expecting them to follow, not appearing overly friendly or hostile. Acting more resolved she walked slow and calmly. This would likely prove another case of eliminating a suspect—an essential part of investigation.

Her sparse apartment decorated with furniture having seen its best days in the seventies was devout of paintings or photograph. Shades and blinds pulled tight walling an outside world. Dingy walls looked bare and rooms contained mere essentials—no personal articles lying around or displayed.

A traditional dark green sofa with sinking cushions frayed around edges matched a square side chair. A small television occupied a metal stand separating living room by an ugly, oval, braided, brown rug covering part of worn, scuffed hardwood flooring.

A kitchen held a chrome and Formica table and matching chairs with splits in yellow vinyl cushions. Pitted chrome frame was beginning to rust. This style table was popular in the fifties and sixties and had recently returned into style due to retro popularity; but this one was past classic stage and downright beat up.

Candy sat a dented percolator on an ancient range and flipped a gas burner on. She pulled mix-and-match, chipped cups and saucers from a metal overhead cabinet and placed them beside an orange, ceramic sugar container. Setting a half gallon of skim milk out, she retrieved three teaspoons from a metal sink-cabinet drawer.

Soon the pot started doing its happy, popping song. She removed it from heat and poured cups of coffee. Candy's hands never shook or wavered. If anything, she acted unconcerned about their pop-in visit.

"What can I do you for, Sheriff?" Candy flashed him a fake smile, trying to convince him she was nonchalant and happy to help.

"Ms. Wrigley, we understand you had a relationship with Walter Burnette. Tell us about it?" Jaiden spoke soothingly to set her at ease, in case her appearance was merely an act.

She snorted and laughed. Placing hands aside her cup she stared Jaiden in the eye. "I was impressed in by his swarthy, good looks and charming manner. He took advantage of my vulnerability while grieving my father's death. I was an easy target. You see."

She faced Wyatt. "I never dated much. I'm terribly shy. Father was ill for many years. I personally nursed him and worked to pay for a roof over our heads. I covered his medical bills and nursing care while I worked at the shop. I barely afforded rent, clothing and feeding him. He passed on, and I determined to lead a different type life. Walter made me feel beautiful. No one ever did that for me. To him I was a precious treasure. I thought him sincere and believed he loved me. He said he was leaving Carmen, and I'd be his woman—that he'd take care of me. My life was stressful, full of commitments and doing for others. It was a rare treat having someone do for me."

"Did he love you?" Jaiden sat upright, shoulders back.

Candy never met her eye, but continued

staring at Sheriff Gordon. "He didn't love me like a normal man does his woman. Walter wasn't capable of such emotions. He loved me and was sincere at the time. The instant another female crossed his path, it disappeared in a cloud of dreams—my dreams."

"How did you find out he was cheating on you?" Wyatt's voice sounded kind and caring.

"I didn't know. One day Bea stormed into our shop livid shouting about me sleeping with her man—meaning Walter. She heard gossip about Walter and me during an appointment then saw us together and confronted me the following day. He'd slept with both of us at the same time."

"Did it split your arrangement with Bea? How are you handling it?"

"Yes, we decided to dissolve our venture. We'll never be friends after what we said and did. It's the best could've happened career-wise." She shrugged glancing away.

"How so?" Wyatt cocked his head looking perplexed. "You went from being an owner to renting a booth thirty miles away. How was it a good arrangement?"

"Not owning part of our company relieved me of financial and mental stress. Now I go to work and forget finance. I don't mind driving to Bonnyville. It's a scenic, low-traffic ride that allows me to prepare mentally for work and to destress from a day on my feet. Let Bea worry about bills, overhead, ordering and bringing in clientele. I'm happy cutting hair and coming home to forget it. I've not been so stress-free since Father became ill."

"You seeing anyone—since your breakup with Walter?"

"No. I don't care about dating. I'm not cut out for the couple's thing."

"How did he take your breakup?" Wyatt knew but was fishing for her reaction.

"Walter was resilient. Bea and I called him when we had our blow up. She gave him a piece of her mind then handed me the phone. I confronted him about sleeping with her, and we were through. He sounded businesslike and wished me the best." She shook her head staring at the wall. "Don't it beat all? I'd never been in love before. I'm not sure I want to be."

"It sounds like Walter." Wyatt's tone was sympathetic. He cleared his throat. "Where were you on the twenty-third?"

Candy glanced at a calendar hanging on a grease-and-smoke splattered wall. "Let's see. I was at work until five. I drove home, picked up a pizza and watched NCIS on television. I love Gibbs." She produced a genuine smile. "I went to bed early, around ten. I had early appointments the next day."

"Did you speak with anyone that evening? Get any phone calls or visitors?"

"No, I'm not in high demand. You know?" She smirked and screwed her mouth up.

"Do you believe Walter wished you his best, or were those merely perfunctory words?"

Jaiden eyed her though she didn't meet her gaze.

"Hell, I saw him later that day myself, parking at a dive motel at end of town. Mayor Ken's wife was waiting in his car while he checked. Then he pulled around a building, and they went into a unit in back. He never knew I saw them. It don't matter how sincere he felt. I was merely another player in Walter's game of life."

"Yes, we're aware the mayor's ex-wife had an affair with Walter. Was it like the ones with you and Bea? Or was their relationship more?"

"I suspect the same old thing. I've heard many rumors about Walter and one gal or another since our break up. He must've screwed every female in the county."

"Indeed. He got around. Are you still angry with Walter?" Jaiden's words oozed out, trying not to offend, keeping Candy cooperative.

"Why in hell should I be? Obviously nothing real occurred between us. Anger wouldn't solve anything or make it easier." She winced and blinked shrugging her shoulders.

"Were you angry with Bea?" Wyatt patted Candy's hand resting on the tabletop.

"Why? He fooled both of us though she wasn't in love with him. She was simply having fun. But he took advantage of her, too, in a different way."

"Do you own a weapon, Candy?" Jaiden scanned a list of suspects with concealed licenses and registered guns.

"No, I never felt a need to purchase one. No one would steal my shit." She snickered glancing around. "Look at me. I'm not exactly a gal men accost." Candy was plain, not ugly and might be marginally attractive given a makeover.

"Don't put yourself down, Ms. Wrigley. Every pot has a lid. So they say." Wyatt winked and stood. "Walter Burnette certainly was not your lid."

"No. That no-good whore-monger and I weren't well matched."

"Thank you, Ms. Wrigley, for your hospitality." Jaiden followed Wyatt out.

"Candy, if you recall anything that might help, you know where to reach me."

"Sure thing, Sheriff." Candy shut the door behind them.

They left and resumed talking in Wyatt's cruiser as he drove Jaiden to her vehicle. "Thanks for joining me tonight. It was easier for Candy, talking about her affair with Walter, with you around."

"No worries, boss. I'm glad to do it. I was curious to discern her mental state after everything she went through."

"What did you think?" Jaiden figured Candy was off the hook, but sought clarity whether she and Wyatt were on the same page.

"Candy got over hurt and doesn't act emotionally tied to her past or sufficiently angry at Walter or Bea. In fact, she acts far better than I expected."

"So we can mark her off the suspect list, once I check her work schedule out?"

"Indeed." Wyatt leaned across the front seat waving to his deputy as she stepped out and closed the passenger door.

CHAPTER 13

Clay rested his head in hands. Elbows on a table hovered above a thick, dusty book he'd been searching through. His mind was numb. His skull ached, and it throbbed in his temples beneath his palms.

An hour earlier Carlton Fuller assured him he'd do everything in his power to see the matter resolved to Clay's satisfaction. He'd met with Carmen in her office, going over records from her firm's title search. She'd confirmed the intention to help him secure legal title to his homestead, and if he still wanted to sell it, she'd manage it for him. At least he had a sufficient professional team backing him.

County clerk, Sandra Beacon, was filing records in a huge journal she heaved from a bottom shelf atop a chest-tall cabinet. She moaned and lifted a heavy document holder. It thumped landing hard onto a metal-topped storage unit. A thin layer of dust puffed into the air reeking of ancient paperwork and fake, floral air freshener.

Sandra's knees buckled and blood drained visibly from her face. Her eyes rolled behind her lids as she went limp and crumbled.

Clay sprang from his chair rounding a corner of his workspace barely in time to catch the collapsing clerk. He lifted her lightweight body easily and taking a couple steps to where a table was free of debris, gently laid her atop it.

Out cold, Sandra didn't appear breathing. Amid screams and shouts of co-workers, Clay focused on the sick female in front of him. He tilted her head backward, opened her mouth ensuring she had a clear air-passage; and leaving her head propped, he checked her pulse. It was weak, but there. The worst thing—she wasn't breathing. He shouted to whoever might hear.

"Call 911." With his eyes still on the pale woman, he spoke calmly. "Ma'am, I'm a doctor. I'll care for you, and help's coming. Don't be afraid."

He whipped a clean hanky from his jacket pocket, spread it across her opened mouth then held her nose shut. He did quick chest compressions then puffed breath into her lifeless body. Aloud he counted as he worked. With the fire department next door, an emergency crew arrived quickly. Uniformed EMT's rushed in pushing a gurney.

Between puffs keeping his focus on the patient, he explained without looking at emergency workers. "I'm Doctor Clayton Barnes. I was working in her office when she collapsed. She has a weak pulse but isn't breathing. I gave CPR. I'd like to ride with you and continue working on her, if you don't mind."

"Sure thing, doc." The male EMT spoke curtly. They lined one on either side as one of them positioned the portable cot. "Okay, on a count of three, one—two—three."

They lifted Ms. Beacon onto it. Clay resumed working keeping count aloud. EMT's secured her with straps. They pushed it through a hallway and out main doors, lifting it into back of a waiting emergency vehicle. Clay stepped into the van with a male worker and kept up timing steady. A female ran around and started the engine.

On the short ride to the hospital, Clay and the EMT used a defibrillator which finally kick-started her breathing. She gasped and eased in to normal rhythm. Her pulse was stronger but wasn't normal. The EMT connected a line and hung a bag of saline. They pulled to a stop at hospital emergency doors.

A crew of nurses met them at an

entrance. Clay backed away explaining what happened to a nurse in charge. Another worker came running in, having followed the ambulance. She informed a nurse who Sandra Beacon was and sent her purse with her. She'd called the sick woman's husband, and he'd arrive shortly.

An older gentleman in a white lab coat came toward Clay. "I understand you initiated CPR for Mrs. Carnes. Would you mind hanging out a few minutes? I'd like to examine her and start treatment, but want to talk with you before you take off."

Clay shook his hand and nodded. He sat in a waiting area. Folks milling around weren't concerned, obviously knowing each other. Nurses acted professional and caring. Patients waiting for emergency care were well tended and satisfied with their short waits, considering those ahead of them in more dire conditions. It wasn't your typical Chicago Emergency Room with ample space, equipment and personnel to man trauma unit activity; but it was much more serene.

Clay rang Jaiden. "Hey, Jaiden. Boy, it's good hearing your voice. It's a hell of a day. You off anytime soon?"

"Sure. Now. What's up?"

"Could you pick me up at the hospital emergency room? I rode in with a woman who had some sort of attack in the courthouse. I left my car there."

"Of course, I'll come right over. I can't

wait to see you."

"Okay, thanks. See you soon."

The doctor hastened toward him. Clay stood. "How's she doing?"

"She's under control and has come around. She said to thank you for your help. She didn't recall; but a nurse told her a handsome, young stranger brought her in. It gave her a giggle. I suspect a heart attack and am doing tests. Her husband's with her. They need to talk. I want to make sure she's doing okay before we cause any more traumas."

"I'm glad she's in good hands." Clay was impressed with workings of a small town hospital.

"So you're a doctor? Visiting Sweetwater?" The older gentleman with a receding hairline and thick glasses sat beside Clay.

"I grew up here, but haven't lived in Sweetwater since I graduated from high school. I did my surgical residency in Chicago. I returned here to settle my parents' estate."

"Oh, I see. I'm sorry for your loss."

"Thank you. It's been a couple years, but I didn't have time to visit or figure out what to do with my homestead." He winced feeling the pang shoot through his heart at his words.

"This is an amazing place to live. Folks would be thrilled having a new doctor in our area, especially a surgeon. What's your specialty?"

"General surgery."

"Even better. Have you given consideration to sticking around? There's an opening in my practice. I'd welcome you, if you decide to remain in town. The hospital would love to have another surgeon on staff."

"Funny you mentioned it. I'm at a point in my career where I need to decide whether to push for a key role at my hospital in Chicago, or move to a location of my choosing and set up practice. Moving here isn't out of the question. Longer I stay, more I'm warming to the idea." Frustration with his identity, his parents' and the fate of his homestead farm lay heavily on his heart. "A lot of moving pieces need clearing up before I make a decision."

"Well, here's my card. I have office hours on Monday, Wednesday and Friday mornings. Stop by and check out my practice. I'd love having you visit and meet my staff."

"Thanks." Clay grinned pocketing a card Doctor Maines handed him. "I'll do it."

The older doctor returned to his patient's cubbyhole shaking hands with Mr. Beacon with a manly hug. You'd never see that in Chicago. He'd never have the opportunity to know most of his patients, if he kept working there—especially with a promotion. In a small town everyone knew everyone else.

He glanced out a window. Jaiden's pickup truck pulled in. He dragged his weary ass out the door toward his favorite person in the tiny burg.

"Thanks for coming." He climbed in and

leaned over giving her sweet lips a peck.

"Anytime, Doc. You look like you were dragged through streets on a rope. Want to tell me about it?"

"Boy, do I ever?" He patted her slim leg, still encased in her uniform slacks. She looked him in the eye and grinned. Her adorable smile said she enjoyed his touch. Elated, his belly did a happy dance first time all day.

His pounding headache dissipated from adrenaline coursing through his system while he worked on the ill woman. His boggled, confused brain took a respite. Jaiden by his side stalled throbbing from returning.

"How about we grab a couple cold brews at The Ten Mile House? Then I'll buy you dinner at Sadie's Royal Diner? Game?"

"Right now I could stand a cold one. I'll tell you everything I learned. It might be easier if we go through gory details someplace besides my house." His chuckle filled with sadness.

"You're frightening me, Doc." A long-nailed, French manicured hand caressed his thigh. It was an intimate act, but not a sexual one.

He was tightly connecting to the fabulous woman. Thought of leaving her behind soared through his brain burning a painful rail blistering his veins and heart. Quickly as a notion arrived, he shrugged it away forcing it far from his lips. Immediate events needed discussion.

Losing himself bit by bit uncovering

mysterious clues to his parents' pasts forged gaps as wide and deep as the Grand Canyon. Considering options or planning a future was impossible. Clueless about himself, how could he be good for another—especially Jaiden? She deserved the best.

Jaiden parked in front of The Ten Mile House. Clay jumped out and rounded the vehicle, snatching the door and opening it. He helped her climb from the tall truck cab. A sweet spark, from her delicate hand resting in his, warmed cavernous gnawing in his gut. Her brilliant, smiling, exotic face returned a semblance of life to him.

He opened a heavy wooden door, allowing her to step inside first then followed. A soft love song crooned from a jukebox in a corner of the dim lit barroom. Jaiden sidled to an antique bar and propped a thigh over a wooden barstool. She leaned across and greeted a few people drinking there while they half-watched a basketball game on a television mounted at one end.

Justin Henderson limped to their end of the counter and grinned. "Welcome, Jaiden. Clay Barnes, is it you—you old son-of-a-gun?" Justin rounded the end and approached Clay with arms wide. Clay moved into them, and they man-hugged with slaps on backs and chuckles. "Wyatt said you were in town. I hoped to see you. How the hell are you? I hear you're some big-deal surgeon. Right?"

Jaiden grinned. "You know each other?"

"Absolutely, we went through school together. We even played football. I was the runt of a team, but a hell of a kicker. I had two good feet to stand on then." Justin glanced at his prosthesis encased in a cowboy boot matching one on his good foot. He snickered.

"I was sorry to hear about you losing your leg, Justin. It sucks." Clay hated seeing his friend in such a state. It must be tough. Justin had lived a rough life.

"It's what it is. My wild days disappeared with my leg and a crumpled motorcycle scrunched beneath a Fairlane station wagon. I'm doing okay. My substitute allows me to do what I love." He slapped his prosthesis doing a jig.

"This your place?" Clay looked around the tavern filled with tables and chairs, decorated with twinkling lights and beer signs. A scuffed, wooden floor looked well-used, like a crowd danced frequently. It was early for dancing, but a few patrons socialized.

"Yep. I do a fair business. Regulars stop in for a brew on their way home from work. They'll arrive soon. It's a favorite meeting place for friends and neighbors. We're busy. Weekends we're swamped."

"You manage the place and work here too? You still married to that sweet, little brunette who moved to town our senior year?"

"Becky? We were together several years. She and our daughter, Bonnie, died in a house fire a few years ago." Sadness waved through

Justin's eyes and on his expressive face.

Clay's heart stalled. *Wow, Justin had really suffered*. It made Clay's problems seem less horrific. He felt awful for his old buddy. "Wow, man, I don't know what to say. I'm so sorry for your loss."

"Thanks, Clay. I appreciate it. It was rough, and I'll always miss them. Whether we like it or not, life goes on." His head rocked back-and-forth.

"Justin remarried." Jaiden's cheerful lilt helped take the edge off gloom filling air space. "She's a lovely woman. Maybe you know her—Corrie Madison, Levi's kid sister."

He couldn't help the huge smile taking over his face. "No shit? You married Corrie Madison? You son of a gun, she's a real looker. I remember her following the three of you around like a puppy dog. She was so adorable with those long legs, blonde pigtail braids and a face covered with freckles. She had the biggest crush on you. You acted totally oblivious." Clay chortled, slapping Justin's back.

A sheepish grimace on Justin's darkly tanned face was laughable. "Son of a bitch—did everyone around me know about it—everyone but me?"

Jaiden tittered. "Sure sounds that way."

"I'd heard Corrie married some famous dude in New York. Corrie and her husband were mentioned in our high school reunion profiles. I didn't attend due to medical school schedule, but I read every profile about classmates."

"Yeah, her first husband was a scumbag fashion photographer who didn't deserve her. They have a teenage daughter, Morgan, who lives with us. She's a little spitfire like her mama." Pride embellished Justin's tone.

"Well, congratulations are in order. Good for you, man. You and Corrie make a good team."

"I think so." Justin glanced down the stools where a customer raised his glass indicating he needed service. "I need to go take care of business. It's good seeing you, Clay. I hope you make Sweetwater your home, and we have an opportunity to chat again soon."

While they talked Justin had set them up two draft beers. Jaiden picked them up and winked. "Come on, Doc. Let's take a table in a corner where we can converse without being the center of attention." She wiggled and strutted.

Clay followed unable to take eyes off her hypnotizing hips. A table she selected was far away from music and a group carousing bar-side. Once seated, Clay gulped his icy, refreshing drink.

Jaiden eyed him with curiosity. "Okay, Doc?"

"I'm fine. It's heartwarming being welcomed by my old buddy, Justin; and hearing about his love life with Corrie Madison. Corrie and Levi grew up wealthy with a lifestyle far above my family's means; but they are the most down-to-earth people. They never snubbed the rest of us. I liked all of them—Justin, Corrie,

Levi and Wyatt. They treated me like I belonged."

"Yes, they're amazing. They've made me feel at home since moving from Texas. Tell me about your day. Why did you visit the hospital?" She reached for his free hand and covered it with hers. Warmth and compassion oozed from her, easing what ailed him.

"While I was in the courthouse, a county clerk had an attack. I administered CPR and rode in an ambulance with her. I met Dr. Maines. He seemed pleasant and competent. He asked me to stop by his office and chat. He's open to taking me into his practice."

"I'm not surprised. He's talked about visiting his daughter in California. He's worried about his patients while he travels for her wedding. He's getting up there in age. He might consider retiring soon."

It would be convenient if Clay stepped into a practice already doing well. Should he consider sticking around?

"You say it was a county clerk? That's terrible. I hope she's okay. She's a delightful woman. Her poor husband must be scared senseless."

"I guess. He came and was there with her. She was under control. Doc Maines was trying to get her stable enough to perform an angiogram. Hopefully he can fix what ails her while he's in there."

Jaiden smiled and made a note on her pad before slipping it back into her hip pocket.

"Good to know. I'll send her flowers tomorrow. What about your parents and farm?"

He released some tension with a heavy sigh. "Carmen's research was accurate. My parents never owned our farm. Property tax records indicated they moved to Sweetwater claiming the land I grew up on late in 1973. They paid existing, outstanding back-taxes. They moved into a disarrayed home allowing folks to think they inherited it. No one suspected. Neighbors believed what they claimed. They were never questioned. I was born October 2, 1973, seven months after Mom and Dad moved in."

"Sounds like wherever they came from, they settled down to raise a family. Your mom would've been a few month's pregnant." Jaiden looked pensive doing math in her head.

"Even stranger, I discovered my parents weren't who they claimed. They assumed identities for people who died young. Mom's namesake, Betty Carter was born in Harden, Kentucky on April 10, 1954 and died at age five on May 5, 1959. No record existed of her social security number before age fourteen in 1973, and she secured a driver's license the following month. I recognized Mom's signature on an application. It wasn't uncommon back then. Rarely did anyone secure a social security number for a child before minimum fourteen-to-eighteen, when he or she was old enough to take a job. No longer—these days, people build tax shelter investment accounts of one kind or another for children. Accounts require SS numbers."

Jaiden's face went blank and her mouth open. "Wow, she lived her whole life without revealing who she really was." An idea was so strange it bore repeating to clarify.

"Exactly—Dad assumed identity of Wilber Carter, born in Perry County, Kentucky on January 20, 1955 and died at age ten in 1966. Again, no social security number was created before he turned eighteen, when in 1973 Dad secured a one and a driver's license the following month in his assumed name. Applications for both originated in the state capital, Frankfort."

"It sounds like they went to Frankfurt, researched and located two young people's stories. They assumed identities and obtained legal documentation confirming they were these two strangers and lived as these people. Right?" She nodded dumbfounded.

"It appears so. I searched for a marriage certificate. None existed. They didn't marry, but claimed to be."

Jaiden glanced at the floor biting a side of her mouth and nodding. "Okay, but legally they are. Kentucky is a common-law-state. After living together for seven years, they're considered a legally married couple."

"I guess, but it isn't much of a consolation. I've no clue to their actual identities. They were Betty Carter—Barnes and Wilber Barnes. I don't know who I am. I've no idea why they went to great lengths hiding identities—even from me."

"Sure." Sadness flowed from her eyes, along with it awe. She patted his hand, and her thumb absent-mindedly stroked it. "I didn't mean to imply you should be fine with it. If they'd owned the farm, it would legally pass to your mom—his survivor, then to you—their sole heir."

"But it wasn't theirs. I went over Carmen's research. Then I did the same research myself. Everything indicates our land was rightfully left in an estate of Simon Fisher. He lived there then died in 1971. The property was abandoned. With no local relatives, his family mostly resided in California and Montana at that time. Notified by court of his death and inheritance of real estate property several heirs shared ownership. Carmen said based on real estate values back then, Simon's heirs had a minimal financial gain at best. Back taxes were due and would've been paid first. They must've figured it wasn't worth hassle of claiming it."

"So what do you do now?" A look on her face made him want to do the right thing—if he could ascertain what it was.

"I met with Carlton Fuller. He's going to help Carmen trace current heirs. I assume more exist by now. Many original heirs possibly died leaving stake to heirs—children and grandchildren."

"It sounds like an awful chore trying to locate all of them. Did you know Carlton from school?"

"No, but I recall him. He didn't remember me. He and his sister, Dovie, were raised by grandparents. They moved here after their parents died in an accident. Old Mrs. Fuller home-schooled the twins. I saw more of Dovie than Carlton. He was a bookworm, quiet and shy. Some of it was because he was gay, too. It must've been difficult. On another hand, Dovie was a flamboyant, flashy, redheaded flirt. I didn't run in their circle, but she hung out with the Madison kids, Levi and Corrie."

"Seriously? Dovie's back in town, too. She moved a year after Carlton and his partner left Boston to set up their practice in Sweetwater. She's a chef and owns a successful, French restaurant in town. You're right about her personality, but it's more liveliness and zest for life than an obnoxious, flirty thing."

"You know Dovie? My world keeps getting smaller. You're right about her personality." He snickered.

"Dovie lives with my best friend, Moggie Larrs. Mrs. Fuller died. Moggie inherited their homestead. She left the twins a ton of cash, but left the horse farm to Moggie. It was a big debacle at the time, but they got through it. She's a spitfire for sure, but I like the little minx."

"Wow, I've missed a lot, living in Chicago. I'm beginning to realize how out of touch I've become. Being around old chums is somehow right and good. This place certainly

has a draw making leaving difficult. Then you—
." He let pain in his heart show on his face. His
eyes filled with moisture. He should say more
about his sentiments for her, but fear shut his
words down.

"I hope you change your mind about
leaving, but I refuse to be the reason you stay. I
won't stand in the way of your career and
everything you've worked for." She blew out a
puff looking away.

She was so damned beautiful. It was a
miracle she was with him—even if for a short-
term fling. They'd initiated a relationship with
eyes opened.

Clay never figured his heart could get so
involved. Everything became muddled
together—his love for his farm, his childhood
friends, and Jaiden. God, Jaiden was a kind of
woman men dreamed of meeting. Part of him
wanted to pull her tight and never let her go.

His career must be considered, being
running for Chief of General Surgery. The board
would make a decision before long. And he had
an offer in Seattle for a teaching and research
position to evaluate. Another offer came from
Cody, Wyoming and another from a hospital in
Fairbanks, Alaska. That would do wonders for
his career.

Today working on Ms. Beacon, he'd felt
together and alive. And an immediate, definite
connection sparked talking with Doc Maines.
Clay needed to clear his head to think straight.

"So the question remains. Who were

your parents? Where did they come from? And why assume someone's identity."

She clearly had no idea part of his anxiety was about her. "Yes, and I have a notion it's connected to their hidden cash."

CHAPTER 14

Wyatt stepped through a shooting range speaking to a couple friends. He searched around looking for Manley Spence, owner, operator and CEO of The Spence Development Firm.

Earlier stopping at a tiny facility squeezed between a convenient store and a dollar store, an older woman filing in a tall metal cabinet told him where to find Manley. Ugly, pale, green room with heavy, green, metal furniture reminded Wyatt of his days in service. Tan walls held a dusty reproduction of scenery in an ancient, fake-wood, plastic frame. The Spence Development Firm did not dress to impress.

"How's it going?" He asked a man standing behind a shooting booth pushing bullets into a magazine. Wyatt strolled over and shook a hand Manley Spence offered.

"I've seen better days, but I'll survive. I

always do. My company has survived worse. I suppose you're here to talk about Walter Burnette. Right, Sheriff?"

"That's accurate, Manley. The forensic auditor's freeze on Walter's BW loans must've affected your business. Your firm's name was on a list of subscribers to funds."

"Yep, old Walter continues screwing everyone in Sweetwater long after his demise." He slammed ammo into a pistol. Scent of gunpowder, shots ringing and a ping of cartridges hitting inside adjoining firing booths in the outdoor range fit a dreary mood of a cloudy day.

"At least it quit raining—excellent day for practice. Tell me about your relationship with Walter." Wyatt leaned his back against a wall separating Manley's from an empty adjoining booth. His long legs stretched crossing his feet. Hands rested casually on his uniformed belly.

"We had a business relationship. That's it. I wanted to expand my business. I haven't finished a current project—a two hundred home subdivision on Carrey property acquired a few years ago. The bank didn't want to lend anymore cash before it was completed. It's seventy-five percent finished. Walter mentioned a BW loan and confirmed I qualified. I obtained additional funds to purchase the Barnes land and begin development."

"By development you mean?" Wyatt used his calm, slow, southern drawl to keep conversation casual.

"Water, sanitation, roads, sidewalks, and subdividing into plots."

"But you don't have a deal with Clay Barnes." Wyatt eyed him straight on seeking clarity.

Manley looked him matter-of-factly in the eye. "Nope. I should've snatched the piece up quicker, but I low-balled Mr. Barnes on my initial offer. It was enough to spark interest, but not to sign and run with. So the bastard came home to check his place out and make up his mind. Now he's getting sentimental. Carmen tells me he refuses to sell to a developer— maybe even plans to stick around for good."

"You'd still like to purchase his land?" Wyatt glanced sideways.

"I'd love to. It's prime for development. No hills or deep ravines. And it's edge of town, a perfect location. A couple ponds on it lend themselves to enticing high dollars from large home seekers. It would make a lovely community. With Walter's shady practices being under investigation and funds stalled, it's cutting into my business all the way around. I can't move on anything new until it's resolved."

"So you had no idea anything fishy went on with BW loans initiating your lien with Walter?"

"None, but I never drew on the mortgage. It was sitting there, available and approved waiting for my purchase of the Barnes estate."

"I see, so this doesn't really cut into what you have going on. It stalls expansion. Right?" Wyatt stood erect.

A heavy sigh punctuated Manley's words. "You could say that, but with sales getting slow and some of my residential purchasers doing business with Walter, I've had five loans placed on hold with his death."

"I see you own a twenty-two pistol, Mr. Spence—a couple of them, at least." He nodded toward two lying on a shooting table.

"Yep, these babies are handy, all around good weapons. Why?" A blank expression changed to high brows and nods. "Ah, Walter was shot with a twenty-two. Right?"

"Afraid so, Manley. I'll take samples of both your weapons fired with and without your beauty of a silencer." Wyatt fingered a metal device clamped tightly within foam padding of Spence's gun case.

"Sure thing, Wyatt. No problem. I've never used the silencer. It came in a package deal with my Browning. The dealer in Hazard wouldn't break up a set."

Wyatt pulled it from foam and glanced down its barrel. It was clean and barely used. He still wanted a sample shot.

"Tell me more about your interest in the Barnes place."

"Carmen Burnette led me to believe she convinced the heir to sell his farm. He hadn't done anything with it since inheriting it a couple years ago. With Walter's loan in place, I was ready to move forward. I lined up contractor and schedules. Carmen was full of shit. I got pissed. That dude had no intention of selling to me."

"So you're angry with Carmen? What about Walter?"

"Sure, I'm angry but hell, it's business. Too many good deals exist to waste time brooding over lost opportunities. The bitch better play straight if she wants to benefit from The Spence Development Firm's business. No more screwing around."

"Were you angry enough to go after Walter and Carmen?"

He rolled his eyes shaking his head. "Hell no. There's enough going on right now. But I like keeping my pipeline filled and knowing what I'm moving on next. One deal won't kill me. It's a measly twenty-five acres— but a good lying chunk. I generally prefer at least fifty for a subdivision. I'm more pissed because my loan was suspended. The auditor mentioned unusual business practices, and wouldn't guarantee his financial corporation would fund my loan. It could set me back if another great opportunity presents itself."

"Yes. The SEC is involved. Apparently Walter's cooked books somehow, and got away with it for a couple years. A substantial number of loans are involved."

"I'd guess every mortgage to be suspect."

"Don't worry, Manley. You aren't being singled out alone. We're looking into every lead and each mortgagee. I see both your weapons fire ten shots."

"Yes, why? Was Walter shot multiple times?"

Wyatt grinned and nodded.

"Let me guess—ten shots?"

"Good guess. You own any other twenty-twos?" Manley shook his head. Wyatt picked up the first weapon. "I need to fire them for samples. The sooner I examine them in the shop, the quicker we can rule you out as a suspect."

"Have at it, Sheriff." Manley backed a couple steps and leaned against a wall crossing one leg over another.

Wyatt pulled the magazine on a Phoenix HP Twenty-Two-A Semi Auto Pistol Compact with a three-inch barrel. He removed eight bullets leaving two he intended to fire. Wyatt shot first at a blank target without a silencer. He attached it and, looking down adjustable sights, shot a second round. Removing a magazine, he stuffed it into his pocket.

"Nice weapon. Fires easily and has a good balance." Wyatt picked up a Browning Buck Mark Contour Rimfire long rifle pistol, removed a magazine and flicked out eight bullets. Leaving two in, he replaced it and shot first without the silencer, then attached it and launched a second round. "Smooth action."

"Yep, she's a dandy and deadly accuracy, a proficient tool for training new shooters but satisfies needs of a seasoned marksman with incredible versatility. A full-length scope base allows mounting about any reflex, red-dot, prismatic, or magnified optic you choose. If you don't want an optic, Pro-Target sights adjust ensuring you're dialed tight."

Wyatt shoved an empty magazine into his pocket, collected ejected rounds then ambled toward targets he'd fired on. He retrieved them and returned to Manley Spence lounging against a wall observing.

"Clear my name, Sheriff. I've had enough of Walter Burnette for a lifetime." Manley stood erect and offered his hand. Wyatt shook it heartily. No sign of nervousness showed in Manley's dry grip or on his face. Wyatt felt confident he'd prove innocent.

♥♥♥♥

Clay entered The Royal Diner. Sage occupied a window booth alone. He strolled toward her and she waved.

"Good to see you, Clay. Are you alone? Want to join me? I came to town for an errand and hoped Wyatt would be free for lunch. He's tied up investigating."

"As a matter of fact, I'd hoped to take Jaiden to lunch, but she's out on a call."

"It doesn't surprise me. They're

swamped these days, interrogating suspects and people of interest in Walter's murder."

Sadie came rushing over with arms wide snuggling Clay into them with a pat on his back. "My goodness, Clay Barnes, it's a pleasure seeing you. I understand you're a hero. Everyone's talking about how you saved Sandra Beacon at the courthouse." She released him and clapped her hands. Her over-loud voice alerted every diner in her crowded deli, and they spun heads with smiles Clay's way.

"Congratulate Clay Barnes, our hero." Sadie started clapping. First one man, then a woman, then a couple and within a few seconds every customer in The Royal Diner stood giving Clay a hearty round of applause.

His face heated, and his cheeks must've flamed from being in the spotlight. Used to handling pressure, working under stress and excelling regardless what happened around him, he wasn't accustomed to getting accolades for doing what he knew well to do. It was his job. In Sweetwater it was a heroic act.

Humbly he accepted hugs, strong shakes and enthusiastic congratulations from a few. Several people welcomed him home and expressed hope he'd remain in Sweetwater. Finally hoopla wound down, and folks went back to their meals.

"Where's the little man?" Clay chose a bench across from Sage.

"Ty's with Rose at Parsley, Sage, Rose, Mary & Wine—my farm. I snuck off to do running while he slept. I'm taking Rose a sandwich, so she can take a break when I return. How's it going with your house?"

He raked a hand over his brow and into his still-short hair. "Not well. Carmen's trying to track down a long list of heirs. Carlton Fuller is working on legal documents to officially turn the place over to me—assuming they're willing. It's damned frustrating, if you want truth."

"Wyatt said you've discovered other strange facts in your research." Sincerity and caring were written in her eyes. He trusted Sage as he did Wyatt and Jaiden. They meant him no harm.

If anything, they'd do whatever possible to help, so he felt comfortable discussing issues with her. "Jaiden is investigating cash we found. A portion of bills consecutively numbered seems suspicious. I'm hoping she can determine their origin. The money doesn't likely belong to me. There's no way my parents earned that kind of income. Unless they inherited a bundle, their stockpile has a fishy beginning. Until I know, I can't figure out what to do about it."

Sage laughed and patted his hand. "Most folks are concerned about debts after losing a loved one. At least your position is on the positive side financially."

"It's confusing. I never doubted my parents were who they said they were. Why would I?
I've discovered they assumed someone else's identity and lived their lives, starting shortly

before my birth, as other people. It doesn't bode well. They obviously ran from someone or something. Unless I figure out who they really were, I'll never understand who I am. I'm starting to doubt everything about myself." An exasperated sigh eased through his clenched teeth.

Sage handed him a menu. "Nonsense, their identity makes no difference. You were named at birth. That's who you are. You're the man you've grown to be, an upstanding citizen, a skilled surgeon, a good friend, loyal son and a fine man. Everyone has a history. Most children rarely learn about or understand their parents' pasts. Yours is complicated and unique. What you discover has no bearing on you. Stop beating yourself up. You can only control what you can control."

A weight lifted from his shoulders. He breathed his first easy oxygen in days. His whole person began relaxing. "Damn, Sage, I wish I'd talked with you sooner. Jaiden keeps telling me I'm not responsible for my parents, but somehow hearing it from your perspective helps so much more."

She snickered and winked. "It's the flower child coming out in me. I have a soothing effect on troubled folks. Ask my friends Rose, Corrie, Riley or Reggie. Stick with me and before you know it, I'll have you doing yoga and chanting."

He chuckled. "Flower child?"

"Don't laugh. I'm second generation

hippie, born in a commune. My parents moved to the suburbs to give me a proper education, but it stuck with me. My love for nature drove me to Kentucky to start my organic farm."

"I heard you held a high-ranking position at the FDA and lived in New York." Wyatt had told him a bit about his new wife and her past life proudly boasting her accomplishments.

"I was head of a department at the FDA while married to my first husband, Cade, in another life. I'm extremely happy in Sweetwater. Our community welcomed me with open arms. Marrying Wyatt is the best thing ever happened to me, besides our children Hailey and Ty."

The woman continued to worm her way into his heart. Sage was a good person to befriend. "Wyatt says Hailey's closer to you than her own mother."

"Our relationship was rocky at first, but we're extremely close now. Hailey's a daughter I wanted and a wonderful big sister to Ty."

"You and Wyatt are lucky." It warmed his heart seeing how happy she was and how much joy Sage brought his friend, Wyatt.

"There's a lot of luck going around town, Clay. You'll find it too. The townsfolk will welcome you more than they did me. After all, you're a native son of Sweetwater. I've seen how you look at Jaiden Coldwater. Don't tell me there's nothing special going on between you." She arched a brow.

Sadie arrived to take orders. He was glad

for a reprieve.

"Would you mind if I stick my nose into your money's origin? Jaiden will probably get to the end of it, but I love a challenge. It's awhile since I've had a mystery to solve, but I'm a decent sleuth when my head's in a game.

"I'll take whatever help I can get. The cash is stored in a safe deposit box, but here's a list of serial numbers." He pulls his wallet out and handed her a copy of a list he and Jaiden compiled. "Have at it. Worst happens—you don't learn anything. Thanks for offering, Sage. I appreciate it."

"Anytime, Clay, I mean it." Her eyes confirmed her words' authenticity. Over burgers Sage eyed him curiously. "Jaiden tells me you're filling in for Doc Maines. How do you like the small-town doctoring?"

"I didn't think it'd be challenging enough, but I'm enjoying it. It's wonderful working at a practice spending time with patients, getting to know them. Everyone recognizes everyone else and there's a lot of respect. Patients are grateful. Constant running pace of a Chicago hospital is a different world. Doc Maines returns soon from California. I'll have a hard time leaving."

"Maybe he'll ask you to join his practice. He's talked for years about retiring to California near his daughter and her family."

"Maybe. It'd be worth considering, I suppose."

"Are you coming to the fundraiser? Our

hospital direly needs a children's wing. Folks with urgent needs for children go to Lexington, Louisville or Cincinnati for proper care."

"Yes, Dr. Maine's receptionist takes off every-other Friday. Her ten-year-old daughter has leukemia. She goes to Lexington for treatments. It's tough on them, with a long drive there, four hours of treatment, and a long drive home. Yes, I wouldn't miss the event. I bought two tickets from Dr. Maines and am bringing Jaiden. I guess you and Wyatt are attending?"

"Absolutely. Levi Madison and his dad, Senator Garret Madison, bought a couple of tables. Levi gave us tickets. We're bringing a contribution to the fund. Levi's sister, Corrie, and her husband, Justin Henderson, will be there. Rose and her husband, Calvin Coldwater, are coming, too. Cal's Jaiden's brother. Levi and his wife, Riley, will host one table. Garrett and Adelle are hosting another. Jaiden and Cal's mom, Brightleaf Coldwater, will probably be their guest. Have you met Jaiden's family yet? I have no idea who else will attend. They run in a different social circle than Wyatt and I do, but they're dear friends."

"I know everyone you mentioned except Mrs. Coldwater, and I haven't yet had an opportunity to meet Levi's wife, Riley. I'm looking forward to the banquet. Hopefully it'll push a construction fund over the top so they can finish a much-needed wing." Grabbing the bill Sadie left during their conversation and finishing his last bite, he stood. "I'd best run.

Thanks for inviting me for an enjoyable lunch, Sage; and thanks for your help. It's a pleasure."

"Thank you, Clay. I didn't mean for you to pay for my lunch though. It's my treat." She slid from the booth following him out.

"Nonsense, you wouldn't deprive me the pleasure of reciprocating that delightful welcome dinner you cooked for me." He handed the bill with a couple of tens to Sadie at a cash register.

"How was it?" Smiling Sadie made change.

"Fabulous, as usual." Clay placed change she handed him on the table, as a large tip. "Thank you, Sadie."

"Thank you for coming. Sage, kiss your young 'un for me." She winked and returned to her kitchen.

"Definitely, thanks, Sadie." Sage waved and
   stepped out.

CHAPTER 15

Clay was in the office between patients. His cell rang. "Dr. Barnes here."

"Hi, Dr. Barnes, am I glad to talk with you? Sandra Beacon here. I understand you're responsible for saving my life a few days ago. I'm one lucky gal. You were in my office when I had an episode. I tracked you down to thank you." Her voice was energetic and joyful.

"My pleasure, Mrs. Beacon. I'm glad I was in the right place at the right time and happy you're doing well." The pleasant surprise would never have happen in Chicago. It boosted his mood like nothing else could.

"I am; and because of you, I'm going home today. You got me to a hospital before my heart sustained severe injury. They fixed it with a stint, and I've been under observation. They're making sure it's working properly. My family and I are eternally grateful for what you did." Her voice filled with emotion, choked on her words and brought Clay even more satisfaction.

"My pleasure."

"My husband and I want you to come for dinner one night. We'd enjoy welcoming you to our neighborhood and thank you personally for helping me."

"It's not necessary but extremely gracious. Relax and let your body heal. You've gone through severe trauma. You shouldn't cook and entertain me." Regardless, her gesture filled Clay's heart with gratitude and pleasure knowing people like the Beacons existed.

"Nonsense, my husband Larry adores cooking. He'll handle details. And we can have a lovely, casual evening together. It might not be fancy, but Larry makes a delightful meatloaf." He detected disappointed. "I understand you're keeping company with a deputy, Jaiden Coldwater. Bring her along. Larry and I like the sweet, young deputy. How about Wednesday? It gives me a couple days to settle in at home. Please, say you'll come." She sounded hopeful.

How to turn her down?

♥♥♥♥

Dr. Maine's receptionist, Jane Anderson, stepped in while Clay searched through a pile of folders with an exasperated look on his face. "You got a minute, Dr. Barnes?" The apprehensive expression on the subdued woman's face looked like she might cringe, but she stood her ground. Whatever she needed was apparently important. She'd acted shy and backward, since he'd been taking Dr. Maine's patients.

Clay pushed aside a stack of papers, not having found what he needed. "Of course. I'd make time for you if I didn't. Maybe you can help. I've searched for Clare Nelson's file. It's not in this stack. I want to review her last test before her appointment.

Without a word Jane sped to a front room, returning with a smile and a folder in her hand. She laid it atop his stack. "Here you go.

177

Results came in a batch from the hospital lab today, so I had it on my desk to insert the reports for you. They're online too, if you want to pull them up to review pictures on screen."

Relief washed over Clay. Why hadn't he thought to ask before wasting time searching? "Thank you, Jane. You're a blessing around here."

Blushing, she wrung her hands. "That's what I need to talk about. My daughter needs her treatment, so I must take her to Lexington tomorrow. Until the new children's wing is completed, she can't get it in Sweetwater. Dr. Maines is fine with me being out, but I fear you might not fare well without help."

Dr. Maines filled him in on her condition. It hadn't occurred to Clay how it might affect his work.

"That's thoughtful and perceptive of you, Jane. Let's examine tomorrow's schedule. If appointments can move to Monday, let's do it. I don't mind working a hospital shift then one in the office on Monday. I can juggle both. Would it work for you?"

Jane was attractive when she smiled broadly. What he'd considered plain switched to a lovely glow when her eyes engaged. If she went out of her way to apply makeup and fix mousey, brown hair nixing her tight bun in back, she'd look attractive. Likely she didn't have time or strength to bother with either as a single mother with a critically ill child, juggling a full work schedule. His heart went out to the competent woman. No wonder Doc Maines couldn't do without Jane.

Clay had reviewed the checkbook. Doc paid her for a full schedule every week, regardless if she was out every-other Friday.

She came around to stand beside him to provide scheduling input. Together they reviewed it.

"These two are coming in for prescription refills. This one wants a referral to an orthopedic doctor. I can handle these three with phone calls today. If they still want to see you, I'll reschedule for next week."

"Wow. I'll come in and work on reports and handle any emergency calls. Otherwise, it looks like I'm free tomorrow, if you contact these seven and move them to Monday."

"Will do, Doc. Anything else?" She looked like a huge weight had lifted, displaying a casual attitude and lighter step, she picked up the appointment book.

Clay stood beside Jane. With a full heart he gave her a tight side-hug. She smiled gratefully up into his face and wiped a tear from her cheek.

"Well, Doc, good to see you so at home in your temporary digs." Jaiden's Texas drawl spoke with an undertone he couldn't place a finger on. Her shoulder and hip leaned against the door jamb, and her arms and feet crossed.

His heart gave a short jerk then bolted into business with a thud causing a lump to rise in his throat and his forehead to bead up. Damn, she was a gorgeous sight, standing all sexy in her tan uniform decorated with a silver badge, patches and heavy utility belt circling her slim waist holding paraphernalia including a weapon. A deep breath failed to still his racing heartbeat.

Jane wove around where Jaiden propped on her way into a front area. "Excuse me, good to see you, Deputy Coldwater. I was leaving." Her eyes followed her path, not meeting Jaiden's.

Clay finished rounding his desk nearing her and slid his hands around her midriff tugging her against him. She looked upward into his eyes with what resembled confusion, studying his face.

"Did you stop by to make my day? Or do you need medical care?" Clay asked bending his head, delving beneath her ear softly sucking the thin strip of tattooed skin. Her heavily starched collar blocked perfect access to her slim throat. She sighed at connection. His heart did a flip-flop, so he followed the kiss with a teasing bite. Her breast pressed against his belly and even though layers of interrupting fabric blocked contact, clearly her nipples responded.

"A friendly visit, Doc, but I'd love your special treatment, if I had the time and no burly guy with a sour expression waiting to see you in your reception area."

"That's Joe Mason. He's scheduled next. Too bad you don't have time. I'd work you into my agenda." He winked.

A stretch of her neck gave better access,

and he took advantage. She shivered and pushed him away gently. Heat from her hands penetrated his shirt. He wished they were naked, so they could warm the rest of him. He tenderly brought one to his lips kissing pads at tips of her fingers one at a time.

"Later, Doc, I have a couple minutes and wanted to see how it's going. It appears you've made the place your own." A strange undertone filtered her words, but he knew better than to try to read a woman, especially one complex as Jaiden Coldwater.

"I like it here." It was truth and simple, so he left it at that.

"I see." She grinned and pulled away strolling toward the front room. He followed stopping in the middle of the reception area. Jaiden wiggling away took his breath. She opened the outside door and finger-waved pulling it shut.

An unexpected afternoon treat— Turning to the waiting area, he eyed Joe who studied him with a baleful grin. "Come on back, Joe." He went back to his office, but not quick enough to miss a snicker on Joe's face.

♥♥♥♥

Friday Clay sat at Dr. Maines' desk going through files for patients he'd examined; making sure everything was in order. His cell rang. "Hello, Dr. Barnes here."

"Dr. Barnes, it's Jane. Are you busy? My

car won't start. I didn't know who to call."

"I'm working on patient files, but nothing that won't wait. Aren't you driving to Lexington?" He folded binders and looked at a clock. If Jane's daughter didn't get to Lexington in record time, she'd have to wait for treatment on Monday. Christina's condition didn't allow for leeway. She needed medicine now, not later."

"I am, but I've tried everything and can't start my car. Marvin at the repair shop said it sounds like my starter is shot. He's towing it later to repair it. In meantime, I'm in a bind." Desperation in her voice overwhelmed words.

"What's your address, Jane? Work I'm doing can wait. I'll gladly drive you and Christina to Lexington."

"But it will take your whole day. We don't have any way back either." She sounded on a verge of relief but afraid to consider it yet.

"That's no problem. I'll bring files along. I can work in a cafeteria while Christina gets treatment."

"Are you sure, Dr. Barnes? I hate putting you out." There it was. She was beginning to believe help was coming.

"Absolutely, I wouldn't have it any other way." He jotted her address down, grabbed his keys and sped from the building. It would take about ten minutes to reach their home.

Clay was ushering Jane and Christina down steps from their tiny apartment building toward a parking lot and his truck. His arm was around Christina, and a hand rested on her mother's back while they descended. Christina apparently made a clever remark. The threesome laughed and chatted like old friends.

Jaiden slowed the cruiser and pulled to a curb along a road adjoining Jane's apartment complex. Jaiden had spotted his SUV then noticed a joyous threesome walking toward it. Why was Clay with a woman and her daughter, acting like a family?

Clay and Jane huddled together in some chore yesterday in Dr. Maine's office. They'd acted familiar and even conspiratorial. Now this—Clay Barnes was seeing another woman.

They'd not talked about exclusivity. If anything, they'd avoided discussing relationships all together. He was likely leaving town. It was the original plan. He was either returning to Chicago or striking out to some place to establish a new practice and life for himself—somewhere he wanted to be. No chatting about him sticking around, and she'd feared bringing it up, avoiding it like a plague.

Jaiden never meant to fall in love with Dr. Clayton Barnes. She meant to enjoy a short-term fling with a handsome physician. She'd promised herself good sex with no strings.

It hadn't turned out that way. She'd fallen for Clay with body and soul, and was way past a point of no return, hell bent for heartbreak on a speeding bullet. Clay was leaving and splitting her heart with his gas pedal.

Now more than ever, she was certain he'd leave. After all was settled, he'd sell to some farmer and split town for greener pastures. He sure as heck wouldn't want to settle down in town or home his parents lived a life of deception in. They'd lied about everything.

He didn't even know what his name should be. Legally he was Clayton Barnes. But he should be Clayton something-else-entirely. No. Clay would never settle here, especially not with Jaiden.

If he even considered it, an upstanding doctor like Clay would want a stable, normal wife and family. He'd never choose a woman who worked strange hours, lived life fast and hard, and ran toward danger on a daily basis. Clay deserved better—than Jaiden.

He loved kids. The way he'd paid attention to little Ty at Wyatt and Sage's for dinner showed he wanted kids—like Christina. Yeah, Jane Anderson and her daughter Christina were a better fit for a long-term relationship with Clay. Jane could give Clay what he needed—better than Jaiden.

She should make it easy for him. After all, loving the doc, she wanted what was best for him. She would help him get what he needed.

CHAPTER 16

Jaiden entered the bakery with a tinkle from a bell above a door. At a counter Gwen Russo worked. It was past a busy morning rush and before a lunch crowd, so one customer lingered doctoring his coffee. Gwen smiled.

"Good morning, Deputy Jaiden. What's your poison?" She waved a hand in front of her toward glassed displays of assorted donuts, cookies and coffee cakes. Behind her a shelf held rows of fresh-baked bread and a dozen or so iced cakes.

Jaiden allowed herself pleasure of savoring scent of fresh baked goods and sugar. She smiled at a warm greeting from a woman she'd come to interrogate. It wasn't sweet treats Jaiden sought, but clarity on Gwen's and her dad, Joel Russo's roles in Walter Burnette's demise.

"I didn't come for treats, but don't let me leave empty handed. Boys at the station will have my hide if they learn I came to your store and didn't bring goodies for them. I'm here to see you and your dad. Is he around?"

Gwen glanced at a closed door behind her. "He's in back baking. Want me to fetch him, or you want to walk with me?" The coffee purchaser left with his hot brew, and the doorbell clanged. Jaiden glanced around and shrugged.

"Let's go back and have a short chat. You can listen for customers from the back room. Work for you?"

"Fine. Daddy's probably in the middle of a project. This way he won't have to leave half done."

Gwen flipped a countertop allowing Jaiden to step behind a counter with her then led to a back room. Joel Russo was clad like his daughter in white, with an apron covering his front. His arms coated with flour, he kneaded a mound of dough on a stainless steel table. Surprise registered in his eyes attempting a weak smile.

"Deputy Coldwater, I wondered who would show up—you or Wyatt. It was inevitable."

"I'm happy you expected us. It's less awkward, I hope." Jaiden extended a hand then withdrew the gesture awkwardly. "Sorry, I don't suppose it's a good time to shake your hand. Please continue working. I want to interfere with your routine little as possible."

She glanced around at majorly stainless room, with counters heavily laden with enormous pots and bowls. Air smelled delightful. Her belly rumbled and growled. Her hand flew to her abdomen. Embarrassment flushed through her and must've shown on her face.

Gwen and Joel smiled knowingly. Gwen sat a plate of sugar cookies with globs of chocolate melted into centers. She stepped to a gigantic refrigerator and retrieved a bottle, placing milk in front of Jaiden.

She waved Jaiden toward a stool. "Sit, Deputy. Take a load off. Have a snack while we talk."

Jaiden smiled thanks then sat and cracked the bottle open. She nibbled soft cookie and closed her eyes for a second while it melted in her mouth. "Thank you. These taste delightful."

"No problem. We enjoy them, too." Joel continued kneading dough. "What can we help you with, Deputy?"

Gwen sat on a stool near Jaiden and looked nervously like trying to act casual.

"I'm glad you're here. We need to talk." Jaiden sat the bottle down and faced him. "Your name appears on a list of Mr. Burnette's clients who took out BW loans. Can you tell me about it, please?"

Without surprise Joel started talking while continuing to work. "I did indeed indulge in one of those loans. I needed money. Walter provided it—at a high cost, I might add. The son-of-a-bitch and his '*special loan*' for people like me were on the shady side. In other words, folks in a bind with no other options positioned perfectly to line his pockets with gold. I wouldn't put it past old Walter to do illegal business. Is it why you're investigating his BW loans? Weren't they on the up-and-up?" Joel cringed. "Don't tell me his company will foreclose on those liens now he's gone. My business is at stake."

Jaiden's hands shot up. She had no idea how lenders funding Walter Burnette's business, would handle outstanding BW loans. Joel suspected they were indeed less than kosher. It wasn't her place to comment on what might or might not happen now.

"You'll need to work with the lenders to resolve your outstanding debt, Mr. Russo. I've no clue what their intentions are. What I know is you did business with Mr. Burnette. It appears less than satisfactory to you, and you seem anxious. Why?"

"Why?" His flour-coated hands yanked from dough and shot to his hips. "Why—you ask? The son-of-a-bitch Burnette was sniffing around my daughter when she was in his employ. He took advantage of her good nature and innocence."

In peripheral vision Gwen shifted nervously on her stool, but kept silent.

"He got her fired. He screwed me financially with his damned BW loan. The bastard did it to dozens if not hundreds of other innocent citizens of this community. Now he'd dead and gone—murdered. He obviously pissed off the wrong person. He continues screwing us royally long after he's gone. My BW loan is almost paid off, but no doubt lender will call it due. I don't have funds or resources to pay it off flat. Why the hell wouldn't I get upset?" He glared, and she suspected smoke would start filtering from his ears any second.

"Mr. Russo, with all due respect, I'm not here to convince you of Burnette's innocence. I need to determine whether you or your daughter has a motive or opportunity to murder Mr. Burnette. Where were you on the twenty-third?"

"So that's the day the SOB met his maker. I'm surprised angels didn't sing on fountain square in town center—may he never rest in peace. I didn't kill him, but I see why someone would want him dead." He shrugged and his hands flew up slightly. "I don't have an alibi for the twenty-third. I was working in my kitchen most of the day alone. We don't have many customers after one p.m., so the afternoon went slow. I placed dough to slow rise in a refrigerator. Then I went home and spent an afternoon watching games I had taped. I ate a sandwich for dinner alone at home."

"I see. Do you own a weapon?"

"I do. I have a shotgun and a revolver."

"What type revolver?" Jaiden glanced at her list of concealed carry licenses. Joel Russo's name wasn't on it. Flipping to a list of registered guns owned by those she was investigating, she found his name.

He paced to a door and flipped open a cabinet. Pulling out a weapon he strode to Jaiden and laid a small pistol beside her plate of cookies. "This Smith & Wesson model 325 Thunder Ranch revolver is my sole hand gun.

It's registered."

"I see." Jaiden picked it up and flipped a barrel down examining the gun. "Decent, little, six-shooter you have here." She admired simple mechanism of a clean weapon. "When did you fire it last? Where do you keep ammo?" She glanced to Russo with a smile.

"I like it. I keep it in case someone decides to rob my place. It's never happened and not likely to. Ammo's on the shelf next to where I keep her. I haven't practiced in over a year. Do you need to take her for examination? If so, I want a receipt; and I want her back when you're done."

"No, but thanks. It's a 45. Mr. Burnette wasn't shot with a 45. You don't own a 22 do you?"

"No, never have." Russo returned his firing arm to its hiding spot and retrieved his dough. He selected a glob and dropped it into a large, greased, stainless bowl.

"What about you, Ms. Russo? May I call you Gwen?" She swiveled on her stool.

Gwen looked nervous and pale. Her voice cracked. "What . . . what do? You . . . want to know? Dad took out his BW loan before he knew Walter and me—before I knew what kind of man he was. Wally and Carmen shared an office building. I worked for Wally—for both of them for a while. His office was on one side of the lobby, and Carmen's was on the other. He pursued me from the day they hired me until I finally slept with him. Then I found out he was bedding those bitches at the beauty shop. Later on I heard about him slapping it to the mayor's wife. The man-whore was screwing half the women in town. For God's sake, he was the biggest dirt bag I've ever imagined."

"Did you kill him? Did you shoot him in a fit of passion or rage?"

Gwen grinned and shrugged like Jaiden had told a funny joke. "I wish I was woman enough to have done it. He deserved what he got; but no. I didn't do it. I hated the boy-slut. I wish I'd had the guts to shoot him. I lost my job. They repossessed my truck because I couldn't pay. I lost my apartment and had to move in with Dad. I couldn't even keep gas in my old clunker or pay car insurance if Dad hadn't hired me to help at the bakery. I'm a laughing stock."

"Don't beat yourself up about your relationship with Walter. Folks know what a scumbag he was. He hurt enough people. You worked for him and Carmen. If anything, they should pity you—having endured Walter's abuse. It's simply wrong."

"Thank you for saying it." Gwen acted genuinely thankful.

"No problem. I'm a defender of women's rights." The familiar ache filled Jaiden's belly with its bulk.

"Good to know. Were you a victim?"

"Let's say I've suffered at the hands of male libido gone wrong." Jaiden blinked away long-ago memories of a pack of wild boys pawing her clothing in an alley behind school, where she waited for Cal after a winning football game.

"Did you kill Walter? Do you own a 22 pistol?" Jaiden looked her in the eye squarely.

"I do. It's in my bag over there. It's loaded, but I don't have a concealed weapon license. I lay it on my seat when I drive. I don't carry it around all the time. But last night I fired it at a fox chasing Dad's chickens. I brought it in today thinking I'd clean it if I had downtime."

"Do you mind if I take the pistol?" Jaiden stood, hands on hips, feet shoulder width apart.

Gwen looked sad and beaten. She shook her head. "No, help yourself, Deputy." She stayed seated. Jaiden stepped toward the corner, picked up a purse and retrieved a small 22 long-barrel pistol. She carried it to her seat and examined it. "A handsome Browning 1911."

"Thanks. It shoots high velocity ammunition with a ten round capacity single action semi-automatic. The five inch barrel provides good performance for fundamental shooting with easy maintenance."

"Yeah, it's an all-around, effective starter gun. What does she weigh?" Jaiden hefted the gun in her hand.

"It's barely over two pounds."

"Good choice, Gwen. I like it. I need to take it back to the station for processing. We need to prove it's not the murder weapon." She slid Gwen's weapon into a plastic bag pulled from her back pocket.

"I understand. I'd like it back."

"Of course." Jaiden scribbled a receipt and pushed it across a tabletop to Gwen. "So Gwen, this looks bad for you. I'm sure you understand. You have the type gun Walter was shot with. It's recently fired. You were livid with Walter and think he deserved to die. Do you have an alibi?"

Gwen scowled looking disgusted. She blew out a breath asking her head. "Not really. I drove alone to Cincinnati to shop. I used cash for purchases including gas. I returned early evening."

Jaiden picked up her package with Gwen's prize toy in it. "Okay. Until we find some way to clear you, your suspects. Don't leave town without consulting the sheriff. We'll be in touch for further questioning. She marched into the front store leaving father and daughter whispering and wishing she could hear their conversation.

CHAPTER 17

Clay and Jaiden had a pleasant dinner with the Beacons. Sandy looked healthy and hearty, confirming a commitment to her new treadmill which she showed off with pride. Larry acted thrilled at his wife's recovery and extremely grateful for Clay's rescue of her. They were cordial and friendly, making Clay and Jaiden comfortable.

Jaiden forced herself to have fun and enjoy the time she shared with Clay, while it lasted, grateful he'd invited her along instead of his other friend. She wanted all of Clay she could get until it was time to turn him loose.

The next day Clay's phone chirped waking the love birds from sleeping in on Jaiden's day off. Clay rolled toward the bedside table snatching his phone from beside an alarm clock showing nine a.m. "Hello." He managed to not sound groggy.

"Good morning, Clay. Carlton Fuller here."

"Carlton, it's good to hear from you. Does this mean you have news for me? I hope it is good news." Clay sat up on side the bed.

Jaiden, now awake too, ran a delicate, leisurely hand across his bare shoulders then down his back gently massaging. Despite his attention to the phone call, which was undoubtedly important, his body responded immediately to her touch.

"Indeed, Clay. I'm happy to say with Carmen Burnette's help, I've contacted each current heir to your parents' farm and received responses. They've agreed to accept your generous offer to split among them. I need you to stop in and sign final papers. I'll overnight them to descendants so they can sign and return them. We should close the deal within four to five days. I'm in my office all morning, if you want to stop by at your convenience. If I'm tied up, my secretary will have a packet marked where to sign."

"Fantastic, Carlton, you've done a bang-up job. I don't know how to thank you."

Jaiden crawled out of bed. Her hip and shoulder brazed his as she stood. Then she sashayed bare-assed to his bathroom. His breath caught at sight of her in her glory. At the door she glanced over her shoulder. She threw him a knowing smile signaling she read his mind and liked his thinking. She blew him a kiss, and he puckered in response. Then she disappeared behind a closed bathroom door. Running water from a shower filtered through.

He squirmed at a persistent erection pointed at his face. The woman had him by his balls, and he loved it.

"Thank me by sticking around in Sweetwater and bringing me your future business. Howard and I would love being able to spend more time with you." Carlton joked, but sincerity soothed his words. He and his partner, Howard Ross, had hinted earlier, he'd like Clay to move back to their hometown.

"That's gracious. You and Howard transitioned from Boston. Right? Tell me about it."

"Oh, sure. Howard and I've lived together since law school. We graduated from Harvard Law, took the bar exam then opened a practice in Boston. It was successful. Dovie, my twin—you remember her?"

"Of course, how could one forget teasing redheaded cyclone, Dovie Fuller?"

"Dovie married one of her instructors while studying to become a chef in Europe. She globetrotted with her famous husband, working in elegant restaurants all over Asia. Gran lived alone after Gramps passed away. Her health started going south. I worried terribly about her. Howard agreed; family comes first. We sold our practice in Boston, moved here, and opened this office."

"How do you like the small-town living

after working in a big city?" Carlton's story was similar to Clay's, except Clay hadn't lost his heart to anyone in Chicago. The closest he'd come to finding lasting love was with Jaiden. If he stuck around their short-term fling might mature into a beautiful future. He'd bet on it.

"Actually, I love it. Townsfolk have accepted Howard and me with open arms. Old friends immediately made us welcome. Our practice isn't on a scale of our Boston office, but Howard and I are satisfied with our progress. It's a different kind of work. We're able to get close to those we help. They're familiar faces in our everyday life. We're finding it extremely rewarding."

That was what Clay needed to hear. "Thanks for being so forthcoming. I'm considering sticking around. I'll let you know what I decide. You're a huge help, both professionally and personally. Say '*hello*' to Howard for me. I'll stop by in a little while to sign papers."

He headed for the bathroom to join Jaiden and take care of a forceful stiff aching for her touch.

CHAPTER 18

Doctor Maines returned to town a day before the hospital benefit. He and Clay did hospital rounds together. Clay caught him up on patient statuses.

"Patients are in good order. So how did it go for you? How did you like working at my practice and taking my hospital hours?" He studied Clay's reaction.

Clay felt a smile engage his eyes showing off his teeth. He couldn't hide pleasure he'd found caring for these people. "It was a joy. Everyone was accepting and grateful for care I provided. Working at a small, private practice, everything feels personal. I got used to it easily."

Dr. Maines patted his back. They strolled together through the long corridor. "You're a Godsend to me, the last couple weeks. I was able to travel and enjoy my daughter's wedding and spend time with my grandchildren without guilt. Knowing my patients were left in good hands made a difference. Any chance I can convince you to stick around? My practice could handle another physician, especially a general surgeon. It'd allow me to shorten my hours. I want to do it. I'm not a young pup any longer. You know?" Doc Maines grinned.

The handsome, aging gentleman looked full of vigor and healthy. From what Clay understood, even the most vital person's energy and stamina began waning as years went by. Sometimes burn out was a reason, and some elderly sought a more leisurely life. Either way, Dr. Maines offered Clay an opportunity he couldn't turn down without ample consideration.

"It's an enticing offer. I'll need to think on it. Your practice is well staffed and nicely rounded with partners. I've enjoyed working here."

Cynthia Smith was a pediatrician. Dr. Maines handled most adult concerns. Tony Harbor was a dermatologist. Sue Clutch was an oncologist. Ray Bean was an endocrinologist. Harvey Long was an orthopedic specialist and surgeon, and Larry Comet was a cardiologist.

Clay could step right into their circle making a perfect fit.

♥♥♥♥

Wyatt knocked on a heavy, wooden courthouse door when he returned to Mayor Kenneth Bailey's office to pursue a specific line of questioning.

"Enter." A booming voice sounded preoccupied. Kenneth Bailey looked up from a stack of papers he was enthralled in. Surprise registered on his face. "Sheriff, this is a surprise. What can I do for you?" He clasped his hands atop the documents.

"Sorry to bother you again, Mr. Mayor. We've uncovered a piece of information requiring further comment from you." He waved them toward him. Wyatt took a chair.

"Yes. Kenneth, we previously discussed your BW loan with Walter Burnette. However, since then we learned your wife, Heady Bailey, had an affair with Walter."

Like air being let out of a pricked balloon, Kenneth expelled a heavy sigh. "Damn it. I should've gotten it in the open up front. I feared it would return to bite my ass again."

He glanced around looking for a lifeline. Finally meeting Wyatt's eyes he shook his head doubtfully.

"It's true. Heady screwed the bastard. We dealt with problems for several years before she finally admitted how unhappy she was and wanted a divorce. We filed. She moved to Lexington to live with her sister then found a place of her own. I started hearing rumors. You know how it is. People knew we'd split up. They told me things they normally wouldn't share. From what I understand, Heady started seeing Burnette long after I'd initiated a BW loan. They were in no way connected. She must've gotten wind Walter was fooling around with other gals, because she asked for a divorce after breaking it off with him. I suppose you think it provides me a motive to kill Walter, but I never heard about it until she'd moved away. I don't begrudge Heady the divorce. We had issues having nothing to do with Walter. Her fling with him was merely a side effect."

"What about Heady? Was she was angry enough with Walter to want him dead? Is she capable of murder?" Wyatt probed with an even voice.

Kenneth shook his head looking defeated. "I can't see it. Heady is searching for what's missing in her life, but Walter wasn't it. I don't think she ever gave a damn about him. Ask her yourself." He pulled a business card from his lap drawer and wrote her contact information on back.

Wyatt stood and pocketed the slip of paper. "Thanks for your time, Mayor Bailey. I'll follow up with your ex-wife. Sorry to bother you." Wyatt waved toward paperwork on Kenneth's desk.

"Gee thanks. I'm knee deep in budget

analysis. It's my most dreaded job. See you at the benefit tomorrow night." Kenneth waved him out. Wyatt shut the door behind him.

A short drive to Lexington and a quick conversation with Heady Bailey, uncovered nothing of help, but did eliminate her from their suspect list. She owned no weapons and had an air-tight alibi for date of death.

CHAPTER 19

Jaiden and Wyatt knocked on Lisa Russell's apartment door. FANCI Funding Corporation's auditor, Ken Horn, had called Lisa in to work occasionally during the last few weeks to help resolve issues at The Burnett Finance Company, but she was largely unemployed and looking for a job.

Lisa wore a large sweatshirt nearly reaching her knees with a pair of tight leggings. Thick socks rolled around her ankles. Her hair was pulled into a sleek ponytail, and she wore no makeup. She looked fresh and young.

Surprise registered on her face at seeing the sheriff and deputy at her doorstep. She inhabited the rental space above her parents' garage. "Ya 'all come on in." She waved them through into her combination living room, kitchen and dining room. A dry-walled partition of about six-feet-tall separated a section of the small dormer space providing privacy for a bedroom area and bath.

Lisa led them to a kitchen table and pulled out cups matching the one she drank from sitting on the table. Without asking she poured three hot brews from a pot on a counter. She sat them in front of her guests and shoved a tray holding cream and sugar toward them. She plopped down across from them and peeled plastic wrap off a plate of home-baked chocolate-chip cookies.

"Try these. I made them yesterday."

Jaiden helped herself to a cookie, bit and smiled. "They're delicious. Thank you, Lisa."

"You're welcome." Lisa gave Jaiden a satisfied smile then turned toward Wyatt. "What 'cha need, Sheriff?" She sipped coffee, but her eyes never left his.

"Actually, Officer Coldwater uncovered an item we need to discuss. It appears you've gotten automatic payroll deposits from Walter Burnette."

"That's right. There's nothing unusual about getting auto-deposits for earnings." Lisa continued a blank stare into Wyatt's eyes.

"No. They'll turn business over to a permanent management group, eventually. I'm pleased FANCI Funding Corporation continues paying your salary. Some companies leave employees in a lurch in positions like yours."

"Yes, Mr. Horn is generous and considerate of my situation."

"It's a second group of Burnett Finance Company payments to you we need to discuss. Three months after you replaced Gwen Russo, you began receiving substantial additional checks from the corporation every other week. They varied in amount. Each was a good sized sum of cash. What did these payments cover?" Jaiden abandoned her cookie and spoke calmly and succinctly. She finished with her spiel. Her eyes latched onto Lisa's studying her reaction. Jaiden was good at reading people, especially women.

Lisa fidgeted in her seat. She glanced around searching for an answer.

Wyatt studied her response. She acted as though she was looking for a lie to tell. He had enough.

"You knew about Walter's shady business deals. Didn't you, Lisa? You extorted money from Walter to keep quiet about his unlawful BW loans. Correct?"

Her shoulders sank, and she sounded like a balloon with air being let out. Closing her eyes, Lisa shook her head.

"That damned fool had to get himself

shot, ruining everything. He was making a fortune. So was his ex-wife, by bringing him clients and getting kickbacks. He enjoyed full reign of every horny bitch in town. The rutting pig tried to bed me, but I turned him down flat. I made him a proposition of my own. He paid me a percentage of BW loan profits, and I kept my mouth shut."

"Did you kill Walter?" Wyatt spoke calmly. He could've easily been asking for directions. His keen eye never left her face.

"I did not. The shit was worth a lot of money to me—alive. Deceased I receive nothing from him. He was a disgusting human being, but I didn't wish him dead." She looked pissed but sincere.

"Lisa, you obtained over ten-thousand-dollars from Burnette Funding Company through extortion. That's a Class C felony in the state of Kentucky. I'm afraid you're under arrest." Wyatt unlatched handcuffs dangling from his belt. He moved behind Lisa.

She didn't resist, but placed her hands behind allowing him to lock them together. "You're taking that bitch, Carmen in too, right? She received kickbacks from Walter for business referrals when he sold BW loans."

"Funds Carmen obtained paid for referrals, which may be against ethical standards. It's not against state real estate stature. Folks may consider Mrs. Burnette's dealings shady, but she broke no law. So, no; she's not joining you in jail." Jaiden grabbed

Lisa's shoulder and pushed her gently toward the door. Wyatt flicked the coffee pot off and followed the women out.

CHAPTER 20

Clay stopped by Carlton's office and spent an hour going through the huge stack of letters signing each one. Carlton had prepared them for signatures from each heir and their spouses agreeing to a sale. Family members scattered across as far west from California, Wyoming, Montana, Idaho, Oregon and Washington. He explained once paperwork was returned from each heir they'd exchange funds, signing everything else necessary making the Barnes farm finally Clay's.

Clay had made arrangements for cash from his personal savings account in Chicago transferred to a local bank to cover purchase. Soon it would belong to him, and he needed to make a decision what to do with it.

Carlton's secretary had brought him a pitcher of ice water and fresh glasses, a pot of hot coffee, cream and sugar. He sipped while doing the mindless task and his mind wandered to Jaiden's spectacular body sprawled nude sleeping beside him in his bed.

Her scent of jasmine and coconut mixed uniquely with her personal fragrance filled his nostrils. A delectable odor surged joyful sparks through his nervous system. His pulse raced pumping heart throbs through his sensuous mind. He recalled every bare inch of a woman he'd come to think of as his own.

Her dark, tawny skin glowed radiantly by moonlight filtering in through bedroom windows highlighting her beauty and making him crazy with the desire to stroke her satiny skin and kiss every mouthwatering inch of her being.

Jaiden was a strong woman—one with a past and demons driving her, forbidding her to trust easily. A fierce guardian of downtrodden, especially women in peril, was part of what made her a brilliant law enforcement officer. She was the most interesting female Clay had met. He needed her—in his life and his bed.

His phone rang. "Hello, Dr. Barnes here." Clay hadn't glanced at the number. He expected someone calling about his purchase, or a medical issue from a patient, doctor or local hospital.

"Clay, Jim Montovia here. I haven't heard from you. I figured I'd best reach out. How's it going? Have you wrapped up your parents' estate? You ready to head home to Chicago where you belong? The board will meet in the next couple weeks to name a new Head of General Surgery. You are still in running, right? You realize you have a shot at the position, don't you?" Dr. Jim Montovia was his boss in Chicago, and he sounded less than sure of anything he said. "We want you back, Clay. You're a fine doctor and have a fantastic career ahead of you on our staff."

"Thanks, Jim. I apologize for not calling you sooner. Unusual developments have been a trial at best. Things are finally coming together. A few complexities need working out."

"Say you're heading home soon. It would do your chances of snaring the leadership role good if you showed your face before the board meets to discuss it." Clearly Jim stood on Clay's side. Clay felt miserable but couldn't confirm he wanted what Jim offered.

"I doubt it. I've got at least two to three

weeks' worth of issues to resolve before considering returning. In fact, I'm not sure it's what I want anymore. I'm considering moving here. The longer I linger, the closer I come to deciding it's what I want."

Jim's sigh sounded shocked. "I can't imagine you relinquishing this role to become a slow-paced, country-bumpkin doctor."

Clay laughed at Jim's out-of-date description. "It's not like that, Jim; but it's totally different from working at a huge hospital in Chicago. We have running water and penicillin in Sweetwater. In fact, there's a hospital—with beds, bedpans and everything." He chuckled good-heartedly not letting Jim's assumptions sting.

"Damn, son, I'm sorry. I didn't mean it like that. I want what's best for you. You have a real shot at our leadership position, which would spur your career straight to the top, and enable you to secure funding for research and effective assets for your future and to benefit our hospital."

"Thank you, Jim. I understand you want what's best for me. I appreciate your support and patience. It can't be easy letting me take time off. I need to decide what kind of future I want. I've been helping here, filling in for a local surgeon for a couple weeks. I'm shocked how much I enjoy it. I'm getting a realistic look at how my career might unfold in Sweetwater and like what I see."

"Are you sure more isn't going on? A

woman perhaps?" Jim knew Clay well and realized he had no personal ties to Chicago, no social or love life there.

As he spoke Clay's face automatically went into a broad smile, and a lilt in his voice expressed his state of mind more than words. "Perhaps—yes, I've met a woman. She's worth everything. She deserves more than I can give her. To make her mine, I'd willingly move to the edge of the world if she wanted me."

"If she does, does it entail residing in Sweetwater? Any chance you can decide in the next couple weeks? If you want off our short list, I'd like to advise the board so they can give another chap a shot."

"I promise, I'll work on my decision and let you know within a week if I'm returning. Work for you?"

Jim let out a long lungful. "Hell, Clay, I don't have a choice. Do I?"

"I'll call you before the next week is out. Thanks Jim, for lighting a fire under me." Clay felt determined and knew what he needed to do.

While he finished his mundane task, he mulled over benefits of staying vs. going. In every instance, Sweetwater came out on top. He loved his home, especially now remodeled to his taste and modernized. It would soon be one-hundred percent his. He adored working with Dr. Maines and partners, and at the local hospital. He enjoyed being in familiar territory surrounded by old and new friends in a community welcoming him, a native son.

Best of all, he was hopelessly in love with Jaiden Coldwater. Jaiden was the kind of woman a man counted on sticking by his side through thick and thin, giving their relationship her all and expecting the same from him.

She was a priceless piece of heaven. He so wanted to be granted a place on her cloud.

CHAPTER 21

Clay arrived home. His house was in

order. Jaiden was working late, so he wouldn't
see her that evening. When he emptied her
bedroom for remodeling, he had raked drawers
and boxes of items into large plastic crates,
sealed and stored them in a closet. It was a good
time to tackle cartons of old paperwork and
memorabilia his mom had collected.

He opened a bottle of wine and poured a
generous amount into a tall goblet. Taking it to
the living room, he stacked three crates beside
the couch. He opened a large trash bag and
placed it by his side. He would sort through
paperwork tossing trash into a bag, stacking
piles of items to keep or requiring action of
some kind on the coffee table.

An hour later he'd emptied one crate.
Most of its contents were in a large black bag on
the floor. He opened a second crate—much the
same. Old record books where she'd kept track
of income and bills paid monthly, receipts for
payments made, cash register tapes of purchased
items, a few advertisements and newspaper
articles about local events he tossed away. A
stack on the short table contained articles in
reference to his sporting escapades in school
along with a few photographs, mostly of him.
Halfway through, Clay found a book. It didn't
look like a small ledger or calendar books his
mother used for record keeping.

Opening it he read inscriptions on an
inside cover. '*Diary—Mable, January 1972-
March 1973.*'

Mable? Who the hell? Was it Mom—her

real name?

Betty and Wilber Barnes didn't actually exist. The book dropped like he became an apparition and it slipped through his skin. Maybe he was. He certainly wasn't Clay Barnes as he'd always believed.

Glancing at the other box, a deep, cleansing breath failed to fortify him. Not now. I should accomplish at least one thing tonight. I must weed through these cartons. I'll deal with Mable later. He retrieved the small cloth-bound book handling it like a precious jewel. Laying it aside, he focused once again on sorting boxes. An hour later he'd finished. The black bag bulged from weight. He tied the end and dragged it out back where he slipped it into a large garbage can.

Returning to the living room, he refilled his wine glass. He bundled a stack of keepsakes and photos he'd uncovered. Good knowing Mom loved him enough to collect the items, even haphazardly stored throughout her bedroom. He'd treasure them as she had.

There was a small stack of invoices and a safe deposit box key with Sweetwater National Bank printed on it. He cross-checked invoices against utility payments and other bills he'd handled since his mother's passing. No invoices were outstanding, so he tossed them into the trash.

He'd check out the bank box the following day, to discover what other unruly surprises Mom had in store. For tonight, he was alone with her diary, getting to finally know who his mother really was.

"That cute fella came in dad's store again today. He's a dreamboat. Wonder where he lives—not around here. He keeps showing up when I'm behind the counter. Dad would beat the shit out of me if he saw me making eyes at a boy."

So his mother had an eye for an out-of-town fellow. *Dad?* He'd soon learn.

For a few months she wrote regular notes attesting to the *dreamy* boy's periodical stops at her father's store and their short chats. Then something changed.

"Will came in again today. Dad was there, so we couldn't talk. He knows Dad watches him when he's in the store. Dad doesn't trust Will. I don't care. I swoon every time we're alone and can talk. He's the love of my life, and I'd do anything to be with him."

An entry a few days later escalated things. *"Will came in today knowing I'd be alone. We talked for a half hour. He wants me to be his girl. He's got a driver's license now, so he's driving his pa's car. I want to be with him so bad it hurts."*

Then a few days later she wrote more. *"Will watched for Dad to leave before coming in today. We were alone for a long time. He hates it at home and wants me to run away with him. He kissed me, and I was in heaven. I'd do anything to be with him. He's coming back next week and we're going to do it."*

"We did it. We ran away together. Will came in knowing I was alone, at a time when there'd be plenty of cash in the register. We took the money and some he stole from his pa. We left town with his pa's car, heading straight south to Connecticut. We're at a tiny mom-and-pop motel. It's old-fashioned but clean. He's in the bathroom now. I'm waiting for him in bed. I can't wait to give myself to Will. He's the man of my dreams." The entry was dated September 10, 1972.

Clay's parents stole from his father and hers then ran away together. They originated from somewhere north of Connecticut.

"I was born to make love with Will. I feel like a real woman. I'll never leave him—no matter what. We're getting low on cash and trying to conserve. We skipped out of the last motel without paying. We've done it a couple times leaving restaurant bills unpaid. I go to the bathroom. Then he does, and we run out the back to race away in the car. What a thrill! God, I love Will. I'd do anything for him."

Damn, even worse. They stole from regular people.

A week later another entry wrote. *"We robbed a bank and got away without hurting anyone. No one recognized us in our disguises. We cased the place a couple days. Then we did it with no customers around. No one got hurt. It was easy. We're doing it again in another town. It's thrilling, but not as exhilarating as making love with Will."*

Shit, Mom liked robbing banks. Who the hell were the people I called Mom and Dad?

A month later the next entry was written. *"It was easier this time. We knew what we did. It's the same bank, but another town branch. There's one in a city a few miles away. We're going there before stopping for the night. Two hauls in one day should do for a while."*

She wrote again a couple weeks later, dated March 12, 1972. *"We've hit six banks so far and have a stash of dough to show for it. I'm starting to get the hang of it, but nervous too. I'm pregnant, probably due in October. Will says one more, and we can stop. We'll go somewhere to live and raise or baby. I hope it's a boy, and he's cute and smart like Will. He'll be a loving dad."*

Wrong. Dad had been named Will. Will what? He might've had brains but obviously no qualms about law.

He wasn't a good dad. Clay always felt awkward around him, like he resented the boy. Perhaps he held him responsible for their having curtailed their exciting bank bandit lifestyle. Obviously both had enjoyed the occupation.

Clay's dad had acted reserved and standoffish with his own son, worse than with others. Everyone considered him a recluse. If Dad had his way, Mom would've never ventured off the farm. She loved playing piano. The church owned one. She went to services in order to get her music fix. Dad allowed it because she promised never to bring folks home or talk about their lives with people she met.

His dad worked the farm and peddled vegetables and hay. He cut and sold firewood, and occasionally did handyman jobs. Mom cleaned office buildings evenings, took in laundry from a couple of families, and did alterations for a dry cleaner in Sweetwater. Between them, they made enough to scrape by.

Apparently neither sought traditional jobs where social security numbers and identities might come under scrutiny. They'd played it safe with their work lives.

But hey, they had a stash of cash to lean on.

Looking back, he pinpointed incidences when they dipped into the bundle. Money was lean and unexpected bills came their way. They paid for things Clay thought beyond their means. He needed money for sports. He broke his arm resulting in large medical bills. He went to college. They told him they worked extra hours to help out and keep his education funded. They didn't want him graduating with a huge debt to repay. He had a small student loan after graduating from medical school. He'd long since paid it off. Obviously, during these peak financial needs, they'd pilfered the robbery cash.

The consideration made his stomach sour and a tight wad rose to his throat. He swallowed it hard and sighed. He never in his wildest dreams thought his meek, mild mother and quiet, reclusive father were once uninhibited, sinister criminals—bank robbers who enjoyed their chosen career.

They'd given it up for him—or had they? He was a convenient excuse to stop doing what would inevitably land them either in the morgue or prison. She would've grown large with the child, making them easier to track down.

Clay never doubted Mom loved him. Dad did too, in his own way. Having him was a fitting, opportune excuse to halt thievery and settle down. It also helped them appear conventional, like a normal family when they took over someone else's real estate.

Sweetwater was a welcoming community. Undoubtedly citizens had respected Mom and Dad's quiet, private ways. His parents chose well, with their new personas.

Clay slept fitfully and the next morning called the number to Sage's cell. "Good morning, Sage Gordon here, Parsley, Sage, Rose, Mary & Wine. What can I do for you?"

"Sage, it's Clay Barnes. You got a minute?" When he awoke, his gut told him to reach out to Sage.

"Oh, hi, Clay. Sorry about the business spiel. I didn't recognize your number, so assumed it to be business."

"I'm calling to ask a favor. You haven't found any news yet about those bills have you?"

"I have, actually found one sequence. I'll double check it then share the information. It's difficult, because the source has gone out of business long ago. Do you mind if I do a bit more digging before explaining?"

"Hell no, Sage. Do what you think best. I have enough on my mind right now to explode a normal brain. Before I ask you to help I need to know—will Wyatt get upset?"

Jaiden explained some of Sage's past escapades to Clay. She'd gotten in danger in the past, and Wyatt was extremely protective of his wife. He loved her very much. Clay didn't want to throw a ringer into their relationship.

"Wyatt knows I need a challenge and love a mystery. I told him you agreed to let me help investigate the cash. He'd offer too, but he's in the middle of the murder thing and doesn't have a moment to spare. Wyatt knows I can handle myself. I'm a decent amateur sleuth, though he calls me a danger magnet. Anyway, what can I do for you?"

He explained what he learned in his mom's diary. Sage marked dates, names and notations beside a map which she planned to use to figure out which banks the Barnes' had robbed.

"This explains a lot about my parents. It's understandable why they kept private and urged me to act that way too. They never allowed me to bring friends over. They didn't attend my games or even graduation. We had what we needed, but not much else. We lived frugally. I guess they didn't want to attract attention."

"Oh, Clay, I'm sorry. This can't be easy to learn about your parents. It's hard to think of loved one's going wrong."

"Yes, I'm glad you understand. I know you and Wyatt will use discretion. I wouldn't want it out in the public. Carlton and Carmen know about the land deal, but they've sworn to secrecy and in their professions, they'll keep quiet to protect their reputations. Jaiden I'd trust with my life. I don't want anyone else knowing about this, especially if my parents went on a rampage robbing banks in the seventies. I don't believe Dad was aware of Mom's diary. He would've been angry and would've burned it. She hid it stuck in bed springs. I moved them during remodeling and it fell out. I tossed it in a box of junk. I found the notebook when I went through the carton last night."

"Clay, there's one more person I'd like to share with. She might help track the money's source. Reggie Casse is an FBI Special Agent. She'd gladly lend me a hand with resources I don't have access to. Reggie will keep your confidence. Secrecy is required in her career as a Fed."

"I know Reggie. I haven't seen her since senior year in high school. She was a perky, gorgeous gal and dated your husband, if I recall. I can't see her as an agent. You and Reggie are friends? It's a small world."

"We're more like sisters. We went to college together, along with Levi Madison's wife, Riley Powers-Madison. Anyway, I trust Reggie with my life. Let me ask her to help solve our mystery, so you can get past it."

"Sure, if you're certain she won't spread it around. Go for it. And, Sage, I truly appreciate your help. I'd ask Jaiden, and I know she's tried to find the information, but she, like Wyatt, is swamped with the murder case. Poor gal doesn't know if she's coming or going." He smiled picturing Jaiden's exotic face.

"From what I understand, she's doing more coming than going, with you in town. The lady is over the moon for you, Clay. I've not known her long, merely a couple years since she moved here. I've never seen her fall for a man before. She looks all-in to me. Don't you break our Jaiden's heart, now—you hear?" Sage was teasing, but truth in her words impressed him. She was a loyal friend.

"Jaiden puts a smile on my face." It was all he willingly shared. "Thanks, for what you're doing, Sage. Let me know if you find anything, or need more information." He clicked the phone off.

CHAPTER 22

Clay rang Jaiden the day of the fundraiser benefiting the hospital children's wing. Her workload remained heavy with a killing yet unresolved. She'd avoided him since the previous Friday. He'd come close to confronting her a couple times, but she'd distracted him or to cut him off.

It was gnawing at Jaiden's gut, wasting time she could be with him while Clay was in town. She ached to jump his bones nightly and find ecstasy she'd discovered in no other man's arms.

Clay was better off without Jaiden. Distancing herself allowed him to develop a relationship with Jane who fit Clay better. Doubtful he'd reside in Sweetwater though, after recent revelations. He'd take Jane and her daughter wherever his dream-life led.

Jaiden certainly wasn't answer to his long-term needs. She should cut the cord now before it hurt any worse.

Was it even possible? She was suffering pitifully without him.

Typing a report at her desk she glanced around the bullpen. She enjoyed working with these men, especially Sheriff Wyatt Gordon. Wyatt had been a godsend, offering her a position.

Her mom was here now, along with Cal and his bride Rose. Hopefully soon they'd have a family. Jaiden had friends like Sage, Corrie, Justin, Levi, and Riley. Sweetwater was a good town to plant roots.

Moggie, her closest buddy was like a big brother—a brother from another mother. Sure, they'd slept together before Dovie arrived in town stealing his heart. They both knew it was only fun. Neither took it seriously. Dovie was good for her pal, Moggie, and Jaiden liked her.

Her cell rang. "Hey, how you doing? I was thinking of you. What's up?"

"You're attending the fundraiser tonight?" Moggie's thick Kentucky accent sounded lighthearted.

"I was planning to go with Clay, but things have changed. I'm working late. I was about to call him to cancel. He can go without me."

"How late you working? One of my mares is giving birth this evening. Dovie's catering the affair. She'll arrive early and be busy the whole time. I might run over and donate some cash after the foal is born if things go well. Want to go with me? I've got Dovie's ticket, though she doesn't need one."

It had been awhile since Jaiden and Moggie had the opportunity to talk. She could use a chat with her best bud and couldn't resist.

"Sounds like a plan. I'll take my gown to the station. After the little one pops out, give me a buzz. I'll change into my duds and meet you out front. It will give me time to finish reports needing typing and spend time with you. I miss you, Moggie."

"Same here. You sound like you are depressed or worried about something. What's going on?" Concern filtered his words.

"I'll fill you in when I see you." He was medicine she needed. Moggie placed a realistic spin on everything. He'd help clear her head. She'd run home and retrieve her gown and heels at lunch time, in case Moggie's foal was born in time for them to attend part of the affair.

Her cell rang. Wyatt glanced her way without comment, from where he refilled paper in the printer beside her desk. "Deputy Coldwater." She hadn't glanced at the screen.

"Hi, Jaiden. How's your day going? I'm excited about the banquet tonight. It seems years since I last saw you. I miss you. I can't wait to wrap my arms around you on a dance-floor."

Clay's sexy voice slid over sharp edges of her bristly mood easing stress she was harboring. Her shoulders responded relaxing at an image in her mind of Clay snuggled around her, holding her against him while they belly-rubbed to a soft love tune.

No, not what you need. She jolted erect once again tensing.

"Clay, I was about to call you. I have a huge stack of reports to type. I'm going to work over a few hours. Go without me."

Disappointment filled his words. "No kidding? Can't you delay it to tomorrow?"

"Tomorrow's my day off. I don't want to spend it behind a desk." No emotion came with her words.

"I'll wait and we can go together after you finish." His tone said he knew this ploy wouldn't work.

"No, I don't know how long it'll take. I might not make it at all. If I do, it'll be late. You go. You're connected to the hospital and planning to sit with doctors in Doc Maines' partnership. It could prove an important night for you. Besides, Wyatt said Sage has news for you. I understand she's gotten farther than I did concerning your found cash."

Wyatt glanced around at hearing Sage's and his names spoken. He eyed her critically then went back to his task, having heard the full conversation.

"Okay, if you insist. But I miss you awfully. I wish you'd reconsider."

She hated causing disappointment in his voice. It was best. "Okay, good. Hey, why don't

you give my ticket to your office receptionist—
Jane, I believe her name is." *Man,* she was
treading thick water.

"Oh, no need. Dr. Maines gave Jane a
ticket. She's coming anyway and will sit at our
table." No thrill embellished his voice, clearly
looking forward to getting laid by Jaiden.

Too bad.

Men's libidos ruled their brains.

An evening with Jane on a dance floor
would push their relationship forward where it
belonged. Once Clay was bedding a normal gal,
he'd never look back.

"I must go." Jaiden clicked the phone off
without saying goodbye or waiting for
argument. It was rude but might help the break.

She looked up. Wyatt leaned his behind
against the copier, arms and feet crossed
studying her. "You don't need to work late, or
come in tomorrow to finish reports. Do them
Monday." He knew she was snaking out of a
date with Clay.

"I want to finish them."

"You're avoiding Clay. Why?" He saw
through her facade.

"Why do you think? The dude is
destined for other places. He's either heading
back to Chicago, or some location where his
heart leads to build a new practice and life. He
won't stick around after uncovering filth about
his parents." She glanced around making sure
other deputies didn't hear. Most were out on
calls. A couple at desks talked on their phones

with better things to do than listen to her conversation with the boss. "I need to cut ties now and end it."

"What was that bull about Jane?"

She shrugged and glanced away, not meeting his eyes. "I suspect potential between them. She's more Clay's type—stable woman with a child. If he falls for anyone in town, it should be her."

Wyatt chuckled. His hand cupped his chin and slid upward swiping across his forehead. Then he met her eyes leaning on her desk with his palms splayed. "You're a scared little rabbit, running from destiny. Aren't you?"

She glared without speaking, arms crossed in front of her chest.

"Jaiden, if you and Clay mean what it appears you do to each other, you're a damned fool to not see how it plays out. Don't push him toward another woman because you think she's better for him."

"I have no say in it. He's dating her, too, Wyatt. I don't have to push him her way. They're already chummy. I've seen them together. We're not exclusive, never even discussed it. I'm backing out of their way."

His expression clarified Wyatt didn't buy it. He shook his head and sighed. "That's a crock if I ever heard one. What if they come together like you say then decide to reside in Sweetwater? How will you handle it?"

Her heart stopped beating and sunk into her gut. She glanced away, and a tirade of tears

threatened to flow. She blinked them back.
Swallowing hard, she turned toward her friend.

"I don't know. I'll deal, if it happens."

"You think on it. I don't want to lose
you. I'm not sure you could stick around and
watch Clay live with another woman. I believe
you're wrong. I've seen him with you. The
boy's in over his head. Why you think you're
not right for him is beyond me. You're one of
the best women I've had pleasure to know." He
threw his hands in the air and marched to his
office.

CHAPTER 23

The fundraiser was a huge success. Every expensive dinner ticket was sold. The place was packed with elegantly dressed townsfolk milling around a festive room. Two bars served, one from each side, centered with elaborately decorated, linen-covered tables. A stage-glittered displaying backdrop visual of a new children's wing. A row of covered tables sat center stage awaited speakers.

Clay ambled to a bar. Mayor Ken chatted with his date, Carmen Burnette, beautifully clad and hanging from his elbow and on every word, obviously smitten. The couple acted comfortable together and obviously had been an item for a while.

Clay ordered bourbon-on-the-rocks and one for the Mayor. He handed it to him and reached a goblet of red wine to Carmen. "Thank you, Clay, enjoying your evening?"

He shrugged. Ken grinned and winked. "I expected to see dazzling deputy, Jaiden Coldwater on your arm. If I recall a double-wedding at Mane Lane Farm correctly, she dresses up nicely."

"She was coming with me, but cancelled, tied up with work. Jaiden may stop in later for a few minutes."

Carmen's eyes popped wide. "Oh, I hope she's found a break in the case."

"Yes. She and Wyatt are working like fiends solving the crime." Ken turned his date in another direction. "Enjoy, Clay. I spot folks I must speak with."

The couple sauntered toward a group talking with Levi Madison's dad, Senator Garrett Madison and his lovely wife, Adelle. The handsome aging couple presented a perfect image of a political pair.

Clay strolled to his table. It was full except for two chairs reserved for him and Jaiden. Jane sat beside Dr. Maines's wife, Cheryl, who held her husband's hand. Dr. Cynthia Smith introduced her husband, Glenn. Dr. Tony Harbor introduced his fiancée, Carrie. Dr. Sue Clutch was accompanied by her husband, Jay. Dr. Ray Ben and his wife, Rachael sat next to Dr. Harvey Long and wife, Sue. Dr. Larry Comet and his wife, Joy were last in the group.

After a round meeting folks and

explaining why he had no date, he wandered toward Levi Madison's table, where many of his old friends gathered. He did a round of handshakes with men and cheek kisses with women. Wyatt stood at a bar talking with someone.

Levi and Riley made a stunning pair. His tall, lean stature was clad in a dark grey, silk, western-cut suit. A shock of unruly, blonde tresses were forced to submission for the formal occasion. Riley wore a maroon gown with no straps showing off her tiny waist then flowing easily about slim hips. Her dark hair coiffed in curls pinned to a chignon along back of her head. A diamond necklace exhibited her long, slim neck. Sizable studs in her ears matched those around her neck and wrist. He'd known Levi his whole life, and adored him. Riley had relocated from northern Kentucky and he'd recently met her, but she'd charmed him quickly.

Corrie with her tanned skin spent considerable time outdoors riding. Long, blonde curls looked stunning against a dark-green gown clinging to her voluptuous shape. See-through sleeves exposed arms and chest. From bust-down the dress lined in dark green beneath filmy fabric looked elegant like the woman wearing it. A straight neckline across its front plunged to her waist in the rear, showing off her straight back. Contrasting, her husband, Justin Henderson, the love of her life, was short and lean with a wiry appearance and bulky muscles beneath a well-fitted suit. His dark complexion and curly, long hair curled around his face and down his neck to the stiff white collar of his shirt. Together they reminded Clay of fire and ice. Each had both in their systems. Together they were a hot-blooded combination.

Sage was gorgeous in her navy velvet gown, plunging in front and back in deep v's with tiny straps at shoulders. Her slim silhouette displayed a slender runner's body. She'd lost any hint of having produced a son a year before. Clay made his way toward her, and she indicated for him to sit at Wyatt's vacant chair.

"I'm glad to see you."

"Jaiden said you made headway with the money."

She grinned like a little girl getting ready to share confidence with a pal. "I did, and I hope you find it helpful. It's not what you want to hear. From what Wyatt said, you realize your parents orchestrated some illegal activity."

"Yes, I found Mom's diary. They robbed banks before settling in Sweetwater to raise a family." He whispered glancing around.

"Two sequences of bills are from separate branches of a bank—two savings and loans, one in Vermont, the other in New Hampshire. They and their holding company long ago went out of business. FBI records show both unsolved robberies occurred in 1973 and 1974. Does it jive with your mom's diary?"

"Sadly, it does. They apparently robbed several banks. Maybe they'd spent the other cash."

"Thieves were never caught in thirteen burglaries in Connecticut, Maine, New Hampshire and Vermont between late 1960s too early 1970's. They could've done some of them, but not all. MO differed in many cases."

"We've narrowed it to at least these two." Gnawing in his gut would surely rip his insides to shreds. How had he not realized his parents were bald-faced thieves?

"Yes, and the same savings and loan had four branches robbed during that period. MO was the same in those, so I'd bet they did them."

"Okay. We know where the money came from, but they don't exist any longer. What do I do with the dough?"

"I knew you'd ask. I solicited advice from Wyatt and Reggie. Both said turning it over to the Federal Government would deposit it in an evidence locker forever. Institutions it sourced from are long extinct. With your parents gone the trail is cold with no way to prove they committed crimes. You're not required to relinquish the cash."

"Did you learn their true identities? I sure haven't—only Will and Mabel." His shoulders felt heavy carrying a weighty load.

"I'm sorry. If they'd identified suspects, we might've discovered who they were. But they remain a mystery."

Where did it leave him?

"Their true identity will forever remain a secret. I know is their approximate ages, and they were from somewhere north of Vermont—maybe northern Vermont or Maine. One entry says they drove south to do jobs. That's all I have. I've no idea who I am, either."

"Ridiculous, Clay. You are Dr. Clay Barnes, the man you've always been. You're a decent, hard-working, up-standing citizen, regardless what your parents did. They loved you and gave you the best life they could, considering their past. What will you do with their money?"

"I don't know. I don't want it." His hands went up into surrender.

An emcee took a podium encouraging folks to take seats. The program was beginning. An idea hit Clay, and his head cleared more than it had in a couple weeks. A load carried on his shoulders lightened.

"Thank you, Sage—for . . . for everything . . . , especially your forgiving nature. I'm giving the dough to the hospital children's wing." Standing erect with shoulders back.

Sage's smile grew brilliant. "Wow, Clay, it's a wonderful decision, and you've done nothing to forgive. What's in the past can remain there, if you choose to let it. Wyatt, Reggie and Jaiden agree and will use discretion to protect your family's secret. Is it okay with you if I share what I learned with Wyatt?"

He rose to go to his seat. "Sure. Tell him to catch me later after the program if he doesn't think it's a good idea. If I don't hear anything from him about it, I'll turn the money over to the hospital later tonight."

"I'm sure he'll support your decision, Clay." Sage patted his arm as he moved away then worked his way through the crowded ballroom to his chair.

♥♥♥♥

After speeches and consuming the meal Clay sought out Wyatt. At the end of the evening they'd announce how much had been collected. He wanted it to include his tainted funds.

"It's a fine gesture, Clay and a much-needed cause, leaving no guilt for keeping funds from ill-gotten means." Wyatt smiled approvingly.

"Thanks, Wyatt. I wanted your blessing before donating. At least it will do good, instead of collecting dust on a warehouse shelf. Since it's not officially my case or the FBI's, you get to determine its fate." He patted Clay's back then strolled to discuss with Garrett his campaign.

Clay wandered around for a few minutes avoiding his table, tempted to drown sorrows missing Jaiden by asking Jane to dance. She occasionally graced the dance floor with one man or another. He didn't keep track. It didn't matter. He'd merely thought to ask her, so she wouldn't spend an evening sitting alone like a wall flower. She and he were the singles in their group. Thankfully she was busy talking with doctors and their wives. Jane was amusing enough, but not his type.

He hadn't realized he had a type. Then Jaiden came along. She was everything red-blooded men dreamed of wrapped in a glorious, exotic package. His blood ran hot thinking of her, and he wished she'd changed her mind and shown up. He longed to enjoy the rest of his evening with her.

He took a restroom break trying to distract his mind.

Moggie called at half-past nine. Jaiden clicked her laptop off and locked it in her desk drawer. In the dressing room she slipped out of her uniform. The guys were out on patrol or off duty, so she undressed in the middle of the room taking her time. She sprayed her favorite cologne between her breasts then slid a chiffon and satin garment over her head. It fell into place around her curves perfectly.

Her breasts perked to attention beneath a straight cut bodice barely covering them. A cinched waist held a strapless garment in place. A straight skirt had a bit of give falling toward the floor. A slit up back to her knees ensured she'd be able to cut a rug in it. A triple-strand of pearl choker and pearls studs in her ears completed her ensemble.

A pink, satin, four-inch pump propped

on a bench so she could latch the sandal embroidered with pearls on toe and heel. Hiking her skirt, she latched a thigh-belt on, checked her pistol and inserted it in the small holster. One never knew what might happen. Jaiden carried a weapon no matter the costume. An extra loaded magazine slipped into her matching pearl-embroidered clutch. Putting her foot down, she fluffed the skirt, so it fell properly. Then she stowed her uniform in a duffle in her locker.

She stepped outside, and Moggie wolf whistled exiting his pickup truck. He rounded the vehicle and kissed her cheek then gave her a warm hug. "You look amazing. Doc will have a heart attack seeing you."

"At least he's in company of doctors. Besides, he was there all evening. I'm sure by now he's well into his new flame, sweet Jane, the woman who works for Doc Maines." Her stormy attitude ruled by a green wave swept over her seeping into bones and making her heart ache.

Moggie helped her into his truck then they sped away. He grabbed her hand and held it, stalling her quivering insides. "All right, tell me what in hell is going on. I thought you were falling in love. I believe you are. Why push Doc into another filly's arms?"

"He's better off. I'm not the kind of woman he needs. He's a regular guy with ordinary dreams. He wants a home, family, and a normal life. He's cruelly hurt, learning tough things to face about his parents, and is reeling from it. He's trying to decide the next step in his career and has several options. He'll likely return to Chicago to head up a surgery team. If not, he'll move somewhere else. He won't stay in town long after what he's discovered."

"Here's what I think. The past is no one's business. People who know the truth are trusted to use discretion. Whatever it is doesn't need to become public knowledge. Doc can stay if he wants."

"You know how gossip gets around. Everyone knows everything about the others." She sighed heavily.

He parked near a front entrance in a spot another car existed. Neither of them budged. They silently agreed to talk it out in the privacy of his truck.

"So? What if it does? It'll go the rounds and be a hot topic for a while. Some new scandal will come along for folks to talk about. It'll go on a back burner—old news. Folks know Clay Barnes. He's one of their own. They're forgiving and protective with neighbors. You know how they are." Moggie's hand swept one of the stray curls away from her eyes. It came loose from a sloppy knot she'd made of her disobedient locks after releasing her working-style bun at the station. Moving a tress behind her ear, he cupped her chin with a calloused paw.

Smiling she glanced sideways. "They've certainly welcomed me into their fold. I love it in Sweetwater. I'd hate to leave."

"What do you mean, leave? You can't leave. Your family and job are here. I'm here."

"If Clay and Jane continue the affair, it might lead to marriage. They've been dating while I've been sleeping with Clay. I saw them together myself a couple times. Familiarity and ease with each other was obvious. He'll ask her to follow him. She doesn't have much tying her here. It'd be easy for her to go with Clay."

Combating visions controlling her thoughts proved a losing battle. Time to end the conversation, but she'd gotten it off her chest with someone who understood.

"If Clay married Jane and lived in Sweetwater, you couldn't watch. You'd leave your home to escape." Moggie hit it on the nail, and his face flushed with concern linked with an urge to defend her honor. "That ass doesn't know a good woman when he has one." He scowled.

Tears started rolled down her cheeks. She patted them with her palms trying not to smudge her makeup. Thank goodness she'd opted for waterproof mascara.

Moggie pulled her into his husky, muscular arms and laid her head on his shoulder. She cried uninhibited for a few minutes. He pulled out a red and white handkerchief. Taking it, she blew her nose and wadded it on the dashboard. She sat erect and smiled.

"You're the best friend a gal could have.

I love you and appreciate your support. Having you around helps ease burden of facing him tonight."

"I'm here for you, kiddo, right or wrong. But I think you're mistaken about the doc. I think he's a goner for you. If he's cheating on your, I wouldn't mind knocking him around."

"He's not exactly cheating. He's in lust for me, but we never agreed to exclusivity. A steady diet in Jane's bedroom and his hankering for me will wane." She blinked at tears threatening to return.

Moggie rounded the truck and lifted her to the ground.

Clay came from the restroom and needed fresh air before rejoining the party. He stepped out a front door and leaned against the building in darkness of shadows.

A pickup pulled into the lot. The pole lighting in the parking lot shone into the cab of the truck. He didn't recognize a stocky man driving, but the woman in pink beside him caught Clay's eyes instantly. His heart skipped a beat. *Jaiden came after all.*

They sat together appearing to talk. She chatted animatedly with her companion. He reached and fondled her hair. The move appeared natural.

Clay's gut wrenched at sight of another man acting so familiar with Jaiden. He'd begun thinking of her as his. But she wasn't—not really.

They'd slept together and spent every possible minute together, but hadn't discussed exclusivity. She had a right to date whoever she wanted.

Reality shredded his guts. Why hadn't he broached the subject?

Dumb ass.

Beating himself up wouldn't remove Jaiden from an intimate scene with the guy. Clay couldn't take his eyes from them.

He was barely willed his heart to continue beating—not capable of more.

The fella cupped Jaiden's chin. Was he going to kiss her?

Clay stiffened and caught his breath.

He pulled Jaiden into his arms, and she let him, laying her head on his shoulder. He couldn't tell if they continued talking or not. It didn't appear they were kissing, but they were in the shadows. Possible.

Clay's stomach soured. He spun and fled inside. He'd die of humiliation if Jaiden saw him lurking in shadows spying on her with her date.

♥♥♥♥

Clay went to a bar and waited in line for a drink. He'd never needed a shot of bourbon so badly. He glanced toward the door.

The muscular dude escorted his date into

the crowded room with a possessive arm around her shoulder. A hand clasped territorially on top of her bare arm. Jaiden looked relaxed, like it was normal.

Clay was anything but relaxed. Sour juices rolled into a full boil in his belly. If he didn't calm them dinner would upchuck soon.

His turn at service, he leaned on an elbow and placed his order then stuffed a bill into a tip jar. Peripheral vision portrayed lovers mingling through a crowd headed toward Levi's table. Parading through the hoard of people, they spoke quietly with friends.

Reaching their seating area, Jaiden's brother Calvin Coldwater stood. The towering part-Choctaw man stood more than a head taller than his petite, powerful sister. She stepped easily into his arms. In a bear hug he swept her off her feet spinning around while she laughed.

Sitting her lightly down, they turned to his bride. Rose Coldwater was equal in height with her sister-in-law with feminine but muscular arms. She snuggled Jaiden into a warm embrace. The women were obviously close.

They made a striking threesome—Rose with purple hair and a pixy face; Jaiden, dark, glamourous with a horse-head tattoo on the side of her neck; and a tall, powerful, ex-Navy Seal, horse trainer in his sleek, western-cut tuxedo with ebony flowing hair blanketing Cal's broad back to his waist.

Jaiden's date play-punched Levi's shoulder. Levi's dukes sprang up like they were punching it out. They danced laughing and finally drew each other into a friendly man-hug. Obviously they contested for some goal— probably to do with horses or racing. He didn't know enough about the guy yet to guess. If he was Levi's friend, he'd be an okay guy. Of course, Jaiden would fall for someone reputable.

Strolling around their table, they chatted casually with everyone. The chap wasn't a stranger to Corrie Morgan-Lane-Henderson, her husband Justin Henderson or Riley and Levi Madison. Even Senator Garrett and Adelle Madison clearly knew him. They engaged Levi and Jaiden in a round of hearty greetings and smiling conversation. Wyatt and Sage hugged and kissed cheeks with Jaiden and the fellow.

The guy spoke into Jaiden's ear. She nodded and smiled then he strode away.

Sage indicated Wyatt's empty seat since Wyatt was standing nearby in conversation with Levi. Jaiden sat. She and Sage talked for a few minutes. Their conversation altered Jaiden's mood. She looked sad bantering back and forth with her friend.

Occasionally Jaiden scanned the room. Was she watching for him or looking for her date? The dude disappeared. Clay leaned behind someone each time she searched the crowd, not wanting to be caught staring.

He downed a last drink then ducked into a men's room for a breather. His insides ached like he'd swallowed a scalpel shredding him to bits.

He'd begun putting down roots and considered sticking around. He'd have to sell the house for sure now.

No happiness for Clay in Sweetwater watching Jaiden with another guy, knowing texture of her silky skin and taste of her body. He couldn't witness another gent touching and tasting her the way he longed to regularly.

With Jaiden screwing a new male, Clay was back to square one. He needed to sell his farm. He'd told his boss in Chicago he wasn't coming back. So now he had to decide where he wanted to be—where he'd never set eyes on Jaiden Coldwater again.

The idea sent his stomach plummeting, and he couldn't draw fresh air into his lungs. Heavy and tight, he needed to get out of this place, to reconsider other options—Seattle, Cody and Fairbanks. Without Jaiden on his arm, those locations held no fasciation.

Clay strode through a chattering hoard of friends and neighbors, speaking to several he passed—his final goodbyes for most folks. Finally reaching the emcee, he handed him a check for five-hundred-thousand dollars made out to the children's hospital wing foundation.

"I hope the money helps. It's a worthy cause. Sweetwater hospital needs a children's wing."

The man glanced at the slip of paper speechless for a second. He gulped air. "Wow, Dr. Barnes, I don't know what to say. It's exceedingly generous and one of the largest donations we've receive. Would you like us to name part of the facility for you, or your parents?"

Clay cupped the hands holding his offering in his own and patted the top. "It's not necessary—definitely not. Name it after someone deserving, but not me or my family. I'm thrilled doing it for a worthy cause and want it to remain anonymous. Can you see to it?" He looked the fella in the eye.

The gent blinked a couple times then nodded without another word. Clay spun and headed toward an exit. A tug on his arm halted him.

Jane Anderson slipped a hand around his arm and stalled his escape. "Where are you heading? It's early. I hoped we'd have opportunity for a dance."

"I'm sorry, Jane. I need to leave. I'm not good company, anyway." Jane was a fine woman and didn't deserve his foul mood.

"You've been drinking and are slurring your words. I cannot let you leave like this. I'll drive you home. It's the least I can do. You've done so much for me."

"I . . . ah . . ." She had a point. Clay didn't have a number for a local cab company. He could call information or take Jane up on her offer. She was obviously looking for a reason to skip out of the party.

"Sure, thanks. That's nice."

"I'll meet you outside at your truck. I

need to grab my purse from the table and say goodnight." She sped off and disappeared into a crowd.

Clay moseyed outside and to his vehicle. Instead of climbing into the driver's side, he opened doors and braced his butt against a fender. With crossed-ankles and arms, he leaned and closed his eyes. Earth whirled mercilessly, and he felt nauseous.

A soft hand touched his forearm. Blinking, he came alert. Instead of Jane ready to leave before him, Jaiden stood there.

Hands on hips, shoulders back, bosom high, chin up, her accusing eyes glared. She breathed. Her chest rose and fell attracting his eyes, which had developed a mind of their own. He knew well perky, pink centers barely concealed by the low cut of her silky dress.

Saliva formed in his mouth. He swallowed heavily.

Nothing was exciting as peeling sensuous fabrics off Jaiden's hot-blooded physique. His fingers itched to touch her skin, to snake beneath edge of the gown and expose pebbled peaks of pleasure he craved to taste. His groin twitched, and blood began rushing to his member.

He jolted upright and stood erect.

"What the hell is going on, Clay? Where've you been? I arrived over an hour ago and haven't seen hide-nor-hair of you. You avoiding me?"

The gal had moxie. He gave her that.

The spitfire turned intimidating when angered.

She had nerve after showing up with a date to an affair she'd agreed to attend with Clay. Scarcely composed, but even angry her voice was a melody he'd gladly listen to all night.

"Excuse me, Deputy Coldwater." Jane rounded Jaiden and reached for the truck cab door. Clay sprang into action, grabbing it before she did. He opened it and helped Jane into the driver's seat then handed her his keys. "You ready, Clay?"

"Sure thing, Jane." He turned around.

Jaiden huffed and quick-stepped toward the entrance lifting her skirt with her hands in a rush to get far away. He shrugged then climbed into the truck.

"I appreciate you doing this, Jane. I didn't give driving home consideration when I belted down five shots of bourbon. I'm doing a lot of foolish things today." His head lay in his hand propping an elbow against the side door. He focused on throbbing in his temples.

"Don't mention it. After what you did for me last week, I owe you big."

"My pleasure. I couldn't let Christine postpone her treatment."

"Still, I'm grateful."

Pulling into his yard he woke from napping with a jolt. "Oh, wow, sorry. I must've dozed off."

"No problem. You needed it. Can you make it inside alone? I'll call a cab." She shifted the truck into park behind his house and reached for her purse.

"Absolutely not—you'll drive my truck home. I'll take a cab tomorrow to retrieve it. Did you leave your car at the community center? I can drive you to retrieve it tomorrow." He climbed out and slumped against the door talking through an opened window.

"I caught a ride with Dr. and Mrs. Maines, so my car's at home. I'm fine. Are you sure about me borrowing your truck?"

"Funny, it's the one thing I'm sure about." He headed toward the bed calling his name.

The engine revved and crunch of truck tires against gravel backing out of the driveway filled night air.

♥♥♥♥

Sage saw Jaiden rush into the ballroom with tears streaking her cheeks. She sped to a ladies' room without stopping.

"Wyatt, I'll be back. Jaiden's upset. I need to check on her." Her handsome husband nodded with a knowing smile. Understanding her well, he didn't waste time or words telling her to keep out of it—not her business. Her friend was in need, and Sage was hell-bent on helping.

Alone in an elaborately decorated powder room, Jaiden slumped against a countertop heaving hearty sighs with each breath. She was distraught and crying.

"Jaiden, you want to talk about it?" Sage eased toward Jaiden.

Jaiden blew her nose with a wad of paper in her hand. Her eyes filled with tears. Evidence of crying full-force streaked her makeup, though her mascara held its own.

"What's wrong, sweetie? Why are you so upset?" Sage snatched her hand and led her to cushy, fabric-covered chairs surrounded by mirrors on three sides.

"It's Clay."

"What about him? I thought you were an item. He's so under your spell, I'd begun to believe he might chuck it all and move to Sweetwater for you."

"No, he's not. Sure, he enjoyed bedding me with no strings. We never discussed the long haul or exclusivity. That's where I screwed up. I fell for the damned, nerdy doctor and never told him. I should've said I wanted him to myself, and I cared. I should've asked him to stay—or take me with him."

"You'd leave Sweetwater?" Surprised, Sage's eyes went wide.

"I'd do whatever necessary to be with Clay—if he wanted me. But apparently he doesn't."

"Honey, I think you're wrong. What makes you say that?" Sage pushed a stray curl out of Jaiden's eyes.

"He's dating Jane Anderson while sleeping with me. She's more his type. She's a standup woman, a regular gal, hardworking, good mother and she'll make him a decent wife."

Sage hardly believed what she heard. Yes. Clay worked with Jane Anderson. She sat at Clay's table tonight, with the other doctors.

Sage tried recalling seating arrangements. Clay was seated to Jane's left. Jane waltzed with a couple different men, mostly doctors and orderlies from the hospital staff. She couldn't recall them talking together or dancing all evening.

"I'm having a problem pairing Clay and Jane together, even for one night—let along for a lifetime. What makes you say that?"

"Fuck him. Couldn't the bastard have decency to leave town before finding another woman? It's bad enough losing him. Watching him with her is gut-wrenching. I can't do it, Sage. If Clay doesn't take Jane and leave town, I'll have to go. I can't watch day-in and out knowing he's happy with her. It'd kill me inside."

"You didn't arrive with Clay. Did you?" Sage eyed her critically.

"No. I discovered Clay was a two-timing me with Jane. I saw them last Friday together. They acted chummy coming out of her house with her daughter, looking like a happy family. I became jealous and couldn't bear being close to Clay. I knew Jane would attend the benefit tonight. Dr. Maines would ensure she had a ticket even if she couldn't afford one. So I begged off coming with Clay using work as an excuse. Dovie was managing the banquet, so Moggie was on his own. He had a colt being born and wasn't sure he'd make it. After the birth he gave me a ride and a chance to talk with him about my problems. Moggie's a good friend."

"So you came with another man. Does Clay know Moggie? Does he realize he's happily in lust and forever love with Dovie? Does he understand you and Moggie are like brother and sister?"

She snickered recalling her past with Moggie. "Yeah, we are kind of—brother and sister—bad kids who played doctor a little too intimately." She snickered wickedly wiggling her brows. "Clay realizes I have a close friend named Moggie, and he's in love with Dovie. Clay knows Dovie, but I'm not sure he's met Moggie. Why?"

Sage laughed at her joke, knowing their history. "You're a naughty girl, Jaiden. I love it about you." With a serious expression, she placed hands on hips. "Hon, could Clay have gotten the wrong idea? You arrived on Moggie's arm." Cocking her head sideways, she studied Jaiden's reaction. "You stood Clay up then came with another man. It might look differently to Clay."

Jaiden gave her a doubtful sneer.

"I'm saying—." Sage's hands went up in surrender.

Jaiden stared into her eyes and neither

spoke. Sage stayed quiet allowing wheels to spin as Jaiden's thought it over.

Great.

Sage patted Jaiden's hands in her lap, stood, kissed her cheek lightly then left her to think about it.

CHAPTER 24

Jaiden needed room to reflect and sort through emotions. She sought quiet. Women filtered in and out of the restroom. It wasn't a place for this. Instead of heading to a crowded ballroom, she slipped into a kitchen.

Dovie's staff continued preparing trays of delicacies with enticing fragrances wafting the atmosphere. Dovie's mouth soured at the idea of eating. She avoided anyone she knew and slipped out a back door.

The rear building butted to a side of a parking lot. Behind it a church graveyard stood. Jaiden plopped on a fourth step and heaved a sigh of relief.

Finally, privacy.

A starry night sky was lit by a quarter-moon. With thinking to do, she sat alone in quiet. Mulling over every step of what occurred since last Friday her heart ached. Clay hadn't exclusively dated her. She was unable to recall pointing Moggie out to Clay or when they might've met. Possibly he'd mistaken Moggie for a date concluding Jaiden threw him over for another guy.

Still, getting his rocks off elsewhere was wearing a crater-sized ulcer in her belly. Last Friday she'd seen what she saw. No way around it. Clay was at Jane's house. Early morning they exited her home together. He'd spent the night.

Rumbling in her tummy threatened to boil over. She slapped a hand across her middle.

Jaiden hadn't slept the night with Clay in over a week due to her work schedule. He found another source for horizontal refreshment.

Clay and Jane laughed and chatted easily, familiarly like one did with a person they were comfortable with. Clay's hand rested intimately on Jane's back like it belonged, ushering her and her daughter to his vehicle. Clay had helped them into his SUV. Then they chatted merrily as he drove them away on some fun-filled, family outing.

Yep.

Clay and Jane were definitely *bumping uglies*.

A slender, medium-height woman crept between two vehicles into a dark spot at rear of the parking lot. Familiar movement caught Jaiden's eye acting suspiciously. The figure remained motionless, so Jaiden lost track of her in darkness, but continued keeping an eye on the area.

Moments later a female shadow, with hair puffed high and clipped into an elaborate up-do, crept quietly along a line of cars skirting a side of the building toward a far end of the parking lot—where the other strange gal lurked. The puffy-haired shadow appeared searching for someone. Moonlight reflected the side of her face—Carmen Burnette.

Not surprisingly, the mayor had escorted Carmen to the banquet. Rumor had them seeing each other. Tonight's event was a good choice for publicizing their relationship. She must've left the mayor inside, because Carmen was skulking around outside alone.

Carmen came to a stop at the hindmost corner of the community center. She glanced around searching and kept eyeing a phone in her left hand.

The dark figure lunged toward her from behind tossing a strap about her neck yanking her backward. Awkward gurgling sounds eked from her throat.

Jaiden leaped to her feet. She flipped her

long skirt up and retrieved the loaded pistol attached to her thigh. Her dress billowed around her. She raced toward the figures barely visible wrestling in darkness.

With a gush of air outward Carmen was grabbed. A thud—maybe she hit pavement or fell against a surface forcefully.

Why hadn't Carmen called out?
She can't.

Tree shadows in an adjoining cemetery made visibility difficult.

By the time Jaiden reached the two figures Candy Wrigley sat on grass with Carmen Burnette sprawled on her back in front of her. Candy leaned backward with gloved hands gripping a homemade garrote tightly around Carmen's neck. Candy controlled the garrote fashioned from fishing line securely holding large loops at each end.

Carmen's face looked wild and wide-eyed, and her feet kicked awkwardly. Moonlight glistened in her bugging eyes. She tried in vain to suck air suffocating quickly. Blood stained Carmen's neck ineffectively thrashing about.

Jaiden ran fast as her heeled feet would carry her and shouted recognizing what was happening.

"Police. Release her. Now."

Candy refused to let go of her grasp. She transferred controls into one hand then reached to her side. Drawing a pistol from its holster she attempted to aim at Jaiden. She fumbled futilely trying to control her victim and weapon at the same time.

"Damn it, Candy, release her. I mean now. If you don't, I'll shoot your fucking head off." By now Jaiden was within a few feet of them. Her feet braced apart, and her pistol aimed squarely at Candy's head.

Carmen's eyes had closed beginning to lose consciousness. She ceased fighting her attacker and went limp.

Candy didn't comprehend and didn't comply. Jaiden fired a shot in air. Candy jolted. So did Carmen with a heavy inhale of air, bumping Candy's hand. Candy dropped her pistol. Her other hand must've eased on the tight string.

Carmen's fingers slipped between her bloody neck and the string. She ripped it from around her and out of Candy's grasp. Glistening tears began rolling down her cheeks, catching light through trees.

Jaiden side-stepped and kicked the firearm out of Candy's reach. "Put your hands in the air, Candy. Do it."

Candy didn't move, but sat like a dumb animal with a blank expression on her pitiful face. Jaiden kicked her hip hard with a pointed toe. Candy jerked and blinked. Her hands shot up.

Carmen dropped the stringed weapon on the ground and rolled to her knees coughing and gasping. She began trembling as though freezing though the evening was balmy.

A roar of voices came along with

footfalls rushing toward them from the kitchen and front entrances. Wyatt led the charge, yelling for others to keep back. His gun drawn, he approached and discerned the state of affairs.

A quick look at Carmen and he told her to sit. His yell commanded shouting toward the crowd.

"We need a doctor and someone call 911." He squatted beside Carmen and examined her neck. She was breathing okay, so he patted her shoulder. "You're okay, Carmen; but we'll let the EMTs check you out, anyway."

Dr. Maines came running from the crowd. He squatted beside Carmen and began checking her out. Sirens wailing signaled the EMT squad was on its way.

Wyatt strode to where Jaiden stood. Having yanked Candy roughly to her feet, Jaiden cuffed her hands behind her back. Jaiden's purse swung from where it hung attached to the belt of her gown.

"You always carry cuffs?" He snickered.

"Mostly. I choose purses to accommodate them. You?" Jaiden cocked a brow at her boss.

He whipped a pair from the back waistband concealed by his tux jacket. "Afraid so." He snorted proudly.

He motioned for a man in front to join them. Mayor Kenneth Bailey strode over. Spotting Carmen he rushed to her side and began gushing over her protectively.

Carmen's hand cupped his jaw

affectionately. He whipped his jacket off and wrapped it around her quivering shoulders. "I'm fine, Ken, thanks to Deputy Coldwater."

He sat beside her and hugged her to his side. Her head rested on his shoulder. "Thank you so much, deputy. I'm forever in your debt." He smiled at Jaiden.

She saluted him with a couple fingers from where she stood beside Wyatt, still holding her grumbling collar captive.

The EMT's arrived and did the same things Dr. Maines had done. The doctor returned to his wife and friends inside the crowd, leaving them to attend their patient.

Mayor Bailey climbed into an emergency vehicle and sat beside his date lying on the stretcher, having agreed to allow them take her in for a more thorough observation.

Wyatt and Jaiden approached the first responder's vehicle before the back doors closed.

"Carmen, why were you sneaking around in dark by yourself?" Jaiden holstered her weapon into its cozy spot on her thigh.

"I received a text from Ken."

Kenneth Bailey looked confused scrunching his brow and screwing his mouth up. "I didn't text you. I haven't used my phone all evening." He reached around to his hip. "My phone's gone. Someone stole my phone."

Jaiden sprinted two steps to where she had cuffed Candy to a tree. Frisking her she pulled out a slim phone. "This yours, Mayor?"

A glance at it and Kenneth nodded then returned to Carmen. "Baby, I'd never ask you to walk around alone in a spooky location like that."

She blushed scarlet. "I thought maybe you wanted to have a little tryst in a public place. I was up for it if you were. Your language was sexy, and I was hot for you." She showed him the text on her phone. The mayor blushed—a lovely shade of pink.

Wyatt looked like he was groaning inside. He peeled the phone from Carmen's hand. "We're keeping both phones for the time being. It's an attempted murder case, and they're evidence."

"Why did you want me dead?" Carmen asked eyeing the woman who had wrestled her aground helplessly.

Jaiden had moved Candy from the tree and cuffed her hands behind her. She shoved Candy toward the quad car. Nearing the EMT van Candy scowled toward Carmen. Pure hatred spit from her flaming eyes.

"You bitch. Walter said he loved me. He made me feel beautiful and adored for the first time in my life. I believe him. But he never meant to leave you. He ruined my business. Now I'm driving an hour a day for a low-paying job. I can barely pay my rent. He dropped me like a hot potato. Before I blinked an eye, he was screwing the mayor's wife. Even after you and the bastard divorced, you kept banging his brains out—disgusting. I watched and waited for an opportunity to make him pay. You wouldn't leave. You hung around like a loose harlot after the closing. I saw you playing *hide the sausage* with Walter on this desk. The two of you looked like rutting pigs." The scowl on her face was frightening.

A gasp sounded. Carmen understood.

"You acted deliriously joyful about dough you earned in a development deal. You fucked him blind while I watched through a window. Even then you didn't leave so I could get even. You followed him to the Barnes farm. The two of you went into the woods together. You give him head by a pond. Then he took you again like a raw dog on a rickety, old bench. I hope you got splinters in your ass, you stupid cunt. You finally left. I strutted up to the old stud. He smiled and acted all horny, like I came to give it to him good. He wasn't laughing when I pulled my pistol and did it. I laughed while he bled to death. The pig deserved what he got."

Seconds of silence felt like an eternity. Finally Carmen broke it. "Why kill me? You didn't do it that day. I never did you wrong. I didn't even know you and Walter until long after our divorce."

"The thrill of killing Wally helped for a while. Then it wore off, and I grew angry again. He wasn't around to vent my anger on, but you were still here. The dickhead kept returning to you. So you deserve to die like he did." Candy spit toward Carmen, but it fell short on the ground.

Wyatt looked at a weapon Jaiden placed in an evidence pouch. "Candy, where did you get the gun? You don't have a 22 registered."

"My pa died and left it to me. I didn't know he had it. I figured he left me a bunch of junk to clear out. I found the piece and started plotting what to do. Walter needed to pay for the way he treated me. It was a good plan."

Back doors shut, and the ambulance sped away. Wyatt's team of deputies and CSI experts swarmed roping off the attack area, taking photos and notes. Jaiden handed one of them the garrote sealed inside a plastic bag. Wyatt handed over the evidence bag with Candy's pistol in it. He removed Candy's gloves and placed them inside a bag which he handed to the officer collecting evidence.

Jaiden pushed Candy toward Wyatt's vehicle. "Boss, I need a ride home. I came with Moggie figuring Cal and Rose would give me a lift. They left before the action."

"We've got you covered."

He glanced at the crowd and waved to his wife. Sage slipped through the hoard and followed her husband, Jaiden and their prisoner to the cruiser. Jaiden shoved Candy into the back seat and slid in beside her.

Metal glistened dangling from Candy's shirt pocket. Jaiden removed a delicate, silver-colored chain. Holding it up, she examined it. A half opened O ring hung in its middle where it had held a bangle. The catch was broken.

"Boss, we've found more evidence." She

pulled out another baggie and slid the bracelet into it. "Candy, where did this come from?"

Candy glared with her brow cocked and looked along her nose at Jaiden. "Where do you think?"

"It's Carmen Burnette's ankle bracelet. Right?"

"I assume so. I found it on the ground where Walter fell after I shot him. The bitch must've lost it while catering to the old flea bag. The chain made an amusing souvenir."

"Oh, God, Candy, you disgust me." Jaiden dropped the evidence bag in her purse. The woman clearly had makings of a serial killer. At least, she was a psychopath.

Candy sneered looking pleased. She shrugged.

Wyatt helped Sage in the passenger side then climbed into the driver's seat. "Babe, we'll drop you at home then take Candy to the station. Jaiden and I have work to do. It will take a while getting this thing under control. Don't wait up."

Sage snuggled close and slid her arm through his while he drove. Laying her left hand on his thigh and her head against his shoulder she stroked his arm with her free hand. "No worries, Wyatt; but I want you to sleep in tomorrow. If you must work most of the night, you'll need rest. You and Jaiden should both go in late tomorrow. Other deputies can handle the shift."

"Sounds good. It's my day off anyway, but I'll come in if you need me, boss." Would she ever sleep again? She was so pent up. "At least one crime is solved."

"You did well tonight, deputy. You saved a woman's life." Wyatt's broad grin was visible in the moonlight and rearview mirror. "Take your day off. We've got this handled."

Candy let out a loud *hump* sound and shifted in her seat.

♥♥♥♥

Wyatt had swung by her house on the way to the station, after dropping Sage off, so Jaiden had her car. At four a.m., Jaiden wound down from investigating enough to go home for shuteye.

A painful twinge gnawed at her all evening. On the short drive she didn't bother resisting her urge to swing by Jane Anderson's apartment complex. Sage could've been right. So she checked it out to see for herself.

Sure as she was breathing, Clay's SUV parked beside Jane's old sedan in two spaces in front of her unit.

Sage was wrong. Clay went home with Jane.

She'd occasional glimpsed Clay avoiding her last evening. She'd lost track of Jane before escaping out back for a breather.

Knowing Jane drove him, she'd kept hoping he wasn't going to her house. But he did. They slept at Jane's place for a tumble in the hay snuggling bare-assed together under her sheets.

Some breather—she'd stepped into a hornet's nest. Good finally getting to the bottom of Walter Burnette's murder case. It would settle the nervous community down and ease the force's workload.

It didn't solve Jaiden's problems—not by a longshot.

Clay went home with Jane. She'd suspected. Now she knew.

Jaiden had done right begging off their date, leaving the field open for Clay's and Jane's relationship to move forward without her in the mix. Jane was good for Clay.

If it was such a wonderful thing why were her guts being pulled out by the inch? Good for Clay didn't translate to good or Jaiden.

What a dumbass she'd been. Knowing being with Clay was a temporary pleasure, she'd fallen for him hard. It wasn't like Jaiden to put herself out there so completely. Clay drew her out like no other and obviously blinded her to reality. Look what it earned her—a broken heart that might never mend.

She straggled into her house and tossed her bag in a corner then dragged herself to her bedroom. Stripping and showering in blazing hot water did nothing to calm her racing heart or ease a knot her intestines had balled into. She slipped on a tank top and shorts pajama set then wandered into the kitchen.

Too early to cook breakfast, she'd probably up-chuck food, anyway. She didn't want to brew coffee because the aroma would disturb her sleeping mom.

Instead she pulled out a glass and a jug of milk. She sat at a bar pouring.

Brightleaf strolled from her bedroom. She tightened her satin robe belt and smiled at her exhausted daughter.

"You've had quite a night. Haven't you? Adele Madison called to tell me what happened."

She toasted her mother with her glass. "Yep, a doozy of an evening, you should've taken Adele and Garrett up on their invite. You missed the action. I'm dead on my feet."

Brightleaf shook her beautiful head. Silver strands swung about her shoulders. She strolled close with pride in her eyes.

"I wasn't up for rubber chicken and hospital speeches. I'd have worried more watching my feisty, law-dog daughter playing hero. Some things a mother shouldn't witness."

She pecked Jaiden's cheek and started the coffee pot then pulled a glass from a cupboard and joined Jaiden at the bar.

"It seems you're once again Sweetwater's latest heroine. You saved a woman's life and solved a crime, making our community once again a safe place to live. I'm proud of you, Jaiden." Her mom slipped a curl from Jaiden's forehead hooking it behind her ear.

Jaiden tried to return her mother's well-meaning smile. The impossible task brought forth tears she'd held at bay all evening. She was finally in a safe place to release them. Jaiden talked with her mom about anything.

"What's wrong, sweetheart? You should be happy." Brightleaf studied her daughter's reaction with sympathetic eyes. She stood, picked up a decanter of bourbon and two glasses, and brought them to her stool beside Jaiden. "You look like you need this." Brightleaf poured two generous portions and handed one to Jaiden. They clicked glasses and downed shots.

"It's Clay, Ma. He and I started seeing each other even though I knew he'd leave soon. I promised myself I'd enjoy his company while he visited and let him go when time came. It's time; but letting him go gracefully is killing me." Her voice quivered with each word, and tears flowed freely down her cheeks.

Brightleaf cuddled her into her arms. Her head lay on her mother's delicate shoulder.

"I've never seen you happy or satisfied as you've been since Clay Barnes arrived in town. I watched you falling in love. You're happy with him. I didn't realize a hard ending was coming. Why're you letting him go?" She pushed Jaiden back holding her shoulders in gentle hands. "What's going on? Is Clay definitely leaving? Is it a done deal?"

"He's unraveled shocking secrets from his parents' past and discovered they didn't own the home he thought he'd inherited. He made it right rectifying the ownership issue, but reeling with the outrageous reality of his family's history, there's no way he'll want to live in Sweetwater. He's lined things up to market his farm. It won't take long to sell."

"His leaving causes you much grief. Must he go? Have you asked him to stay? Where will he go? Back to Chicago?"

"Doubtful. He was up for a great promotion, but he had no heart in taking it. I don't think he likes Chicago. He has other offers to consider. I haven't spent much time with him over the last week. I've been investigating the homicide. He's chosen a position by now."

"You don't know which he prefers? Would you go with him?"

"I love it in Sweetwater. I've made a difference since coming here. You, Cal and Rose are my family; and you're here. It'd be hard leaving you, but if Clay asked, I'd follow him anywhere."

Brightleaf smiled, too soon.

"He hasn't asked and doesn't care about me like I care for him."

"What gives you the idea? You said yourself you haven't spent much time with him lately. Maybe he was waiting until you're together."

"No, Clay's seeing someone else. It's my fault. I never asked him to see exclusively me. He's dating a woman who is a much better fit for him. She's a fine lady and a hard-working, single mother. I've seen the three of them together. They make a lovely, happy family."

Brightleaf scowled and emitted a frustrated sigh. "You saw them together? And he never told you anything about dating the other woman? You sure? Certain you haven't misconstrued a situation?"

"No, Ma, I'd love being mistaken, but Clay's with the gal. I've seen them together more than once. It's serious. I broke our date last night, then arrived late catching a ride with Moggie. Dovie was tied up with catering the affair. Clay hooked up with her again at the banquet. They left together. I drove by her place on my way home. His vehicle is parked in front of her apartment. He spent the night. That's enough evidence for me."

Tears flooded out again, and she laid her head on her mom's shoulder. Her body heaved, and she allowed tears full reign.

Brightleaf stroked her back and held her tenderly. She felt like a bird with a broke wing.

"Jaiden, I don't think it's over. I don't believe it. No man you're capable of loving so deeply would treat you this cruel or be so oblivious to your feelings for him. There must be more to it. You'd never fall for a dishonorable person. Follow your soul. If your heart wants the man, open to hearing what he has to say." She pushed Jaiden away so she could see her face. "Promise you won't shut down."

"Ma, my heart is breaking. I'm too weak to do anything more than wallow in pain." She stood, gulped the last of her bourbon, rinsed her glasses then strode toward her bedroom and hopefully silence of sleep. Surely she was exhausted enough to collapse into oblivion when her head hit a pillow.

CHAPTER 25

Clay awoke early. A heavy burden had lifted leaving freedom in its wake. The cash was gone, and he liked where it landed. Though he was still reeling from Jaiden's new direction, he was energized by moving forward and ready to take action.

After a quick shower and coffee, he jumped in a cab he'd called and rode to Jane's apartment complex. She and Charlotte would likely sleep in since it wasn't a school day. Not wanting to disturb their morning routine, taking his SUV, he drove to town.

A quick stop at a bank where he had deposited the found money and conversation with a manager assured the hospital would have no issues obtaining funds from his check.

Having refused the job in Chicago, he had racked his brain deciding which offer to accept. A few interesting options existed.

Cody, Wyoming, short on surgical staff, presented a decent bonus package. The lovely area east of Yellowstone and north of multiple hot springs, located within driving distance of major landmarks. Winters were brutal, however.

Seattle, Washington tempted him with his own lab and research backing plus a surgical staff position. It sounded inviting, except he wasn't fond of the city's prevailing weather.

Denver, Colorado, one of the prettiest cities he'd ever visited surrounded by snowcapped mountain ranges, had a lot to offer. A mecca for young, outdoorsy type, a tremendous amount of winter and summer activities made available in and around the city.

San Diego, California provided a key position on staff, with promise if his first surgical year went well he'd be in line for head-of-surgery the next time the role opened. The gorgeous, modern town filled with exciting nightlife and fabulous restaurants. The ocean being a marvelous advantage combined with ideal weather, made San Diego difficult to turn down.

Last on his short list was Fairbanks, Alaska. They wanted him for Chief-of-General-Surgery and presented him lab use and research funding. The understaffed location sold him hard on an available position, providing a house and airplane for patient care and personal use. Apparently jetting around the wilderness was required. Living and working in Alaska would challenge him and provide an adventure. It sounded intriguing, but not without Jaiden.

Everything he thought of, his mind brought Jaiden into the mix. He couldn't help himself.

She'd never indicated she wanted Clay for the long haul—the opposite. They'd agreed to a convenient fling with no commitment or strings. His head had agreed to it.

Then his heart deserted him and did what it pleased. His heart was pleased with Jaiden.

Damn.

He'd fallen like a lead balloon for her. He'd never get over this.

He had no choice.

Jaiden forced his hand. . She'd gotten a better offer. She blatantly broke her date with him then came to the same event with another man.

She'd avoided Clay the last week. Sure. She was busy. But they could've stolen a few minutes here and there, if willing. She'd probably spent time with her new fella.

It was Clay's freaking fault. He should've told Jaiden how he felt and explained. Despite what they'd agreed he'd fallen in love with her. He should have told her outright he wanted an exclusive, serious relationship with her. He should've done it when he realized he was permanently under her spell.

Too late—she was with someone else. They were intimate and familiar with each other. She'd found what Clay wanted to give her with another man.

Last evening Dr. Maines asked Clay to accept a fellowship at Sweetwater Memorial with full surgical rights. He had full agreement from the other partners in his medical firm to bring Clay into their practice. Clay would at some point in the not too far future, replace Dr. Maines completely when he retired.

It proved a pipe dream—living and working in Sweetwater, spending the rest of his life with Jaiden. If it were a reality, he'd accept the position in a heartbeat. Sweetwater had more benefits than all others on the table.

It was a moot point. Jaiden didn't want him. He couldn't accept.

He had to make a decision. Time had come. Bids needed answered.

He parked in a lot at Cabaret De' Fuller, Dovie Fuller's restaurant, to have lunch with Wyatt and Levi. Struggling with his decision, he wanted their opinions to help determine where his future lay.

Entering the semi-dark, elegantly designed restaurant was like walking into a French café. Delightful fragrances filled the air. He glanced around a fairly crowded room. Spotting Levi's shaggy, blonde head sitting across from the silver-haired sheriff, he strode to their linen covered, candle-lit table.

"Wow, this is some joint. Dovie did well." He shook Levi's and Wyatt's hands and slid into an empty seat.

"Wait until you sample the food. I never thought I'd like French food, but Dovie has converted me." Wyatt laughed. The waiter arrived with menus and filled water goblets for the threesome.

"She's quite a chef and made a name for herself since moving here. She catered our double-wedding last year when Riley and I married, and Corrie and Justin tied the knot. She catered the girls' shower before that. Since then, Dovie is the go-to person for a banquet or catered meals in Sweetwater."

"Didn't she marry some famous chef? I saw them on a cable show while I was in med school." He glanced at a menu and his mouth watered.

Wyatt sat his water glass down. "Yeah, she was married. The son-of-a-bitch cheated on her. She left him. He followed and stalked her. He killed one guy and aimed a pot shot at Sage. Dovie's better off without the asshole."

Clay had always liked the little, redheaded spitfire. Her bark was worse than her bite. He had doubted rumors about her playing fast and loose with boys. She flirted, and guys loved to brag. But Clay couldn't think of one male he suspected of being with Dovie. He'd assumed she used a bad reputation as a device to keep them at bay, rather than drag them into her web.

"She sure is. You remember her grandmother's ranch hand, Moggie Larrs? Dovie had a thing for Moggie as a teenager. He was an adult at the time. She went away to college then chef school, studied in France where she married her cheating hubby, then traveled all over Asia with him before realizing she needed out of the relationship. She relocated here. She and Moggie fell in love. They've lived together since before her grandmother died."

"What happened to the Fuller House Farm? Carlton is an attorney. He handled my real estate deal. Dovie owns and runs this restaurant. Did they hire someone to manage the horse racing and breeding business?"

"No, in fact they don't own it. Mrs. Fuller was a smart, old geezer. She knew her twins had no interest in the farm. Carlton would've turned it into a subdivision or sold it for a factory site." Levi shook his head disapproving such an idea.

"Wow, that's a lot of land and prime real estate. It's in a perfect location, and lays ideally for grazing racers. Who owns it if not Carlton and Dovie?"

"Mrs. Fuller bequeathed the farm and horse industry business to Moggie Larrs." Levi grinned approvingly.

It was a shock, but made perfect sense. No skin off his teeth. He was having enough trouble figuring out his own real estate issues. "Wow, I bet everyone was shocked."

"Yes. In fact, Carlton started to contest her will. He and Dovie were on the outs about it. It nearly drove Dovie and Moggie apart. They seem really happy together, now they've resolved differences. They had it tough, losing their parents so young. It's good seeing Dovie and Carlton starting a new family."

"Yes, I see Carlton lives with his college sweetheart and husband, Howard. You say

Dovie has a lover, Moggie. Are they planning a wedding?" Clay would've long since left town, so it didn't matter.

The waiter arrived and began taking orders. One-by-one the men gave him direction.

Clay glanced toward a back hallway—leading to a kitchen, restrooms and offices. Dovie's flaming, red hair was difficult to miss. She stepped from a door closing it behind her and leaned her behind against it. A man strolled toward her from the kitchen.

He eased up against her, pressing front of his jeans into her lap and his chest against her breasts. His hands went around her head, tilting her face. He bent and took her in a long, lingering kiss. They pulled apart for an instance speaking quietly, their faces so near they surely felt each other's breath. She smiled radiantly with her arms locked around the guy's neck. He kissed her again. This time Clay thought they'd surely suffocate before coming up for air.

Clay's stomach rumbled, but not from hunger. Anger built, and he gulped air allowing his lungs to expand. His fists balled at his sides, appalled.

The jackass playboy cheated on Jaiden. The dude had gall, kissing Dovie in the open. Anyone in her restaurant could see.

"Excuse me." He laid his napkin on his seat and rose from the table. His stride was purposeful sprinting long steps toward the hallway.

The lovers broke apart. With a quick

laugh at words one of them uttered, Dovie exited a door Clay figured led to the kitchen.

Clay's steps quickened not wanting the dude to escape. He entered the narrow, darker corridor, getting a better glimpse at the player who messed with Dovie and Jaiden. Handsome in a rough way with thick, muscular shoulders and arms, his waist was short and tight. His physique was one developed from manual labor instead of gym workouts. Wearing tight, denim jeans with a western cut, his button-up shirt sported pearl snaps and a pointy collar.

The stranger ambled toward the dining room, taking a couple of easy steps forward. Clay rushed him grabbing the shorter, stronger man by his shirt and shoving him squarely against a wall.

Shocked registered. The fella gasped and his mouth opened. "What the—?"

Clay slammed his head against a wall behind him, leaning into him and holding him down. "You dirty, cheating, man-whore, how many women around this town are fooled believing you sincere? You're itching to dip into as many pairs of panties as you can. You disgust me. You don't deserve her."

The stockier man's fists sprang up trying to push Clay off and defend his self. "What the hell, man? What in tarnation's wrong with you? My love life isn't your business. Get the fuck off me." He shoved Clay and caught him off balance. Clay stumbled back a step releasing the grip on his shirt. "Who're you and what the hell's wrong with you?"

Seeing commotion, Wyatt and Levi rushed into the hallway. "What's going on?"

"This little prick was messing with Dovie." Clay waved toward the stranger.

"So?" Wyatt's head ducked between his shoulders and bobbed up looking confused.

"You said yourself, Dovie's spoken for. She has a man. This SOB needs to leave her alone. He's screwing around with Jaiden too. What're you—the Sweetwater boy-toy of the day?" His words spat toward the stranger.

He glared with hands on his hips, batted his eyes a couple times then shook his head looking to the side. Shoulders back, he extended his hand to Clay with a snide snicker. "I'm Moggie Larrs. You're Clay Barnes, right?"

Clay looked dumbfounded. Levi and Wyatt snickered. Levi patted his shoulders. "It's true, Clay. It's time you two met. Moggie's the best friend Jaiden Coldwater ever had, but he's faithful as stars to Dovie."

"But . . . but Jaiden was your date last night." Clay looked at Moggie sideways, not completely sold yet.

Moggie laughed still holding his hand out to Clay. "No, man, I gave my buddy a ride and a shoulder to cry on last night. You had another date. Soon as Jaiden told you she couldn't come with you, you invited the Anderson chick. Watching you together was killing Jaiden. You're sleeping around on her, and she's stayed faithful to you." His head rocked sideways.

"I wasn't with Jane. She came with Dr. and Mrs. Maines. Jane sat at our table. She was Doc Maines' guest."

"Jaiden was extremely upset. You went home with that gal last night. I called to check on her earlier. She's bummed out still. She says you spent the night with Jane." Moggie's piercing eyes drilled holes through Clay.

"I didn't go home with Jane. I got drunk watching you and Jaiden together. Jane was generous enough to drive me. Then she drove my SUV home." Confusing—was he wrong about Jaiden? Why would she think he was with Jane?

"You better clear this up with Jaiden. You don't owe me anything, but Jaiden deserves an explanation. That little filly is miserable thinking you're seeing another gal the whole time you bedded her. She thinks you're making plans to start a new life with your woman and her kid, like a perfect, ready-made family." Moggie's words filtered what sounded like loathing.

He deserved it. Revolted at the idea he might've inadvertently hurt Jaiden. Even if she didn't want him for the long-haul, she didn't deserve to think their time together meant nothing to him. Rare and precious; he didn't want to hurt her.

He shook Moggie's extended hand. Turning to Levi and Wyatt, his brows went up. Worry must've registered on his face. They looked sympathetic and backed up.

"Sorry about lunch, guys. I've got to go." He fumbled for his wallet. "Let me get it."

Levi shoved him toward the front door. "Go do what you have to, Clay. Don't worry about lunch. I've got it."

Wyatt clapped Levi's back. "That so? Moggie, you might as well join us. Clay already ordered a steak."

Clay glanced over his shoulder exiting and saw him wrap an arm around Moggie's shoulders. While the door shut behind him in his rush Moggie's voice followed.

"Sounds good. I can eat steak."

Clay had making up to do with Jaiden. One thing for her to think he was leaving town, and another completely for her to think he was cheating on her. It would never do.

❤❤❤❤

Clay hadn't been to Jaiden's home, she shared with her mother, Brightleaf Coldwater. He'd never even met her mother. He parked in their driveway. With no windows on a garage, he couldn't be certain Jaiden was home.

He'd heard about last night's bust. Gossip got around in Sweetwater. It filtered air like a fine mist when he stopped at the bank that morning.

Jaiden had solved Walter Burnette's murder, saved Carmen's life, and was a town heroine. Pride filled his chest with more than oxygen. Part of him wished he'd hung out longer, so he'd have been able to watch, but he was thankful he'd missed watching the woman he loved run headfirst into danger.

He rang the front door of her brick, ranch house. Chimes sounded inside. Curtains open but blinds kept him from seeing through a large, plate-glass window. Rustling inside then a lilting voice announced, "I'll be right there."

A stunning, older woman standing about shoulder-high to Clay opened the door. She cocked her head aside eyeing him through a screen door. Her silky mane of silver tresses flowed with movement reaching her waistline. Lovely, high cheekbones and deep pools of darkness for eyes, her smile displayed a perfect set of glistening whites. She moved with grace backing away while pushing the door open.

"Please, Mr. Barnes, do come in." Her voice was musical and warm like a soft song. It sounded vaguely like Jaiden's.

Clay stepped into a living room furnished in a modern design. A puffy white couch was accented with navy chairs in oddball shapes still managing to look inviting for sitting.

"Please, come with me." Mrs. Coldwater led through a wide doorway into a dining area. A large floral arrangement centered a glass-topped table. To his left a kitchen separated by a broad island. She pointed toward several unique metal and white leather stools lined along the bar section. "Sit. Have coffee with me."

Clay sat quietly. The elegant woman

went about a menial task. A door behind him creaked. Then a voice he longed for finally came.

"Mom, was that the doorbell? I . . . ."

He spun finding Jaiden staring with her mouth opened. She looked adorable with no makeup on and sleep in her eyes. Her hair loosely was tied at the nape of her neck. A white tank top stretched over braless breasts peeking through thin fabric. Cutoff jeans frayed, so they tickled tops of her slender thighs. Purple nail polish adorned toes of her bare feet.

"Clay, what . . . what're you doing here?" She stood statue still.

"Mr. Barnes is about to have coffee with your mother." Mrs. Coldwater spoke from behind him. Here's a cup for each of you. Why don't you take it to the patio?" Taking her cup, Brightleaf disappeared along a hallway, shutting a door behind her.

"Clay?"

He stood, picked up both cups of coffee then exited French doors though a dining room to a patio.

"I'm not going to start by disappointing or disobeying your mother." He placed the cups on a glass-topped picnic table.

She shrugged then paddled slowly toward him. "What do you want?"

He pointed to a chair, and she sat. He shut the door and propped against another chair facing her. Leaning toward his knees he reached for her hands.

She didn't jerk away. They tremored while heating his palms. Soft and silky, he wanted to bring them to his lips to touch and kiss. That would never do—not now—not with Jaiden in a precarious temper. Explaining took precedence to his yearnings.

"Jaiden, I've screwed things up royally with you. I'm so damned sorry for it. I've hurt you unintentionally, and I'll never forgive myself."

"Look, Clay, you must live your life the way you want. I'm a big girl. I knew what I was getting into with you." Her sad face looked resolved.

"No, it's my fault. I wallowed in my problems, consumed with guilt about my parents, about who I am, what I want and where my future leads. I was so damned self-centered. I let you down and hurt you. I'm eternally sorry."

"Look, you can't regret loving someone. No need to apologize." She broke a hand free and back-swiped a tear with it.

"I'll never be sorry for falling in love. I'm head-over-heels and want to shout it from the tallest building. I can hardly breathe." He blinked back moisture pooling in his eyes.

She ripped her other hand free and patted his nervously. "I'm happy for you, Clay. You've apologized. Now please, leave." She hugged her waist with her arms and stood.

"No." He didn't bother standing.

Her head tilted, and she propped her

hands on her slim hips glaring. "What do you mean? No?"

"I'm not done. We're not done." He reached for her hands. She shook them in air and turned her back on him.

Her tiny behind was every bit as enticing as her front. Clay longed to rest his hands on her hips and pull her toward him to kiss her there.

Another time.

"I met your Moggie today. He's quite a man. I saw him and didn't know who he was. I thought he was your lover. He was at Dovie's restaurant kissing her. I thought he was cheating on you. I almost punched his lights out."

She snickered and spun to study him for a couple minutes. Neither spoke. Then she guffawed.

"Wish I'd been a bug on a wall, watching you go after Moggie. You might be taller than him, but the old cowboy can hold his own. He's a tough son-of-a-gun. Did he hit you back?" She surveyed his face critically, not hiding her snide snicker.

"There was no punching, only shoving and shouting obscenities. Levi and Wyatt broke us up. We had a short talk, enough for Moggie to set me straight. He told me I'd hurt you. It kills me, Jaiden. I can't live with hurting you."

She shrugged giving it little importance. "You have to live your life, Clay. You can't change because of me. You've apologized. I understand. Now go."

"You're right. I can't. It's time I got

things out in the open. I don't expect you to love me. But I will never stop loving you, Jaiden." He stood meeting her eyes.

Her head jerked forward looking dumbfounded, and her mouth fell open. "What? I meant you should be with Jane. You love and need her. The three of you are a beautiful family. Enjoy it. Don't feel guilty. I knew the first time we slept together no strings were attached. You were free to see whoever you liked. Go, be with Jane. Live your life, here or wherever you decide to relocate." Again she hugged her waist, but this time she turned her back.

This was a turn of events he hadn't expected. It must be what Moggie referred to. "What in hell are you talking about?" He ran two steps between them. Immediately behind her, his arms went around her, refusing to release her though she fought him at first. When she stopped struggling, he kissed the top of her head pulling her tighter against him. Her trembling body was warm and pliable. Her silky skin invited his hands to roam.

"What's this nonsense about Jane? You mean Jane Anderson?"

Jaiden nodded vehemently but silently. He nipped at her neck, and she shivered. He smiled.

"Jane works for the doctors—for me. I'm not seeing Jane. I've kept faithful to you. I'm loyal to you, Jaiden. I can't think of another woman besides you. You consume me."

Lynda Rees

She struggled locked in his embrace. "I saw you. You, Jane and her daughter were laughing and going out together, all happy like a perfect family. And you went home with her last night. Maybe you got drunk, but that's no excuse for sleeping with her. I saw your SUV at her place around four a.m. I puked bile thinking of you lying naked in her bed, with her curled up to you." She shivered. He kept kissing along her shoulder and down her arm.

"I didn't sleep with Jane—never. I saw you with Moggie and thought you tossed me aside for a better offer. You jilted me last night, you know. I got drunk. Jane saw me leaving and offered to drive me home—to my home. She dropped me off and drove my vehicle home. I retrieved it earlier today. I didn't even knock to say good morning. I picked it up and went on about my business."

"But I saw you before with her—with her and her daughter, really early morning. I . . . I, ah . . . thought—." Her head tilted trying to look him in the face. He loosened his grip on her allowing her to turn within a circle of his embrace.

He thought for a second then it dawned. "Oh hell, I drove Jane and Charlotte to Lexington last Friday. Her car broke down and it was early morning. Charlotte needed treatment, and I was free. You must've seen us leave. Honestly, sweetie, there's nothing but a working friendship between Jane Anderson and me."

Her face tilted toward his, and she mulled over his words. Remaining patient, he gave her time to understand. She sighed heavily.

"Well, at least that's one item cleared up. But you're still leaving. You have financials wrapped up. The farm is in your name. You're free to sell it and remodeling is completed. There's nothing holding you. You have offers for incredible jobs. Have you decided which one you'll accept?"

He smiled at the most beautiful creature he'd ever met. "Not completely. I turned down Chicago. Cody and Denver are too cold in winter. Alaska sounds like a cold thrill, but it might prove worth facing brutal winters for a year or so to experience it. It would provide excellent opportunities for snuggling for warmth with my woman. I can't imagine living in Alaska without the love of my life. No offers entice me without my lover beside me."

"I thought you said you and Jane aren't lovers." Her brow wrinkled in a most adorable way. It caused tiny lines on sides of her eyes. He wanted to kiss them away.

"We aren't. Jane's not the woman I'm talking about. I'm desperately in love with a Sweetwater deputy. I doubt she'd be pried from roots so diligently planted here. Does it mean I'm destined to live without her? Would she by chance consent to marry a small-town surgeon and live on his tiny farm?"

Jaiden cocked her head. One brow rose, and she squirreled her mouth up. Her arms fell loose and free.

"He hasn't asked her. He hasn't even said those three little words." Her lower lip protruded enough it drove him mad wanting to suck it into his mouth.

"You mean a four letter word?" His voice teased, and she smiled. Sparkle in his eyes jolted his heart into overdrive.

"Spit it out, buster." She backed up. He released her.

Clay bent and came onto one knee. Taking Jaiden's hand he stared into a pool of deep, coffee-browns he'd forever lose himself in.

"Jaiden, marry me. I love you with every atom in my body. Make me the happiest man alive. I promise to cherish you forever. You own my soul. Say you'll be my future."

Clay pulled his wallet out, flipped it open and retrieved a slim, gold ring. "This is my mother's wedding ring. They never formally married, but it's closest I have to a promise of a long life together. My parents weren't traditional—anything but. However, I know for sure they loved each other and me. Marry me. Wear this until we can find a jeweler later today to select a proper engagement ring."

"I'm honored to wear your mother's band. I'd be the happiest woman on earth marrying you. You said small-town doctor. Are you staying here?"

"If you'll have me, I am." He nodded. He slipped the simple jewelry onto her finger.

She tugged him to his feet. Holding both his wrists, her eyes focused on his. "It's a life sentence, doc. You up for it?"

"I'm sure you can keep me up, Jaiden; and I'm praying for a long, long life sentence."

THE END

Note: If you enjoyed this story, I'd love to hear from you. Take a moment to give me a review.
https://amazon.com/author/lyndarees **Amazon**

https://www.bookbub.com/profile/lynda-rees
Bookbub

https://www.goodreads.com/author/show/171874
00.Lynda_Rees **Goodreads**

If you liked this book, you will enjoy God

Father's Day. An excerpt is included for you.

GOD FATHER'S DAY by Lynda Rees

Justin has it all—a profitable law career and a superficial affair with a wealthy heiress. Her father wants him to marry her and manage his dynasty. That's fine with Justin, since he believes love is an illusion and only useful as a tool to get ahead.

Justin's dad, Richard, becomes critically ill and Justin rushes to his side to care for him and make the most of the time they have left together. Richard confesses a dangerous history haunts him and he's not the man Justin thinks him to be.

Revaluating who he is and what he wants from life, Justin loses his heart to a different type woman. Becky distrusts men due to a complicated history, but Justin's grief breaks down her wall. She can't compete with his rich fiancé. Stalked by her ex, she believes Justin betrayed her. The past endangers their lives and futures when a hit man seeks his next victim.

Get it at https://amazon.com/author/lyndarees

About Lynda Rees

Lynda is a storyteller, an award-winning novelist, and a free-spirited dreamer with workaholic tendencies and a passion for writing romance. Her dreams come true, blessing her with a supportive family. Whatever crazy adventure Lynda congers up, her loving Mike is by her side. A diverse background, visits to exotic locations, and curiosity about how history effects today's world fuels her writing. Born in the splendor of the Appalachian Mountains as a coal miner's daughter and part Cherokee, she grew up in northern Kentucky when Newport prospered as a mecca for gambling and prostitution.

Published in contemporary, suspense, romance, and historical fiction, children's middle-grade fiction, advertising copy, and freelance, Lynda is an active member of several professional writing organizations and volunteer judge of professional writing events.

Author's Note:

I hope you enjoy my work and we become lifelong friends. Time for romance!

Lynda Rees, The Murder Guru
Love is a dangerous mystery. Enjoy the ride!

Book Deals, Exclusive Content and FREE reads—

Find out how:
Website: https://lyndareesauthor.com/
Write and ask me for your FREE copy of Leah's Story, a short story and prologue to The Bloodline Series.
lyndareesauthor@gmail.com

Also By Lynda Rees

Historical Romance:
> *Gold Lust Conspiracy*

Romantic Suspense:
The Bloodline Series:
> *Parsley, Sage, Rose, Mary & Wine*
> *Blood & Studs*
> *Hot Blooded*
> *Blood of Champions*
> *Bloodlines & Lies*
> *Horseshoes & Roses*
> *The Bloodline Trail*
> *Real Money*
> *The Bourbon Trail*

Single Titles:
> *Operation Second Chance*
> *2nd Chance Ranch*
> *God Father's Day*
> *Madam Mom*

Reggie Chronicles:
> *Hart's Girls #1*
> *Heart of the Matter #2*
> *Magnolia Blossoms #3*

Children's Titles:
> *Freckle Face & Blondie*
> *The Thinking Tree*
> *Co-author Harley Nelson*

NO FEAR and No Fear Learning & Activity Book

Latest NEWS and Purchase Links at my website: https://lyndareesauthor.com/